MURDER IN IRELAND

&

OTHER STORIES

MURDER IN IRELAND

&

OTHER STORIES

Tom O'Mara

 www.trafford.com
North America & international
toll-free: 1 888 232 4444 (USA & Canada)
fax: 812 355 4082

CONTENTS

CONTENTS

MURDER IN IRELAND

I n the sleepy town of Sligo, a few miles north of Galway, along the Irish Sea a terrible secret was about to be uncovered, a secret held for decades by Brits and Irish authorities alike, a secret the Taylor boys would bring to light through murder.

In the dawn of the day that would alter their lives forever the Taylor boys argued if they would be wrong to do what Mom asked. In the end, the boys agreed with Mom. They had to act. The deed had to be done. They couldn't live as cowards. They had to grow up, gain stature in the community and among their friends. "The rewards are more than worth it," Uncle Billy said.

"Squash your fears.... Remember this army murdered your grandfather and his brother," Mom told her boys as they started on their journey, rifles at the ready, into the center of town at 4AM, the best time to attack according to a military manual on guerrilla warfare their Mom had studied and Uncle Billy confirmed." "Remember, these men are here to squash our freedom, to defend the Crown, to help keep those murderous tyrants in power" Mom told the boys as they left on their mission of murder.

In the cold dawn with mud gathering on their boots the boys, Uncle Billy and several men from Dublin left their Mom's barn and headed south... They walked with a purposeful strides, touching the ground as quietly as possible as they got closer to the garrison so their targets would not sound an alarm. The men in front were trained as snipers by Her Majesty's military and handled killing the guard dogs with ease.

Their main target was the garrison of British soldiers on the outskirts of town, a troop of British soldiers garrisoned along the coastal highway in a new facility, making them a more or less permanent peacekeeping force, sent at the request of Political leaders in the North of Ireland, over the objections of many citizens in the South as a means of calming the fears of the Protestants in the area of attack by the Catholics, even though the only IRA attack in the past 20 years was during a dispute between two large families of Catholics over land rights for a 300 acre parcel of rich farm land.

Her oldest boy, Sean, got to the entrance of the barracks first. He waved his brothers Seamus and Patrick to move forward. Uncle Billy and his friends entered from the other end of the barracks after silencing the two guards at the gate to the compound.

"Lock and Load" they signaled one another as they moved toward doing the deed planned for the last three days. Then, with the speed of an eagle swooping down on its prey, they silenced the sleeping troopers with weapons equipped with silencers, killing the 25 soldiers manning the garrison. Those who moaned and cried for mercy after being wounded were simply executed with a single bullet from a pistol with a silencer by Uncle Billy.

A second wave of conspirators brought in the gas from the garage, sprayed it along the walls and all over the men lying in distorted ways on the ground and in their beds, a look of shock or surprise or a kind of vague peacefulness locked on their faces. The back door was opened. A match was tossed and the flames started to engulf the bodies and barracks. Ten minutes later a bomb blew up the ordinance locked in the station.

The boys back tracked to a road through the woods where a truck waited, tossing their weapons and boots into the truck for disposal at sea. Back home, the boys quickly changed into the older yellow and black rubber boots they used on the farm, cheering as ordinance left in the barracks exploded in a second roar that lit up the night sky and shook their home.

Uncle Billy and his "Dubliners" drove to his boat after dropping the boys back home to tell Mom all was well. With a couple of bags of guns and boots and rubber gloves on his boat Uncle Billy and his "Dubliner's" headed out to sea. A mile out Uncle Billy put a couple of bricks into one of the bags, wrapped it in sturdy high test fishing line and tossed it into the sea.

"Those bastards will never find this evidence," he said to the wind. A smile filled his face as the group toasted to the successful killing of troops that didn't belong in the South and killed his kin and father when he was a young man. A few minutes later another boat pulled up next to his. His friends from Dublin tipped their hats to him and were gone.

Breakfast was very satisfying that Sunday morning as the Taylor boys told Mom the details of the raid and the pain shown on the faces of the British soldiers left dead, burning in flames on the barracks floor that morning.

"They didn't know what hit'em Mom. I felt like Rambo," Seamus said.

By noon the town of Spittal swarmed with British soldiers and police investigators of the Irish Republic at the main station in Galway, a few miles distant from the crime scene, as well as Scotland Yard investigators. By dinner time every crime fighting resource in the Republic and the United Kingdom would have secured the crime scene, giving the soldier's remains the privacy and respect they deserved as they were photographed and put into body bags before transport to military coroners in London.

After a hearty breakfast the Taylor boys went out to the golf course, spending their time caddying for visitors from New York. They liked to caddy for Yanks of Irish Descent. The boys loved the Yanks seeking to experience a bit of their homeland because the Yanks tipped better than the folks who came over from Europe and considered the Irish their poor cousins in the world they felt was dominated by the newly formed European Union.

"Yanks see our boys as their long lost relatives, the ones left behind. The relatives living in the misery of occupation and struggling to make ends meet while enduring the occupation of the British – those slimy bastards who have spent generations putting the Irish in their place and pounding into their brains as often as they could that the Brits were superior and the Irish were lucky to polish their boots," Uncle Billy often explained to the boys when the occupation of Ireland came up in conversations as they carried his bags down a fairway watching him practice for the pro tour with his coach, Kevin Riley.

The Sligo News top reporter, Tommy O'Riley, took graphic pictures of the "crispy critters" as he referred to the dead and burned bodies of the British soldiers left behind in the Spittal barracks on that "bloody" Sunday as the British Guardian, a paper friendly to the U.K., referred to the victims of "vicious thugs."

When the police asked O'Riley how he got to the scene of the crime before the fire department, he said: "I got a call from someone to go check out the slaughter of the troops at the barracks."

"A terrorist act," the Queen told a reporter for the Guardian from one of her offices in Buckingham Palace. "We will find these cold blooded killers and hang them high on London Bridge," a distracted Queen told the reporters on CNN that afternoon. "No one will escape our justice. We will find these vermin, these mindless creatures who executed some of our finest young men, citizens dedicated to our safety and security as they slept. It is simply outrageous," the Queen was saying when her security detail took her forcefully from the room in the palace where she was giving an interview to the BBC. In fact, The Queen was carried into a secured area of Buckingham Palace, her guards closing the bomb blast proof door as the sound of explosions filled the main floor of Buckingham palace.

Outside Buckingham palace guards were cut down by men in a van with machine guns, followed by a van with an open top filled with men firing rockets into the palace and a third van with men tossing hand grenades into the guard boxes in front of the palace and the clusters of police and soldiers who came running in the direction of the exploding ordinance.

Before the third truck passed out of sight of the front gate of Buckingham Palace, two bodies were dumped onto the street from the back of the van. These men were later identified as soldiers missing from the Spittal barracks on the night the barracks was attacked and burned.

The three trucks drove at a high speed and did not stop for the pedestrians who scattered when the gun fire broke out. The same breaking news report on BBC reported a Lear Jet crashed into the Queen's palace in Scotland where the Prince and his "Bride to be" were spending the weekend with friends and family before the Royal Nuptials. "Fortunately," a talking head on the BBC said, "the future king and his friends had left early for a picnic and were not harmed. Sadly, several of the staff at the palace perished in the attack. Ten were injured and are in local hospitals. Doctors say they will all be fine."

In two days, enemies of the Crown have murdered 27 soldiers stationed in Spittal, 18 soldiers at Buckingham Palace, 3 London policemen and 4 servants at the palace in Scotland.

"It has truly been a sad and horrible Sunday in the history of nation" Harold Gamey, lead talking head for BBC in times of national trouble reported in an unusually grave voice as the photos of the fires burning at Buckingham Palace and the bodies of guards lying dead on the ground in front of the palace were shown on the evening news, followed by photos of fires burning in the small town of Spital, Ireland.

THE INVESTIGATION

Captain Tony O'Rourke was the best murder investigator in Ireland. He had solved 100% of the murders assigned to him over the past 20 years.

His secret was simple:" I don't exclude anyone or anything. After an exhaustive study of all the details, the murderer simply emerges. Investigating a murder is a bit like searching for oil: the oil explodes out the hole when the drillers hit the pool of the ugly black stuff. As the poet said, "Murder will out."

"Look," Captain O'Rourke told his team assembled in Sligo that afternoon: "A crime this great has to be talked about. Someone has to be bragging about these murders. They can't keep quiet. Who could? Keep your ears open. Make whatever deals feel right to get these vermin out of their holes. Okay. Get to every informant, every IRA and terrorist cell you can. We want these killers. There is no sleep for anyone until these bastards are dead or in irons. Clear?"

"Yes Sir!" his team replied in a loud, clear voice before breaking into groups of four to study different aspects of the murders assigned to them.

As Captain O'Rourke was directing his men to "get the bastards", Mary Taylor walked slowly into the confessional at St. Margaret on the Sea Catholic Church across the street from her tavern. She wasn't sure she should confess to inciting her boys to murder those thieving bastards, but she felt the action was okay as long as she wasn't doing it just for her own benefit. Raised a god-fearing woman, by strict Roman Catholic parents, Mary Taylor waited in line to confess her sins to the one priest in the Parish known to share her hatred of the British forces occupying Ireland.

"How dare those bastards put a barracks of soldiers in our free South of Ireland, Father" Mary started her confession.

"Now, Mary, this is not a political forum. Confess your sins and let the rest of the parish get home before midnight," Fr. Clooney replied.

"Oh. You're not supposed to say my name."

"It was only a guess, don't you know."

"Really?"

"Aye! So could you get on with it," Fr. Clooney continued as he looked at the security camera view of the folks in line waiting for confession, concerned that the long line would make him late for the regular weekly dinner with his peers.

"I have to confess I know the lads who killed those soldiers on Sunday. More than that, Father, I encouraged them. I helped them. I even made them a fine breakfast after they murdered those bastards. I didn't kill anyone though so, tell me father, what am I guilty of anyway?"

"Well, Mary," the priest said slowly," this is bit more than the usual list of sins I hear in this box, so be still while I figure this out and don't tell anyone else. As my grand dad used to say, "Loose lips sink ships" Grandpa served in the Royal Navy you know and said that sentence so many times he nearly drove me mad with it. So, say the rosary every day and come back in a week."

"Okay, Father.

"Thanks for the courage to get those bastards murdered," Mary said as she started to say her rosary the next morning. When she got back home that night she made the boys a chocolate cake to celebrate their attack on the Crown.

Fr. Clooney listened to the mundane sins of his flock for the next hour but he could not get the confession of Mary Taylor out of his mind. "I have to do something. I can't just forget this kind of a mass murder in my parish. It's just not right."

Still, Fr. Clooney knew his vows. He had said he would not break the seal of confession unless, of course, it could save a life or the person who confessed said he could tell the story; although, even that was a bit tricky for a Catholic priest. "It is too bad we don't have group reconciliation like in the States instead of the old fashioned one on one confession in this parish," he told his fellow priests over dinner that night.

Inspector O'Rourke knocked on the parish door just after dinner. He joined the priests for coffee and a bit of brandy "to beat back the night's chill" the Inspector said as he accepted a good sized spot of brandy from the assembly of priests.

"What brings you all together tonight?" the Inspector said. Did anyone confess to these killings and you have to figure out what penance to give?" O'Rourke asked.

"Oh Yeah," There was a line around the church for confession and all sorts of folks admitted to the killing of those policemen as an act of God's mercy," Fr. Clooney said, half smiling as he took a swig from a freshly poured glass of brandy.

"There is no love for the Brits in this town, Inspector," another priest offered.

"I guess that would be too easy," O'Rourke responded, "but worth a shot. I'm guessing there are no breakers of the seal of confession in this group. Still. It would be the right thing to do, to turn in the killers of these innocent soldiers, wouldn't it?"

"Not really, Inspector," the oldest priest said, as he raised his cane and pointed it toward O'Rourke. "These fellows were here in violation of the treaty the South and the North and England signed several years ago. The people of the village don't like them being here. Most want these British soldiers gone and view them as an army of occupation rather than a force for good in our community, don't you know."

"I know they're hated, at best tolerated because they are well armed and organized. The local folks aren't the ones most likely to murder in such a systematic fashion. It's got to be a truly well organized gang of murderers that pulled off this murder with such military precision."

"Well that leaves out our flocks, Inspector. These are simple folk. Fisherman, factory workers not trained in the ways of members of special-forces or other military specialties. These folks are hard working and god fearing people. They wouldn't have the skill to pull off this kind of cold blooded mass murder. Of that I am dead certain," Monsignor Kelly assured Inspector O'Rourke.

"Who then could have done this so deep in the land of the Republic?" O'Rourke continued.

"What makes you think it was a professional hit, "Inspector.

"Ah, that's a good question so let me share what I can.

First, the killers erased all the company dogs, and hid the dogs out of sight so no one wandering around the compound or the night guard would think anything was wrong. Some of the dogs were left in the middle of the yard with a bits of blankets or sail pulled over part of them so no one would get as suspicious as they would if "ALL" the dogs simply disappeared.

So these guys planned their assault and they planned it well. Then, these guys executed the policemen with weapons with silencers. No shots were heard in town. The tavern owner next door slept through the murders. He didn't wake up or call emergency services until the ordinance in the building exploded at 4:30 or so. In addition, these guys murdered the soldiers without any resistance. The soldiers did not fire a shot. They were completely surprised and killed in seconds – completely unable to call for help or to fight back. It was as cold blooded a murder as I have ever seen," Captain O'Rourke said.

A silence filled the room as the priests considered the malice and cold-blooded nature of the men who must have taken the lives of the soldiers in the barracks. Such raw hatred had not been seen in these parts for a century or more.

"Are these murders related to the attack on the Queen, Inspector" the elderly priest sitting quietly in the corner, a book open on his lap, asked in a near whisper.

"Ah. You must be a reader of detective stories, "Inspector O'Rourke responded.

"In truth, we don't know. It's too early to connect the killers in London with anyone here. But we have to wonder why both attacks happened so close together. Coincidence? We don't know. But I will certainly be looking for any connection between folks in town and known members of the IRA in England and Ireland.

"And retired soldiers, I suppose, are also suspects," the elderly priest continued.

"Aye, that's logical, "Inspector O'Rourke responded.

"It's early in the investigation. And, gentlemen, I would certainly hope you will be telling your flocks that mass murders are simply not condoned by Holy Mother Church any more than child abuse," Inspector O'Rourke said as he rose to leave.

"Thanks for the brandy. Let me know if you hear anything that could help us find these murdering bastards," Inspector O'Rourke commented as he shook hands all around before leaving the room to go back to the crime scene and pick through the rubble with a crack crew of forensic scientists that had helped him crack all the complex murder cases he had solved over a 20 year span of service as a homicide investigator.

"You think those will help, Inspector" Sergeant Molly McGuire asked after they got in the car.

"No, Molly, I don't think so. The old guy won't even mention it in his sermon. He seemed to be smiling and celebrating as I described every detail of the murder. He not only admired their handy work but he was pleased that we were puzzled and not sure if the attack on the Queen and this barracks in the back waters of Ireland are related. Check him out Molly. I'm betting he has a kissing cousin or two still tied up with the old IRA hardliners who would kill British soldiers and coppers for fun."

Tuesday: 7AM

Sergeant Molly McQuire went for her morning run so she could process all the information that had been gathered the day before by the forensic folks. It was very confusing and suggested many directions of investigation. A run always seemed to clear her head and energize her. Often during these runs she would start to fit parts of a case together calling those details to an answering machine on her computer as she ran along the road.

Spital was a lovely place for a run. The Sea on her right was running with white caps this morning, the wind invigorating and the steady rhythm of the waves on morning felt particularly soothing to Molly's psyche. Molly had long legs. She wore her hair in a pony tail and dressed in a baggy camouflage suit from her time in the British army.

She was two miles into her five mile run, passing along the coastal road near the Church when a van pulled up twenty feet in front of her. A man stepped out of the van with what appeared to be a stun gun at his side and yelled at her: "Get over here girl," he said as he raised the weapon to fire in Molly's direction.

Molly seemed to trip, rolling off on her right side. The man smiled, thinking "another easy catch" and dropped the weapon as he moved toward her. Molly pulled out her weapon, fired twice, dropping the man with two rounds to the chest. He fell back into the van.

The man in the passenger seat jumped out with a pistol in hand: Molly fired twice and hit him in the chest. The driver yelled "God Dammit!" and hit the gas.

Up on her knees, Molly fired three rounds, hitting the rear tires of the van causing it to veer sharply to the right just as a large truck turned the corner. When the van hit the truck, its front end was flattened.

When Molly got to the scene she saw the driver was unconscious, his life saved by a seat belt. In the back seat she found two young girls tied with ropes and duck tape across their mouths.

When the troops arrived a few minutes later, Molly was sitting with the girls, assuring them they would be returned home. One girl used her phone to call her parents. The other girl used the truck driver's phone.

O'Rourke arrived less than a minute after the EMTs, fire, police and military commandos.

"Some shooting Sergeant," Danny O'Shea said after he surveyed the two men on the ground.

"Thanks," Molly said, smiling in the direction of the detective O'Shea, a fellow she secretly hoped would notice her ever since she arrived in town to investigate the murders at the garrison.

"So these girls were grabbed from the road just a half hour ago while they were walking to Church. Is that it Molly?"

"Aye, Sir. They were walking along when the truck pulled up ahead of them. Two men got out and fired stun guns at them. Then they picked them up, tied them up and tossed them in the back seat of the van. They wanted to do the same thing with me, but, as you can see, I was not so easy."

"Indeed. And the girls told you they heard these guys saying they would sell them for a pretty price."

"Yes Sir."

"Okay. So you stumbled onto a trafficking ring. Get warrants and arrange a raid within the hour at the locations on their driver's license and at the house of the owner of the van. They are probably others young women at that plane and friend of these pieces of crap involved. We don't want anyone alerted. Do you want to be a part of it?"

"God, Yes."

Okay. O'Shea, you and Sergeant McQuire get a raiding party together. I want a hit on these bastards within the hour."

"Sir."

An hour later, two squads of police raided the apartment of the first man who tried to grab Sergeant McQuire and the farm owned by the man in the passenger seat who also felt the sting of the red headed firebrand on the murder investigation squad.

When the investigators got back from the raid, they had six men and two women in handcuffs, plus 20 young girls who had been held, trafficked and forced into prostitution by the gang of 8 in custody and their partners.

Molly and Danny O'Shea went to lunch at "Patty's Pub"-- a popular watering hole for locals and tourists across the road from the Church on the coast road after everyone was booked and the girls put in touch with their parents by phone. Social Services would get the girls home.

"That was a good morning, Molly. God you are one hell of a shot. How did you get so good?"

"My Dad taught me. He was constable before he became a prosecutor. He made us all learn to shoot. He thought it would make us safer when we got older."

"He was sure right about that. Where is your Dad, now?"

"Heaven" Molly said as she took a bite of her burger.

"I'm sorry," O'Shea said.

"Me too," Molly replied after drinking a bit of diet coke. "Dad was murdered. It happened right in front of me and my brother. I was 12. My brother was 14. He shot and killed the murderer with my Dad's pistol as the killer fled the scene. He is a soldier now. He loves it. And, me, you know, I'm a homicide expert."

"My life is a bit quieter than yours, "O'Shea replied. "My folks are still alive, living in Dublin where Dad is a conductor on a trolley and Mom is a legal secretary. I became a cop by accident. I met a fellow when I was playing soccer that ran a special squad for the Dublin police. I wanted to be a professional soccer player. I got into the minors, cracked my ankle and it never healed right. I just couldn't make it as a pro. He suggested I take the exam. I passed and here I am."

"How do you like it?" Molly asked.

"I love it. Days like today are really good; the bad guys are behind bars and their victims are going home to parents who will cry for joy for years that they are back in their arms -- Too romantic?"

"Kind of sweet, actually..."

"Right... let's get out of here. We got bad guys to catch"

"Okay, let's do it," Molly smiled as she punched Danny O'Shea softly in the arm.

2PM

"Molly", O'Rourke called out as she entered the precinct. "Guess what we found in the back that van – a couple of the guns that killed those soldiers. These bastards either bought them or used them. We are busy sweating the 8 we caught in Galway but the driver from the van is still out cold. Doctors will call us as soon as he comes too. He really whacked his head on the mirror. Of course he'd be okay if he had worn his seat belt."

"But crooks never wear seat belts, "Molly said in a mechanical voice.

"Smart Ass --- so, you have been listening."

"Yes Sir," Molly joked.

"By the way, that was some shooting this morning. We have to get you into the annual shooting contest. Okay...Now-Get over to the hospital and interrogate that bastard when he comes to – we want the guy who sold him those guns. Take O'Shea so we don't run into any crap from the locals. He is well liked over there his Captain tells me. You know let's get beyond that territorial baloney. Any trouble with some egomaniac, call me. I mean it. I want this bastard to talk."

"Yes Sir," Molly saluted with a big smile.

Watching the two detectives walking out of the station O'Rourke thought –'I guess they'll be an item and in a couple of years I'll have to be a godfather. God that kid will be a great detective – might even shoot straight.'

The Driver of the van was still pretty groggy when Molly and Danny arrived so they met with his ER doctor.

"You might get something coherent from him," the ER doctor said, "but I suspect he is still pretty confused. He hit his head pretty hard on the front window. Don't be too long, unless you have to. I don't want this bastard to block you from finding the rest of the trafficking gang. It was a gang of young girl traffickers you caught this morning, wasn't it?"

"Aye Doctor, it was. We really got lucky. But now it looks like this bastard may have been part of the gang that murdered all those soldiers on Monday. They had guns in the truck that matched the guns used for the raid. We really want to get information from this guy, Doctor," Molly said.

"In that case, Danny I'll just close the drapes to his room and tell the nursing staff to let you stay as long as you want. Say hello to your Mom and tell her my Mom will turn 65 next month. We'll be hoping your Mom can come to the party. It's going to be a surprise. Even Erin is bringing her family from Australia for the party."

"We'll be there John. Just let me know when," Danny said as the ER doctor left the room, closing the door, putting a "No Visitors" sign on the door.

"John? And how does the detective from Dublin's Mom know the ER Doctor from Galway, Danny boy."

"Ah. Ever the detective, Molly McQuire, it's a long story."

"No rush. Eduardo is still out cold. Take your time. Spell it out."

"Pushy detective, you are."

"Aye: That's what we do, we detectives. We detect."

"Ok, if you must know. John was a Doctor working with Doctors without borders in the Congo. I was in the Royal Marines. We got attacked while there to protect the hospital from the bad guys raiding the place, stealing drugs and medicines they needed for their wounded, kidnapping doctors and nurses to help fix their wounded and, of course, to kill a few more of the wounded in the hospital who happened to be under the medical care of Doctors like John Dolan.

One night they attacked, I saved John's life, got wounded in the process. John cleaned up my wounds when the firefight was over. We both loved soccer so we ended up chatting up the history of soccer and debating the greats of the game after lights out when the facility was on high alert.

When I got back my Mom called his Mom and came down to meet her. They got along. Starting to chat and 10 years later they remain mates, calling each other once a week to catch up on their boys. I understand they complain about how we have not gotten married and delivered them some fine grandchildren to spoil."

"Mothers are so unreasonable. To think their boys could be still be free of a partner at age – what are you now, Danny, 30 or so."

"I'm only 29 Girl."

"Girl is it. And I'm all of 28."

"And single. Can't imagine why?" Danny replied as they squared off, eyeball to eyeball as if they were center ring and ready to duke it out in a battle to the death.

"Water....I want some water, God Dammit," Eduardo kept repeating.

Molly and Danny turned to the criminal and shouted: "Shut up" in the same tone and pitch, sounding like a well rehearsed chorus of two.

"Eduardo Santoni," Molly began, pronouncing his name in an elongated way with a quiet, sinister sounding tone. "You will get your water when you tell us what we want to know about the guy you bought the guns from that we found in your trunk. And, if you don't tell us, Sergeant Dan here is prepared to start breaking your fingers, one by one, until you tell us. Why? Those guns were used to kill – to murder while they slept – some of our colleagues. Do you understand what I just told you Eduarrrdo?"

Eduardo looked at Danny's right hand. The scalpel in his hand looked like a five foot sword, something that could chop off his head and the glare from Danny strongly suggested Danny was not playing around. He looked like a man ready to take Eduardo apart, piece by piece, just as Eduardo had done when he was a young drug dealer in Juarez, Mexico, working for one of the cartels a few years earlier. He knew the glare, the look in the face of a man who was ready to simply rip a body apart until the information was gathered that his leaders wanted.

"Sure. I'll tell you. The guy is no one. He was just looking to make a few Euros selling those rifles to us. Our boss liked large caliber, modern weapons and we got them for less than $500 Euros per weapon."

"What was his name? Where did you meet him? Molly continued.

"Some water?

Danny handed the prisoner a paper glass of water. He sipped slowly as he calculated how much to say and how much not to say.

"Okay. His name was Bill Taylor. We met him a bit south of Sligo, on the ocean front road, just before we snatched the two girls you found in the back of the van, a few minutes before my friends tried to snatch some red headed bitch who shot them both. Amazing – a bimbo with a gun who knew how to use it; both guys died. She shot them down like dogs in the street. Cold –a cold hearted bitch she was. A hell of a shot she was, but cold."

"Really," Danny said. Could you recognize her if you saw her again, Eduarrrdo?"

"No. I was in the driver's seat. My view was blocked. Then she shot out my tires, didn't she?"

"She did," Molly said.

"Some shooting," Eduardo continued.

"Okay Eduarrrdo," Molly continued, "who put you in touch with this Taylor guy?"

"I don't really know. Our boss told us to meet him, get the guns and give him $5,000 US. We just did what he said."

"What about the girls on the road. Why them?"

"We were heading home and grabbed them; that's what we do."

"Is the farm and apartment in Galway the only place you hold these girls," Danny asked.

"Yeah; that's right," Eduardo replied.

"Okay. Danny let's go. We got to get this Taylor guy."

"What did he look like, Eduardo?" Danny asked.

"Look like: he was very tall, thin, red hair, about 45, maybe younger. He smelled of fish. He was probably a fisherman or just came back from an early morning bit of catching."

Turning to leave, Molly hesitated. Danny looked puzzled. Molly took a pair of blue surgical gloves from her coat pocket, slowly putting them on as she walked toward Eduardo's bed.

She looked down the man cuffed to his bed, grabbing his hair and pushing up on his chin in one quick step. Pushing up on his jaw, Molly glared at the six foot muscle man who tried to kidnap her.

"Just wanted you to know asshole, I'm the woman your guys tried to snatch this morning. I'm the copper who will see your ass is put in a small room for the rest of your life. If I could, I'd stand you in front of a firing squad and blow your low life ass to hell."

Molly and Danny told the officers outside the door to keep Eduardo hand cuffed to the bed and not have any visitors. No nurses or doctors in the room without both police officers assigned to the room present when the medical folks were in the room. "Don't mess this one up, Billy," Danny told the new officer. This bastard is one of the guys who murdered the boys in Sligo.

"If he tries to escape, I'll shoot him dead a couple of times, Danny."

"Good work, Billy."

4PM

O'Rourke started the briefing of the investigating team with some startling news.

"I'm happy to say our London medical examiner has some good news for us. They found some DNA on the body of one of the soldiers tossed from the van in front of Buckingham palace. It seems someone spit on one of our boys – one of the two soldiers missing from the garrison here in Sligo. The spit had the DNA of a man named Billy Taylor, a former Special Forces officer who served in the Middle East and other places. He lives here in Sligo. And, his finger prints were found on the sack with the guns taken from the slavers who tried to take our Molly McQuire while she was jogging along the Irish Sea. No luck there..."

"You can see from this photo on the big screen that Billy Taylor is one sturdy guy. He is well trained, considered armed and very dangerous. We intend to pick him up right after this meeting. We have debated the best way to do it and decided we will send in Molly and Danny. They have been mentioned as the key investigators on the case so they won't be surprised and may not feel threatened when Molly and Danny show up to ask questions because they have been questioning all sorts of people in town. We'll give them a word to say if the SWAT team should invade the house."

"Molly and Danny I want you to wear vests under your jackets, just in case. This is a pretty dangerous guy and he could be volatile. We were going to break down the doors but his sister, Mary Taylor; a local librarian and part time bartender at the family tavern, Patty's, and her sons may be there at dinner time.. This will get us a chance to – what do they call it Danny "reconnoiter" – check out the state of the house from the inside."

"Actually Captain, we used to call the point man "bacon and eggs because we figured the point man would be the first thing the enemy would see before breakfast," Danny O'Shea replied.

Everyone laughed a nervous laugh as they left the room to gear up for the assault on Billy Taylor's house.

Billy Taylor's house was only 8 doors down from the temporary quarters that O'Rourke and his team were using, so Danny and Molly decided to walk.

"You know, Molly, I don't want to sound like the macho man here, but this is really a bad guy. He's got skills that I'm not sure even a tough guy like me can overcome. I'm beginning to think we should have said No and demand the full scale breach by SWAT."

"Oh, come on, Danny, this is the best way to find out how tough it will be to breach the place. He doesn't know he's a suspect. We've got a solid reason to say hello and maybe, just maybe, we can save his sister from the trauma of full scale breach, a hostage situation and, ultimately, a shoot out that might just get her killed."

"You are a Rottweiler, McQuire. I don't want to get on your bad side."

"Better not, big boy. You should see my brother in action."

Danny knocked on the door and waited, feeling the calm that used to come over him just before he went into a firefight, knowing there was no alternative and the best way to stay alive was to stay "attuned to the environment" as his training officer repeated over and over again when he went through sniper training.

"Mr. Taylor," Molly asked.

"Yes."

"Mr. Taylor, Officers O'Shea and McQuire would like to have a word with you. Do you have a few minutes?"

"Sure: always happy to help the police when I can. Come on in, we can talk in the kitchen if you don't mind."

"No. Not at all," Danny said as they followed Billy Taylor down the hall toward the kitchen.

"This is my sister, Mary," Billy said.

"Hi," Molly said as she and Danny shook hands with Mary Taylor.

"We won't be long, Mr. Taylor."

"So, Mr. Taylor, it seems you were out fishing early this morning off shore from Church about the time Molly here was accosted by three guys in a van, and we wondered if you saw any other cars along the road. We think there were others and Rory Dolan told us he saw you out fishing in the area. Was he mistaken?"

"Wait a minute," Mary said. "You were accosted on the road near the church, this morning?"

"Aye," Molly replied. "It was okay. I outran them; just some drunken boys trying to give a running girl a hard time. It was nothing until they hit their brakes and turned into oncoming traffic. Sadly, the boys are all in hospital. Lots of broken bones, they'll live. Maybe they won't drive drunk again."

"Tough way to learn that lesson," Billy said as he turned off the stove.

"That deserves a cup of tea," Mary said, as she got up to organize cups and saucers.

"Aye: but in answer to your question. I didn't see much traffic. It was foggy. I did see Dolan. We swapped a few fish stories and he was really jealous of the big bass sharing its last gasp with us on my deck. Great fish dinner when Mary puts together our weekly dinner with the boys and we swap stories about how to make a bit more cash from the fishing store and Patty's, of course. This town will be crawling with tourists in June and we need to be ready. It's only a few weeks and then it's back to dull and boring."

"Well that's it then," Danny said.

"It was good meeting you Ms. Taylor."

"Mrs. If you don't mind, officer."

"My apology," Danny said as he turned to Molly.

Molly pulled her gun and said to Billy, "On the ground, now, Bill Taylor" as she kicked him in the groin. As Billy leaned forward, Danny smacked him in his Adam's-Apple with his foot. In seconds the Swat Team filled the kitchen with weapons drawn with one of the men kneeling on Billy's back as another put hand cuffs on him.

Molly turned to Mrs. Taylor starting to say, "I'm sorry" but Mary Taylor's face was filled with rage and she was plunging a large butcher knife at Molly's heart as she yelled "Bitch". The knife started to penetrate the Kevlar vest, but caused no harm to Molly because it got stuck in a chest pocket sized doll Molly had bought as a gift for her niece.

Molly swung as hard as she could with her right arm catching Mary Taylor in the Adams-Apple with such force that Mary fell back to the floor pulling the butcher knife with her. She was quickly subdued and put in hand cuffs.

"You Okay," Danny asked holding Molly by the shoulders.

"I think so. Look. The knife stuck in my gift for my niece, Rosie."

"You can always get a new Doll,"

"Yeah, but I'm never going to give up this one. This doll is going to be in my breast pocket every hour of every day I'm on duty."

"Lucky Doll," Danny said before he realized it.

"Oh. Oh. Romance reigns in the Homicide room" one of the SWAT guys said.

Everyone laughed, except Danny who looked at Molly and shrugged, raising his hands in the sign of surrender: "Couldn't help myself", he whispered.

"You will PAY," Molly whispered back.

7pm

As Molly and Danny walked back to the station, Danny put his hand softly on her shoulder and said, "Look, I like you. I can't help it. Is it going to be a problem or am I just out in left field and dumb as a box of rocks?"

Molly stopped, turned slightly left, stared Danny straight in the eye and kissed him softly: "You're not dumb at all. I'd say if O'Rourke lets us off when we get back we'll both get lucky."

"Damn, I like that idea Molly." They started to run hand in hand back to the office, quickly dropping to the ground after a black or tan car pulled up in front of the station, tossing a bag or explosives and what appeared as hand grenades automatic weapons fired into the building. The exploding hand grenades hit a gas-line, enhancing the power of the explosion, shattering windows for on many houses.

Danny pulled a driver getting into his car out of his car. Molly got in the passenger seat and they took off in pursuit of the truck while Molly called 911:" request all units on the coast road of Sligo to stop the Fed Ex delivery truck heading toward Galway along the coast road. Sergeants O'Shea and McQuire are pursuing in a green Volvo. The guys in the truck are armed with automatic weapons and hand grenades. They just blew up the command center on the Sligo road next to the liquor store.

It's a bad one. Send all the help you can muster. There were a dozen men and women in the office when we left a half hour ago."

The 911 operator replied: "Are you or your partner injured?"

"No. We are okay. SWAT is right behind us with a couple of prisoners in tow."

"Can we get helicopter support, now?"

"It's been dispatched. They are 10 minutes out from Galway."

"Great. Advise when you know the extent of the damage at the command post, Please."

"OK."

"Okay, Molly, show us what a good shot you are. Get that damned truck's tires so we can put these bastards in irons," Danny ordered as he raced along at 80 mph, getting to within 100 feet of the bomber's truck. When their car went airborne because of a bump in the road Molly got off three shots – one of the shots hit the left rear tire of the murderer's truck. The truck swerved, turned on its side and started to roll off the road.

"Magnificent! My God What a shot! - in the air no less!"

"It was easier in the air. There was no road bumps to interfere with my aim'" Molly said in such a calm, matter of fact fashion, Danny started to laugh so hard he almost drove them off the road as he braked their borrowed Volvo.

Danny and Molly got to the wreck at the same time as the SWAT team. The officers moved cautiously toward the wreck because the SWAT commander said: "Careful, these bastards are well armed."

"It's okay sir" the point man moving behind a bulletproof shield shouted from the wreck. The driver looks dead. The guy in the back is breathing but there are no guns in sight."

The shooter in the back of the truck was pulled out and cuffed after a couple of the team kicked him. The corpse was pulled from the front seat before the coroner got there because the detectives wanted to find out who he was and capture any evidence that might be in his pockets

"Damn. They're both Taylors. They must be Mary Taylor's boys or brothers," Danny said as he and Molly compared the driver licenses on the two murderers.

"Molly," the SWAT team yelled out. "We got a bag of weapons in the back. These bastards were ready to hold off an army."

Within the hour two SWAT teams invaded the other Taylor household on a heavily wooded road near the Church overlooking on Irish Sea. Swat gathered up the girl friend of the eldest, Billy Taylor – a boy named after his Uncle Billy – his godfather.

With the Taylor family in jail, guarded by the soldiers assigned to replace the murdered garrison, Molly and Danny headed back to the gutted headquarters to learn who had been hurt and see what they could do to help the survivors.

"Damn, the Gods are conspiring against us," Danny said.

"Yeah, but at least we're still here. I'm wondering if O'Rourke is still with us. And what happened to the Taylor folks. Did they attack headquarters to kill them or because they wanted to kill us; you know, the police."

"We'll know soon enough, Molly."

They could see the flashing lights from a mile away. Fire and police and EMT filled the streets and the main road in front of the temporary murder squad headquarters. By the time Molly and Danny got there the building that was still smoldering from the fire and explosion they had seen as they came back from the interview and arrest of Billy and Mary Taylor.

"Do you have a list of casualties?" Molly asked an officer filling in a form at the site, but before she could look at it, Captain O'Rourke yelled, "Hey McQuire. Where you been? Christ it's been a mess here. Where's O'Shea?"

"We got what's left of the Taylor family in custody. How did we do here, Sir?"

"Well we lost three of ours – Graham, O'Neil and Cameron. I was in the bathroom and the explosion tossed me into the tub so all the debris hit the old iron lady and didn't break any of my bones."

"Damn lucky, Sir!"

"Aye, and damn funny too the way I went flying and ended up with a door on top of the tub. Not my time, I guess."

"Guess not, Sir," Danny said.

"Okay, here's what I want you two to do. Go over to the garrison and question Billy and Mary Taylor. Then, go question the son and girlfriend we snatched at the house. All the records we have gathered so far are on a server you can access with your normal passwords. They blew up the building but they didn't destroy any of the evidence or the leads we have developed; that "cloud thing" invented by some Yank saved our inputs. -- Molly, we need to find out about their London connection. We want the bastards who attacked the queen. See if Taylor will share information. Offer him a bigger cell or a cell with a relative instead of some crazed Arab who can't speak English or some psycho killer who just might rip out his throat in the night. You know the routine."

"We are on it, Sir. Come on Danny."

"That's right, follow your leader Danny," O'Rourke called out.

"No leader here, Sir. We're equals – Sergeants both."

"So you are," O'Rourke said as both he and Molly smiled, winking at one another, mutually amused by Danny's defense of his position and his dignity.

"Ah, sure and you defended yourself well," Molly mused as they walked down road to their car, under a full moon, in a cloudless sky, the sounds of the Irish Sea in their ears.

"He knows. He's amused," Danny said.

"About what?" Molly laughed.

"Us, of course; he knows we are going to date, marry, have kids, and retire with 20 years to form a PI firm and he's going to be god father to our first born."

"He knows all this because of a light kiss away from him and everyone else."

"Aye, Molly, he knows. The thing is: do you know?"

"I'm not sure yet, Danny me boy because I don't know what kind of a lover you are or if you snore and roll around in bed so much I won't be able to settle in and sleep peacefully with happy dreams that are not interrupted by noisy farts and window rattling snores."

Putting his arm over her shoulder, Danny stopped, felt her turn into him and they shared a lingering kiss, her tongue and his tongue simply roaming and probing the other's mouth.

"So how loud do you snore? Molly asked.

"You'll soon find out," Danny laughed.

"Indeed, I will," Molly chuckled as she squeezed his ass and ran to get to the driver's seat of their squad car.

As they approached the Garrison they noticed the grounds had been fortified. A tank stood at the front gate and a jeep with a machine gun on a turret stood on the other side of the road.

They were escorted to the prisoners by a full bird colonel, a battle hardened chap in his late forties with the posture and muscular structure of a man who worked hard at keeping in shape so he could survive the rigors of any assignment he might be asked to perform for the benefit of his country.

"They said they want a barrister. I told them terrorists don't get the advice of counsel. If I had my way they would face firing squad in the morning and I'd make sure they were dead with a bullet to the head if the firing squad left them alive. And, to finish off my point, I told them they were like rats in the sewer, deserving less pity than a rat."

"And, did they say anything, Colonel," Danny asked.

"No. These are hard core killers. No conscience. No interest in salvation. We should just toss them in a hole for a week. Then they'll talk."

"Danny, you take Billy and I'll take Mary – she is pissed at me for that blow to her neck. Maybe the rage will work for us."

"Billy it is. See you in hour or so."

By the time Molly and Danny got back to the station, Captain O'Rourke had the results of the forensic team assigned to tear the Taylor homes apart; to seek DNA evidence as well any writings or other information that could help O'Rourke catch all the people behind the murders.

The interrogation of Mary Taylor

Mary Taylor sat upright in a hard wooden chair with a smirk on her face, her hands attached to an old wooden table standing in the middle of the room, bolted to the floor. The walls of the room were pea green – "disgusting and a sign of the taste in these pigs," she planned to tell her boys when she got out of this ugly place.

Molly watched Mary for a few minutes from a one way window, noting she let her hands rest quietly on her legs and her breathing did not appear to be labored. It seems she had prepared for this moment for some time because she was not as bewildered looking as most suspects plucked from their home by armed soldiers.

Molly walked slowly into the room. She stood behind her chair at the other side of the table for a few seconds, pulled the chair back and sat down. Quietly she laid a brown file folder on the table.

"So Mary Taylor, are you wondering why you are here?"

"No. It's the usual nonsense of the Brits- false information, false imprisonment crappola of the Imperial House of Windsor, a bit like Lord Nelson's time except today you use guns and tanks instead of cannon and swords. Big Deal: I took a swipe at you with a knife. I was defending my brother, that's all."

"Ah. You're a historian then. Fine. Here's a bit of history – a bit more recent than Lord Nelson's attack on Irish people hundreds of years ago. The other day, soldiers stationed here were murdered by some murderous bastards while they slept. Cowards always kill the sleeping don't they?"

"Do they?" Mary snapped, her face going from placid to hostile, from a smirk to a sneer.

"In this case, yes. They were well organized cowards, however. They killed the dogs before the attack with well placed shots, probably from a considerable distance. Sharp shooters for sure, probably trained as assassins from the accuracy of the shots. They even got close and covered the dogs with various kinds of cloth and tarps so any passing guard would think the dog was asleep, not dead. So they were trained in stealth."

"Ah. So it was an inside job then. Some mad Brit killing another bunch of Brits. No one from the outside could get that close to guard dogs, could they?"

"We are investigating that, however, you are here because you were in your brother's home when he was arrested for selling some of the guns used to kill those sleeping soldiers. Did you know your brother was a gun runner, a man who worked with thugs who steal Irish girls off the streets and traffic them into dens for prostitution?"

With a look of sadness, Mary's shoulders sagged for a moment before returning to their elevated position.

"My brother is a fisherman and a tavern operator. He doesn't sell guns and girls. It's fantasy. You have information that is simply bogus. I've known him all my life. We have coffee together every day and dinner together with my family every Sunday. You are just wrong. Billy would never do that sort of thing."

"Well Mary he does. Here are the pictures of the weapons he sold to these three traffickers; two were killed in gun fight with the police and the third is in the hospital when he crashed his van into a large truck on the coast road near the church in the center of Sligo. Here's another photo of their truck and the two young Irish girls they had tied up in the back seat after they kidnapped them as they walked to church that same morning."

Mary leaned back in her chair, placing her right hand on her chin, taking deep breaths. Her eyes looking back and forth from the pictures of the dead men and the two young Irish girls dressed in their Sunday best as they innocently walked to Church when these three brutes snatched them from the road.

"It can' be true. I won't believe it unless Billy tells me it's true."

"Oh. It's true. Take a look," Molly said as she turned on her iPad.

"This video of the accident shows clearly the girls, the kidnappers and, of course, the black bag with weapons these bastards bought from your brother Billy. How do we know Billy had the weapons and sold them to these bastards? We have Billy's finger print on the bag and the weapons. We have the testimony and ID of Billy by the bastard that survived and we found the $5,000 US dollars in Billy's house that the survivor of the car crash told us he paid Billy for the weapons."

"Baloney: This is all made up. I want to talk to Billy."

"You are not going to see Billy until arraignment when you and Billy are charged with conspiring to kill those soldiers in the garrison."

Molly's phone rang. She saw it was Captain O'Rourke and left the room.

"Get anywhere with that woman, Molly?"

"No Sir. She is a cool one. Just hates Britain and won't agree that her brother is the bastard who sold the guns to the kidnappers. But she'll crack. She wants to see her brother. Should we do that?"

"No. In fact, give her a hot meal and come over to her house. I want to show you something."

"You're in the field, Sir?"

"Yes. I still know how to clear a crime scene. This you need to see. Come over right now. Put the Colonel on so I can make it clear we want Mary Taylor well fed and rested when you get back in a couple of hours."

"Yes Sir."

"Coronel, this is Chief Inspector O'Rourke. We need you to feed that woman a good lunch. Hot food and coffee would be best. We need her to be well rested and wide awake. After you give that order, you need to come with Molly over to the Taylor House. We found something that you might be able help us understand. See you in a few."

"Very well," the Coronel replied into the dial tone.

THE INTERROGATION OF BILLY TAYLOR

Danny approached Billy Taylor with a bit of nervousness because, like Billy, he had been trained by counter terrorists folks in the art of deception.

"Mr. Taylor," Danny began. "There is no point in giving you a polygraph because like me you have been trained to cheat the machine. So we won't waste our time on that sort of nonsense."

"Good", Billy Taylor replied, "I don't want to stay here any longer than I have to. You guys have wasted enough time on me and my sister already. Treating us like criminals in front of my nephew and sister is about as offensive as one could be. Pure stupidity, if you ask me," Billy finished as he flared his nostrils and slammed his free hand on the table.

"Ah Billy, me lad, you are such a bad actor. You think I'd waste my time with toilet tissue like you if I didn't have to? No way. So sit back and listen to the crimes we are going to convict you of committing in a ruthless and cowardly way."

"Cowardly, my ass, you little crapper," Billy shot back. "I'd eat a little shit like you for breakfast if I those two apes hadn't put the cuffs on me and tied me to the floor with chains attached to concrete blocks."

"I get it. You're a bad guy. You beat up all the little guys on the playground. No wonder your file from the SAS says you were retired for being too bloody brutal to prisoners, drinking too much and flattening too many citizens."

"Those things are petty theft compared to what we have you on today. You are being charged with the murder and conspiracy to murder British soldiers as they slept in their barracks in Sligo, as well as selling guns to criminals, aiding and abetting in the commission of crime defined as trafficking in young Irish girls. You are going to go away forever, at a minimum. You might be shot by a firing squad or hung by the neck until dead. Personally, I'd have you drawn and quartered, with your head on a pike on London Bridge."

"What Nonsense Detective are you talking about? I did none of those things. I'm a fisherman who owns a bar with my sister. I don't kill people and I certainly don't traffic in young girls. I leave that for the clergy. You must be mad? I want a barrister. I want out of here."

"Sorry Billy, I can't do that because we have evidence that links you to the murder weapons used by the killers of our soldiers as well as the men captured for trafficking who said you sold them the weapons we found in their van on the coast road."

"You believe slackers like that rather than a man who owns property, runs a legitimate business and is known throughout these parts as an honest, hard working man who goes to Mass every Sunday with his widowed sister her children," Billy replied as he shook his head to signify absolute disbelief in the evidence that Detective Sergeant Danny O'Shea just presented to him.

"I didn't know your sister was a widow. I thought her husband was a drunk who just walked away on day and had never been heard from again. How do you know he is dead?"

"It's just a figure of speech. At any rate, he is dead to us."

"So, you deny all the evidence."

"I do".

"Well, Billy, I am sorry to hear that because unlike you, DNA evidence does not lie and fingerprints don't lie. We have matched your DNA to the bag carrying the weapons used to kill our soldiers. We have your fingerprints on the weapons found in the bag. We even have your DNA on one of the bodies of one of the soldiers you helped murder. It seems you had to spit on the pants of one of the soldiers after he was shot and killed by you and your band of cutthroats."

"I need to piss."

"Great. We'll' get you a can," Danny said as he quietly closed the file on Billy Taylor and left the interrogation as he whispered into his ear–"Into the ground you go-- asshole."

Noon at Mary Taylor's house:

Captain O'Rourke was looking over the Irish Sea on the porch of Mary Taylor's house when Molly drove up. Mary had inherited the home from her folks – an inheritance from her Mom and Stepfather when they passed leaving her and Billy to raise each other. She was 18 and he was 16 when their Mom and Stepdad passed. On the table in front of him was an evidence bag with a surprising find inside Mary's house.

"Hey, Molly, how did the interrogation go with Mrs. Taylor?"

"You know Sir she is a bit of a surprise. No sense of intimidation. No Fear. She just looks on the questioning as if she wasn't there, as if she wasn't the suspect and, frankly, she appears to be a bit bored with the whole process. She is angry with the Crown but not afraid. It's not like most of the suspects I've encountered, but, Sir, I'm convinced there is something going on with her, something I need to crack through before I can get her attention and, hopefully, her confession."

"Hm. Tell me, Molly, where is the colonel."

"He'll be along. He was yelling at some private who did not salute him in the manner he felt was correct. Man, is he a stickler and what a mouth. He belongs in the jungle that one, give him a spear and canteen of water in search of a tiger to wrestle to the ground and kill with his bare hands. He is really, really aggressive for a guy in his 40s."

"Well, look at this evidence bag. We found these 10 dog tags from British soldiers in her bedroom on the mantle. They were in a glass jar, next to another glass jar with a frog on a spit. We checked them out and, to our surprise, they match the names and serial numbers of British soldiers who have either been found dead in alleys in Dublin or simply disappeared. There is one dog tag for each soldier who died in each year over a ten year span – starting 32 years ago. It's got to be more than a coincidence, don't you think?"

"Sure is strange, Sir. Are you thinking someone in her family – maybe her brother Billy or a friend – starting killing a soldier a year until they stopped?"

"Well, Molly, I'm thinking she might be the killer. She could be the classic serial killer who keeps a trophy from each kill."

"But why would she stop? Why would she start?"

"Ah. That's my little genius of a detective. She started for one simple reason – revenge."

"Revenge, Sir."

"Yes. Our little Mary lost her father when she was ten years old. She was walking with her Dad on a crowded street one holiday weekend. They were going to meet her Mom and brother Billy who were buying some clothes for the new school year. Apparently, a man raced by them with two soldiers in pursuit. One of the soldiers foolishly fired his weapon at the running man – some IRA scumbag who had just murdered another soldier by throwing a hand grenade into a police car parked on the corner with a window open. Anyway, the soldier fired, missed, killed her father with a shot to the neck and kept running past Mary and her father. No one stopped to help. The little Mary, holding her father's hand, watched as he simply fell to the ground and died."

"Jesus, Sir. How horrible it must have been for her."

"Indeed," Captain O'Rourke continued. "Her Mom was just approaching when the shot rang out. She saw her husband fall and came running. He was dead when she got to him or pretty soon thereafter – the action report doesn't spell that detail out. It just said, 'Mr. Taylor was dead, his head cradled in his wife's arms when they police arrived on the scene.' The soldier who fired his weapon, killing Mr. Taylor was never found. There was no ammunition or weapon missing in the unit on duty in that section of the city at that time. It was 1976, August."

"The shooter was never found."

"Are thinking she grew up and decided to find the shooter?"

"I am."

"That's quite a conclusion, Sir."

"It is. Still, I can't seem to shake it. These dog tags really suggest I may be on the right track. It would not be the first time revenge was the motivator for murder."

"Well, Sir, do you want me to probe this with Mary?"

"I do."

"Okay, Sir, but let me play the devil's advocate for a minute."

"Okay."

"How did Mary overcome these guys? She is a woman of small stature – 5 feet 4 inches at most and she only weighs about 120 pounds, if that. She wasn't trained in hand to hand combat, as far as we know. I suppose she could have lured them into an alley and killed them with a small caliber weapon as they used both their hands to pull down her panties or to unzip their trousers. How were they shot, Sir?"

"Smart girl, you are. They were all shot in the chest, at close range with what appears to have been a German luger of the WWII vintage. Three shots to the chest and one to the throat are present in each case when the bodies were found. Four bodies were never found."

"Boy that's pretty brutal and very thorough. It seems really personal, as if the killer knew these men. So, Captain, you are thinking she is taking revenge for the man who shot her dad in the throat when she was child. Why did she stop? That doesn't seem right."

"Yes. I have thought of that. These kinds of crazies don't usually stop unless they are in jail or die. However, if she started this kind of murder when she was 16 and married when she was 26 she could have stopped because she moved from Dublin to Sligo with her husband, started a family and just didn't have a chance to get back to Dublin to continue killing. At any rate, Molly, I want you to go in there and see what you can extract from her. As far as I'm concerned she is a lot more deadly than we thought."

"Okay Sir, but I don't know. I like her for an accomplice at the garrison but not a participant. She just doesn't seem to have the agility or strength to march through the woods in the night and execute these soldiers. Her brother is certainly a logical candidate for the murders, but she just doesn't seem to fit the profile of the killers."

"Sergeant -- Get in there and turn that woman into a killer."

Molly decided to walk back to the jail. She was tired and wanted to get her thoughts all lined up before turning on Mary Taylor and treat her as a hostile witness, a liar and, perhaps, a serial killer turned mother and barkeep.

The colonel saw her walking, stopped his car and walked back with her.

"So, Molly do you really think Captain O'Rourke is right? Is she the serial killer we have been searching for all these years?"

"Captain O'Rourke is smart guy, Sir. He has been doing this for 2 decades and if he sees the pattern and can leap to the conclusion she could be the killer, it is definitely worth investigating. He is a very cautious guy. I've watched him for 6-years now and he does not leap to conclusions."

"One of those boys was in my unit when I was a young man and just getting to know that the military was for me. He was a farmer from up in Scotland, 20 -years of age, a great runner and he boxed like a professional. We loved him because he really knew how to tell a story. And, of course, the women loved him. His Scottish accent was the closer. His name was Cameron Braddock, a private on his first week of R & R after graduating from training. We were all shocked that he was killed in such a brutal way and left naked in an alley in Dublin."

"What year was that Colonel?"

"1980—August."

"I'm sorry Colonel. I'll see if I can get her to talk about him."

"Please. Molly, if you find this lady is the killer of Cameron I'll make sure no one shoots her until she stands trial – at least, I'll try. The men will be ready to drop her in a hole if she is the one."

"Colonel, if she killed those soldiers, I'll get her in the top security, civilian prison faster than you can say, "Fire in the hole!"

Molly excused herself and walked over to Danny O'Shea sitting on a big stone near the entrance to the garrison looking out over the Sea, trying to get past his frustrating conversation with Billy Taylor.

"Molly, me girl, you look awfully good.'

"Thanks big boy. You look a bit befuddled."

"Ah, that is the word. This Billy is a brick. He's been trained by SAS to be as revealing as this big old fat stone that I am resting my arse on."

"And a lovely arse it is, Sergeant."

"You are a snotty girl, sometimes."

"It's my most endearing quality."

"Really?"

"Yep--Wouldn't you agree?"

"Nope-I'd say your most endearing quality is your nose and the way you hair bounces on your shoulders as you run."

"Oh, you noticed. You weren't looking at my butt on the highway this morning."

"Nah -- Your hair got me"

"You are a find, Danny me boy," she said as she wrapped her arms around his waist.

"Later, later girl, we've still got a lot to do."

"That can wait," she said, kissing him the ear.

They shared a Hershey bar as they walked back to the interrogation rooms, planning their vacation when they finish this case.

"Bermuda it is – if you not a snoring machine that keeps me awake" she said as they parted, Danny on his way to interrogate Billy Taylor and Molly off to get Mary Taylor to commit a series of murders that still mystified police and military investigators.

3PM

"So, Mary, did you have a good lunch. Are you full?"

"I'm fine, but I'm ready to leave. I want to be home to make my boys dinner when they get back from fishing."

"Ah, Well, Mary, that's not going to happen because we found these dog tags in your bedroom, in a jar on the mantle, like some kind of trophy. And, imagine our surprise when we discovered these men were all killed in the same way by the same gun up in Dublin, once a year, starting when you were 16 years of age. Coincidence?"

Mary took a sip of tea. Slowly she sat back in her chair and stared in expressionless way at Molly for nearly two minutes. Molly simply leaned back and said nothing.

"Ah. So you guys have planted evidence in my room. Another bloody trap by a government that has as little interest in the truth as a tiger has in mercy when it's hungry and spots a baby deer sleeping. How do you live with yourself?"

"I sleep very soundly, except when I am seeking the killer of an innocent child. Still. Mary, you may as well know your fingerprints are the only finger prints on these dog tags, just your fingerprints and those of the soldier who was murdered."

"Modern technology can do wonders, can't it," Mary replied as soon as Molly finished.

"Of course, I forgot, Mary, you know all about murder. You saw your dad murdered didn't you?"

"You are a bitch," Mary yelled at the Sergeant, tossing her tea cup on the floor.

"I'm sorry. Is that why you started killing all these soldiers – one a year, in August, on the anniversary of your Dad's death by gun shot?"

"I never shot anybody."

"Okay. Have it your way. Tell me, then, how did you come to have these dog tags in your bedroom? Did you date these men?"

"I'd never date a copper or a soldier. Those bastards let my Daddy's killer off. They never really investigated. My Daddy was as important to them – to people like you and the soldier who shot Daddy -- as a cat run over by a police car. When the American's starting calling you guys "Pigs" I cheered and said, Amen."

"Really, Mary, such language from a woman who goes to Communion every day at the Church across the street from your home is very surprising, but not really un-expected because you are the killer of many fine young men who had only one desire –to serve their country. And don't give me that innocent or angry look you have down cold because Mary you have just proved to me that you are a liar – and, a murderer."

"Oh please. Charge me or let me go. I'm tired of your games."

"Well that's too bad because I have here a picture of a private Cameron Braddock taken by a fellow soldier two days before his body was found in an alley dumpster in Dublin with three holes in his chest and one hole in his throat. Recognize the girl?"

"Not really."

"Well I'm surprised because that is a picture of you at age 21. You were with the private. The picture was taken by a soldier and friend of Private Braddock. That soldier is the Colonel at this garrison. He was in training with Private Braddock – Come on Mary, we have other pictures of you from that period of time. It's you, alright. You made a mistake. A dumb one that would not have been discovered unless, of course, your need for revenge caused you to plan and execute the murder of the garrison in Sligo a few days ago. You got greedy and we are going to hang you by the neck until dead – in the tower without cameras or publicity or debate. Your miserable life will be ended—and soon" Molly said as she closed the file, got up slowly, took her tea cup and left.

When Molly returned in an hour, she turned off the one way mirror. Mary Taylor's face turned white as a ghost when she saw her sons, Seamus and Liam and her brother, Billy, in orange jump suits worn by prisoners, handcuffed to one another.

Molly returned the mirror to one-way just after Mary Taylor blew the boys and her brother a kiss. A tear rose in her left eye, then her right eye, when the vision of her loved ones ended. She closed her eyes, leaned back in her chair and started to moan in a soft and definite way, in the way a loved one often reacts late at night when memory of a terrible death of a lover or a parent or a child penetrates the conscious mind at an unexpected moment. She rocked back and forth, left to right, right to left, as Molly watched in silence knowing her murder suspect had begun to fully comprehend the consequences of her revenge, of her nearly lifelong hatred of the Crown, a hate turned white hot when some unknown soldier fired down a street, murdered her father, and ran by seeking the murderer of a fellow soldier without one moment's compassion for her father, her mother, her brother or her.

Molly left. Outside Danny told her Billy was going to prison. He would be charged in the morning with murder, gun running, trafficking and kidnapping. "He'll get out in a box. Good riddance"

"Aye" Molly replied.

10AM

When Molly walked in on Mary in the morning, she saw a new woman.

The cockiness was gone. The rage was still present but the sense she was going to get out of jail that day seemed gone from her general demeanor. Her bright green jump suit with Prisoner stenciled in dark black block letters on the front, back and along the sides of each leggings stood in sharp contrast to the 51 year old woman in the summer dress, decorated with flowers with a bit of a plunging neckline seated in the room a day earlier. Seated next to Mary was her barrister, a young woman, well known in town that frequented Mary's tavern on Friday for dance and song in search of a husband – Patricia Flaherty?

"I am Mary's attorney."

"Of course you are," Molly replied with a great deal of derision and impatience in her voice.

"So, are the games done now, Mary?"

"My client."

"I didn't ask you a question," Molly continued.

"Yeah. Okay. No more games, but no more conversation until you tell me what will happen to my boys and my brother. I'm not going to make your life easy if you don't give them a good deal."

"Fine," Molly said in disgust. "What do you want? What do you have to trade? It had better be good or you will die in a cell after a lifetime of seeing the world at 11PM for one hour per day for exercise with no visitors and one shower a week. No TV. No books. No movies, just memories."

"You can't do that," her lawyer said.

"For the murder of British soldiers in such a blood thirsty and cold manner I can put this scum in a prison like the Black Hole in Calcutta and no one will care."

"Shut-up or leave," Mary told her lawyer.

"Here's what I want," Molly continued.

"First, I want to know about the murders of young soldiers for ten years when you were a young woman in Dublin. Second, I want to know where the bodies of the four boys you murdered in Dublin are buried. Third, I want the gun you used to murder those boys. Fourth, I want to know where the body of your "Missing" husband is buried. Fifth, I want the names of the IRA members who helped Billy kill all those soldiers in this town."

Her attorney looked at Mary with a look of shock on her face. "Mary is not a serial killer. She's not an IRA member. What are you talking about?"

"Look, Attorney Flaherty, you apparently don't know anything about the vicious nature of this woman. She makes the Mr. Hyde look like a choir boy."

"Okay," Mary said after nearly three minutes of silence as she closed her eyes and took deep breaths.

"I'll tell you as much as I remember but not until I get an agreement, signed by the President of Ireland stating that my boys will not get more than 5-years in a minimum security prison and my brother Billy won't be executed."

The following morning, Mary Taylor, signed the following statement:

"When I was a young girl my Daddy was murdered by a British soldier and no one did anything about it. No one was punished. The government acted as if my Daddy was just a goat run down on the road, a being of no importance, a death that did not require a thorough police inquiry. My brother Bill y and I were raised by our Mom who, being a woman of few skills, married a terrible man by the name of Walter Cronin. He beat her when he got drunk. Billy, a strong boy at 14 fought him off when he came after me for sex one night when he came home drunk. When he passed out on the kitchen floor, we cut his throat and dragged his body out to the back yard. We dug a hole and cleaned up. When Mom got up in the morning, she was surprised to see him gone. We told her nothing. She went to work at a dress shop, made a modest living, but kept us together. I was 12 and Billy was 14 when we murdered that drunken bastard.

Mom lived a difficult life, took care of us as best she could and made sure we studied hard and finished school.

Mom always said, "Education will save you from the kind of life I've had to live. Mom died of consumption – TB - when Billy and I were in our twenties. Her death was blessing because she suffered so.

When did I start taking my revenge for the death of my Daddy at the hands of an anonymous British Soldier? I got the idea from a television program about murder and revenge. It made sense. I liked the balance. I felt if I killed one of those British soldiers I could give my Daddy the justice he deserved.

I was sixteen when I killed the first soldier. I went to a bar on the main street where the soldiers often partied on a Saturday. It was called Patty's – the same name we called our tavern here in Sligo. I just picked up a soldier. He was a little drunk and not particularly handsome so he was grateful for any good looking girl who took a notice. We went in the alley down the block. While he was tugging on his zipper, I shot him in the chest three times. Then I shot him in the throat.

The gun was in my purse – a German luger I had taken from my stepfather's tool shed after we killed him. He had it from the war or some friend. I don't really remember. He was such a lying creep so I never knew if anything he said was true or false. I left the body naked in the alley and walked away, slipping into the crowd on the street. I wore a red wig and I had a second coat under my outfit. About a block from the alleyway where I left his body I took off my outer layer, put it into a shopping bag in my purse and went home.

I didn't tell anyone what I had done. I didn't tell Billy until 6 years later when I asked him if he knew anyone in the IRA. He knew a few guys and he gave me a number to call. I called and told them there would be the body of a British soldier in a particular alley on the next Saturday and I'd like them to remove it so the police don't start investigating. I was getting nervous but I couldn't stop killing these guys.

I would go to Daddy's grave the day after every execution to cry and tell him his death was going to be revenged soon, that I loved him and missed him. He was a really good man, a funny man who cared for us and loved us as if we were irreplaceable vases from the Ming Dynasty that are in the British Museum protected by an army of security police.

When ten soldiers were dead, I decided to stop killing. It was like the movies of WWII when the Germans used to kill ten civilians for every soldier occupying a town that was killed by the insurgents in France. I just decided Daddy was revenged.

I met my husband, Jeremy O'Flaherty, a handsome young man with great prospects. He was going to be an architect when he finished university training a few months after we met. His father and mother treated me very well and they seemed to be a loving couple.

We married and our twins, Seamus and Liam, were born. We were both very happy. His parents were very supportive. Sadly, his parents were killed in a terrible car crash on a country road while they were on vacation. A truck had a blowout, swerved into their car and drove them down a hill. The police said they died instantly or as close to instantly as they could imagine.

We were devastated. Our hearts were simply broken. For ten years they had been a wonderful part of our life. With their death, Jeremy became a different man.

A year later, Jeremy took his inheritance, sold everything in Dublin, and moved us to Sligo. We thought the change would be good for us and the boys. He always wanted to own a tavern / restaurant so we bought what today is "Patty's" here in town.

We had enough to buy a small farm of 40 acres and the tavern. We had a house, a barn, goats and a couple of miniature horses for the boys to learn responsibility and ride. It was an idyllic life. We had everything we had ever dreamed of for ourselves. Billy moved here from Dublin and worked as the bartender in Patty's. He had a winning way with the folks in town and the tourists who came here in the summer. We prospered and felt blessed. Our childhood was nightmare, but it seemed to be over. We could finally begin to plan for the future with a kind of certainty that we had never experienced before.

Sadly, Jeremy took to the drink –"The scourge of the race," his Dad used to say. He went from a happy man to a crazy man. He would get up at three in the morning; get us all into the parlor. There, with a brandy bottle in hand, he would rail against the government and the church and the rest of humanity calling his fellows a bunch of worms who belonged in the lowest pit of Hell because they had so little pity or compassion. He would pass out. We would go back to bed.

In the morning, he would ask "What Happened. How did I end up on the floor?"

In time, he got violent. He gave me a black eye one night and he tossed Seamus against the wall – a wee lad – when he came to my aid. One stormy night with lots of lighting and thunder I had him chase me to the barn. I wanted to get him away from the house and the boys. In the barn, I shot him with the luger I hid there. Three bullets to the chest and one to the throat ended his life and his torture of me and the boys. I tossed him in a hole and buried him behind the barn.

In the morning the boys asked where their Daddy was.

I said, "He's gone fishing."

After a year they stopped asking. The police shrugged their shoulders. "He's become a drunk, probably drowned in that storm," one detective told me. No one really seemed to care. They just went about their business catching the car thieves and little fish too dumb to avoid prosecution.

I'll give you the names of the IRA conspirators for the Sligo barracks when I get the letter signed by the President of Ireland that assures me that Billy will not be executed, serve his life term in a minimum security prison and my boys will not serve more than 5 years in a minimum security prison. My boys killed no one; they only took the men and guns out to sea on Billy's boat. They know nothing about that night or my history."

Mary signed with a flourish- her signature nearly as large as that of John Hancock on the U. S. Declaration of Independence.

A week later the President of Ireland signed a letter agreeing to all of Mary's demands with one proviso – if they escaped from prison they would serve the balance of their lives in a maximum security prison when captured.

Within a few days, the men responsible for the murders in Sligo and the attack on the Queen at Buckingham Palace were captured. Mary was placed in a cell by herself, only leaving the cell at 11PM for one hour in an exercise yard about the size of basketball court, surrounded by 40-foot walls, under the supervision of two armed guards. Her court date was private. Her punishment life without the possibility of parole, no visitors and no meals shared with other prisoner. Her doctor, if needed, would take care of her in her cell.

Within a year it was reported that Mary Taylor hung herself from her barred window and was buried in an unmarked grave near the prison. Her death was not investigated. No one but her brother and her sons ever asked if she was the victim of revenge, murdered by the guards in the military prison in which she was confined – a serial killer of 10 soldiers, a co-conspirator in the murder of 26 soldiers in the barracks in Sligo and an attack on the Queen and Royal Family at Buckingham Palace in London.

Molly and Danny O'Shea were married before they went on a two week vacation in Bermuda.

Three months after the confession of Mary Taylor.

On the last day of their honeymoon in Bermuda, Molly and Danny planned to eat a leisurely breakfast after a morning romp in the sheets, a ritual incorporated in their routine since they landed in Bermuda. Their room on the top floor of the hotel overlooked the ocean, facing east so the two early risers could sit on the deck, drink their coffee and watch the sun rise after their frolic.

"So, Danny, what are we going to do when we get home? Are we going to have to join the 4 to 12 shift so we can romp at the start of the day? It might be a good idea; the morning has been so luscious these last two weeks. I hate to see it end."

"Aye, let's go for the night shift when we get home. It's where the action is most of the time anyway, isn't it?"

"It is Danny me boy, my love, my husband... I love saying "my husband".

"Well then Wifey --why won't you change your name to O'Shea?"

"I can't! It doesn't seem right. I like my name and my heritage, but if it's such a big deal when the O'Shea family gathers I'll use the hyphen that's so popular these days. I'll change it when we get back, even though changing all the paperwork is a big pain in the arse."

"Really... you'll do that for me?"

"Nah... you silly man, "she laughed, as she wrapped herself around Danny, got up, put a towel around herself and wandered off to shower.

When they got to their usual table for their last breakfast in Paradise, they found it occupied by very handsome fellow, dressed in a business suit, with a rather large man standing a few feet behind him with his back to a wall so he could get a full view of the room.

Molly turned to Danny and said, "Armed guy on the wall."

"I see him," Danny said quietly as he picked up a steak knife from the buffet tray and folded it behind his right wrist so he was ready to put the knife in the heart of the gunman if there was trouble brewing.

The hostess greeted them and said, "The man at your table is the British Consul for Bermuda. He asked to join you this morning and we did not think you would mind. He is here quite often. A very big tipper and very well thought of on the island."

Danny handed her the knife saying, "This was on the floor."

When the pleasantries were over, the British Consul, Byron Higgins, handed Molly an envelope, with a return address of "Buckingham Palace".

Inside was an invitation to join the Queen and her family for lunch in two days time at Buckingham Palace.

"I've been instructed to have you put on board a private jet sent by the Queen so you will be in London on time for the event. I hope it will be convenient for you," Mr. Higgins said.

"Why in heaven's name would he Queen want to see us," Molly said.

"Ah. Ever the detective, I see," Mr. Higgins replied.

"What's on the menu," Danny asked, with a straight face that made both of them laugh.

"I don't really know, Mr. Higgins," replied. "But I've heard the chef in the Palace is one of Europe's finest, so if you want something special because of dietary concerns, I'm sure it can handled."

"Oh. I meant for breakfast, today," Danny said.

When they arrived in London, a car picked them up and took them to the palace. They were escorted to the guest wing and given a very spacious suite. Exhausted from the travel and time change, they fell sound asleep and didn't wake until nearly 10:30 in the morning.

Their light breakfast was followed by dressing in the uniforms provided for them, uniforms that were normal for them to wear on state occasions.

When they entered the dining room, Queen Elizabeth and her husband came over to greet them. The Queen even gave them both an unexpected hug, something she seldom did.

"Molly, you will sit between me and Kate, William's wife. We really want to talk to you. You did a wonderful thing finding the men who tried to kill us and killed all those young men in the service of the nation. We are very, very grateful."

"We – Danny and I were lucky to be working with the best detectives in the Empire, Your Majesty."

"Of course, the others helped but you cracked the murders of all the cold cases when you got Mary Taylor to confess and reveal all the gruesome details of her murdering life."

Around the table was Captain O'Rourke, Commissioner O'Hara of the Irish Constabulary, Prince William and Harry and Phillip, husband to the Queen, but the Queen, Kate and Molly virtually ignored the men as the Queen asked and Molly explained how they cracked the case. The queen wanted all the details, even the feelings that Molly felt when she realized what a monster she was staring at when Mary Taylor confessed to brutally murdering those young soldiers.

When Molly finished, Queen Elizabeth asked, "Did the President of Ireland keep his word and give those murders with 5 years in minimum security?"

"No, your majesty: his note was never published anywhere. We made it up. And when she signed the confession, they were all sentenced to life in solitary confinement to be served in prison in the Falklands. They will never see the light of day again."

"So, Molly, who knows about the phony note from the President of Ireland to Mary Taylor?" the Queen asked in a very quiet voice.

"Just Danny, me and Captain O'Rourke now you and Princess Kate," your Majesty.

"Good. That is all who need to ever know."

The Queen stood and said, "Danny, will you and Molly come with me."

The three walked out arm in arm to a library just behind the private dining room of the family. When they emerged, Danny had copy of the complete works of Chaucer – his favorite English writer- and Molly had a first edition of Sherlock Holmes by Sir Arthur Conan Doyle – her favorite author since she was 10 years of age.

The Commissioner, Captain O'Rourke, Molly and Danny flew back to Galway on the same Royal's plane they flew in on from Bermuda. There a few police cruisers met them and drove them home. As they parted, captain O'Rourke said, "I don't expect to see you two before 10 in the morning – and that's an order."

Molly and Danny decided to spend the evening at Molly's apartment because they had not yet moved in together and she wanted to spend their first night back in Ireland as a married couple in her place,

"besides," she told Danny, "I've got more clothing choices to make than you and my bed is harder."

On Molly's voice mail was a message from her Mom explaining how she had broken her ankle and could not attend the luncheon that the Queen had graciously invited her to attend."

"Call and tell me all. I want to hear it from you not read about in some newspaper. Love you both."

10:00 AM

Everyone in the office rose to cheer the couple when they got back to their desks. They bowed and laughed. Danny said the "Queen Mum said to tell you all that you are all the best that England has to keep a lid on the bad guys. She was very grateful for your skills...."

"Okay, "Captain O'Rourke said: "Let's go solve a few murders. Molly you drew the first of the day. Sara will get you up to speed on the way to the crime scene."

Sara Hogan had worked with Molly on many cases in the past three years and they had become close friends because both women were single. Sara was five years older than Molly, a single Mom with a ten year old daughter and an ex who had simply disappeared. He was smiling and happy when he left for work 3 years earlier, but he never came home. The Police could find no trace of him. Only his van was found parked near the electronics warehouse he managed in the heart of Galway. His case had gone cold for more than 2 years. All leads were simply dead ends. He was like the man who evaporated or fell into the Bermuda Triangle.

As they rolled out, Molly asked: "Any news on Ed while we were gone?"

"Nope: same old, same old. Honey doesn't ask me anymore. She just seems to accept that her Dad is gone. Yesterday she asked if Dad was with God. I told her I hope so. How was Bermuda?"

"It worked for us, Sara. Not dreary; Lots of sun and sand and foods to put a couple of inches on my waist. God I'll need to run hard for the next two weeks, unless, of course, I'm pregnant..."

They were laughing as they turned the corner of a typical middle class street in Galway.

The officers on the street said, "Pretty open and shut, Lieutenant. The mother killed her son as he was reading his paper after breakfast. The shotgun was on the ground between her and her son when we arrived. She said: "I killed him. He had to die."

"Who is he," Sara asked.

"The local priest, a Father Corcoran is the victim. He's been here for ages."

"Why did he have to die?"

"Ah. She discovered her son was a predator of youngsters. She found all sorts of photos and decided he had to burn in Hell."

"Well this any easy one, but there will be quite a roar in the press when this gets out," Molly said.

"Welcome back to the Emerald Isle," Sara quipped.

"Aye," Molly said with a sigh as she stepped into the hallway of the home, spying the elderly lady sitting quietly in her chair, praying the rosary, staring at the corpse of her son.

"Mrs. Corcoran, I'm Lieutenant Mc Quire. I understand that you told Officer Harris you murdered your son with the shot gun on the floor. Is that true?"

"Yes."

"Can you tell me why?"

"No. I told the officer. Can you take me to jail now?"

"Sure. Officer Harris please place Mrs. Corcoran under arrest and take her to holding. We'll be along after we inventory the scene."

Officer Harris and Molly helped the 70 year old Mrs. Corcoran up from the chair. Molly noticed her small hands were soft as a goose down pillow, her skin wrinkled and sagging, he eyes set in a sadness that was often present when a victim or doer were taken into custody or brought out on a stretcher to an awaiting ambulance for transport to a hospital.

For an hour Sara and Molly sifted through the contents of the home, finding the pornographic films and videos that apparently drove Mrs. Corcoran to execute her son piled neatly on top of his desk in a converted closet on the second floor where cameras and a large computer screen had been set up by a bar with fine scotch and three very thick leather chairs set for viewing.

Molly took a call from Danny: "So, an old lady killed a priest. Is that it, Molly?"

"It's much sadder. The mother of the priest killed her son because he had a porno collection with lots of young boys. She just took a shotgun and killed him, both barrels at point blank range in his dining room. We're going to interrogate her. It's just so sad. I wish I were with you on the beach."

"Aye, darling, that would be best. Meet for lunch?"

"Oh yeah – see you at Jenny's at noon."

"Okay, love."

Mrs. Corcoran sat quietly in the interrogation room, sipping slowly on a cup of tea, regularly running her hand over her lap to straighten out her dress, turning her head from side to side, her shoulders hunched over. She had a pad of paper and a pencil in front of her but she had not used it when Molly entered the room at 10:30.

"So, Mrs. Corcoran, why did you do it? Why did you shoot the reverend?"

"I had to. He was evil. Possessed by the devil, he was. I had to send him to hell to get my Patrick free."

"You freed Patrick?"

"Yes. I killed his devil. Now, he can go to Heaven and I can see him when I go to Heaven."

"And how do you know the Reverend was possessed?"

"Those photos upstairs tell it all; only a devil would have such filth in his house."

"Mrs. Corcoran, would you please write down everything that happened this morning in the house of your son?"

"Of course," she said as she picked up her pencil and started to write in a clear hand like the nuns had taught her to write in a fine, cursive way while under their care in grammar school.

"Well, Captain," Molly said as she turned her report," there goes a 70 year old woman who just killed her son because he was possessed by the Devil and by killing him she was able to get her son's soul back into the state of grace. Thus, she said, I will see him in Paradise."

"Pretty crazy."

"Aye, Captain, pretty crazy and really sad."

"Going to lunch with Danny?"

"Aye-- He is waiting for me at Jenny's. You want to join us?"

"No. I'm on a diet. Brought a diet bar and diet drink for lunch. I got to get the gut down. Besides you newlyweds don't want the old school teacher interfering with the conversation about where you're going to live and so on and so on," Captain O'Rourke joked.

"Sir. We can always use a negotiator."

"Right: Now don't forget our conference this afternoon at three."

BATTLING BOOZE IN MANHATTAN

After a Monday night football party in a Midtown bar, I woke up when an A-train came to a screeching halt; brought back to life by the ear splitting racket caused when subway brakes scraped against metal rails filling the air with red sparks. Thank god it was the 51st Street platform on the East Side of New York City. Clearly, this wake up alarm is the best wake up alarm in the city; thoroughly obnoxious, loud and rude enough to awaken unconscious commuters or guys like me who need to come to after too much partying with friends.

My tongue felt like sandpaper and my head pounded like a jackhammer. I needed a drink, immediate relief, but there was no bar open at this early hour. I had no wallet, cash or credit cards. Someone – for sure not a friend – had plucked them from me while I was unconscious on the bench at the center of the platform reserved for seniors and handicapped waiting for a train. A clock said 5AM. It could have been broken, of course. After all I was in Manhattan.

How did this happen to a great guy like me? I was a happy go lucky salesmen of suits and ties for America's top executives, suits made by special tailors brought to New York from Hong Kong to satisfy a need for hand crafted, custom suits – a necessity for executives who roamed the board rooms of corporate America, especially the ad guys and bankers who hustled on the streets of Midtown where I plied my trade. It didn't seem possible; my pants, my shoes and my tie taken while I slept. Jesus, these guys have no mercy. Happily I wasn't in Minnesota and it wasn't the dead of winter – just the tail end.

I only planned on two drinks then home to sleep off my overseas trip; instead, I was laying on a bench in my shorts on a subway platform. There was no one on the platform, so I skulked off toward by office just three blocks from the station. Thank god the streets were still dark. The office building security guard, Morris, saw me approaching the building

He smiled and waved to meet him at the side door.

"Been partying again, Joey."

"Oh Yeah!"

"She must have been some greedy chick, taking your pants like that."

"Unsatisfied and demanding and demanding: I had a 3 hour boner because she insisted I take all the Viagra she had in her medicine chest."

"Some guys have all the luck, Joey."

"Morris, I'll make you a deal. Get me to my office and I'll hook you up with her as soon as I get my wallet back from her."

"Don't do me any favors, Joey. She is clearly one bad ass crook."

I took the keys gratefully and sauntered over to the elevator, punched the button for the fortieth floor, leaned into the back wall of the elevator listening to "swoosh" from the new elevator. I was eager to get to the office, shower, get some cash and, if I was careful before I went out, get a bit of brandy in my coffee.

When I turned on my computer an hour later I saw an email I had written to myself from London on Friday: "Got to stop drinking. It's killing me, but what would I do with clients if I quit. I'd be so dull I'd get fired and then I'd really be in trouble. Take pills. Drink less. That's the answer."

Morris was all smiles when I came down from my office, all cleaned up, in a 3 piece suit, wearing highly polished shoes. I gave him the keys to the office and $20 bucks from the stash in my office safe where, luckily, I found my wallet and credit card. Apparently I had left them in the safe before going off to a Monday night football party at our neighborhood bar.

"Want a coffee, Morris?"

"Sure, Mr. J. (He always called me Mr. J. when I gave him a twenty) "Make it black and a strawberry bagel, buttered, if they have one. Otherwise, any flavor will do, but not toasted. I've got a microwave."

"Okay. See you in an hour or so."

Walking south on Third Avenue, I headed for a diner across the street from Smith & Wolensky, my favorite watering hole, a place with Martinis that made the hair on my feet stand up, "Great booze, great steaks that's S & M," I said to the world at large as I bought my paper and headed across the street to the diner.

I hesitated before I entered looking in a showroom window to check out my appearance. I wondered if there was any permanent taint of the night of craziness showing. My eyes still looked too red; Vicine had not taken the red out. My head was pounding and I could see a vein pulsating in my neck or was it my carotid getting ready to explode and send me to the level of Hell reserved for drunks and those who had no sense of discipline and debauched themselves into Hell at a young age…. Dante still ran through my brain even though I'd dumped the religion bit and the holy rollers of my upbringing before I got out of high school after having sex with Diane Woolston on Jones Beach after her junior pro. Sex was great and lightning did not strike me dead after that first great ejaculation into a womb instead of a sheet or a pillow.

Looking closer I saw I was still a formidable figure: six foot, 200 pounds, no belly showing, plenty of golden blond hair, a square jaw, no black eyes or scars on my Norwegian face. I was a sleek, muscular Viking – a good replica of the genetic disposition granted me by my ancestors. I guess I was really drunk last night; otherwise no one could have robbed and stripped me on a subway platform, maybe on a train. I wished I could remember.

Halfway through an omelet, coffee and orange juice my cell phone rang. It was Buzz, a fellow who took me to an AA meeting a few weeks ago after I'd called and asked if someone could come over and get those deadly dragons out of my apartment because they were tearing at my flesh and I couldn't figure out how to get rid of them.

Buzz and his buddy, Harry, came over. Buzz was six foot four or five and Harry looked like professional boxer with hands the size of hams.

They were good to me. They gave me a drink of bourbon. It helped. My body stopped shaking and the dragons started to fade as I downed the third shot.

Buzz had not seen a dragon in his apartment since he stopped drinking when he was 25 years old some 20 years earlier. Back then he said he was sleeping on top of heating grates in NYC in the winter so he wouldn't freeze to death. "Sadly, I wasn't careful enough. What drunk is? I lost several toes frost bite because I forgot to get my whole body, including my feet, on top of the grill."

Harry got sober in jail after a DUI almost killed him and his four year old daughter. He was sober, he said, for 10 years now, married to another woman and had sole custody of his daughter because her Mom died of an overdose.

"Hey Joey, what's up," Buzz said as he walked over to table and sat down.

"Buzz, I'm losing it."

"Really?"

"God, I can't believe I said that."

"Is it true?"

"Yep," I said as the tears streamed down my face. "I can't face it anymore," I yelled like some lunatic on the street.

The whole restaurant looked at me and a cop on the end got up and started toward us.

Buzz looked up. He said to the police officer, "Billy-- how's the family?"

"Good Buzz, thanks. What's with your friend?"

"Bad night…"

"Want a ride to Bellevue? I could take a few minutes. We could check him in. No arrest on his record. Does he have insurance," he asked Buzz as if I wasn't even there.

"What do you think, Joey? Want to go away for awhile?" Buzz asked.

"I can't. Not today."

"You sure?"

"Not Bellevue, okay, somewhere else."

"Okay. Do you want to go home or to a sober house in Midtown?"

I stared into space, turning the idea over in my head of going home or going somewhere with people who would keep me from drinking for awhile, a place where I could eat and sleep without fear of the shakes and sweats and the pain in the brain that seemed to demolish my resolve not to drink, to stay sober when I wake up in the middle of the night with a pounding heart and the sweats and the shakes.

"What about my job?"

"Call in sick. The flu bug is big right now. In a week you'll be fit as a fiddle, won't he Billy."

"You bet. Five days and you'll feel like a new man. Sure beats getting sick all over the conference table in front of clients or getting cuffed and tossed into holding downtown. Been there yet?"

"Oh yeah, I've been there. Okay. Let's go."

In the patrol car, I called the office and told them I had the flu. I left the message on the answering machine. It was 7:30 AM. No one was in the office yet. It felt a bit cowardly but I was starting to shake again when Buzz gave me a drink.

"It's the last till the sober house," he said.

A perky young woman with blond hair and blue eyes, an angel as I saw it, greeted us at the front desk.

She and Buzz spoke for a few minutes while I sat down at a table with a nurse who took my vital signs then asked me to blow into a breathalyzer like the cops use to test drunk drivers. I was over the legal limit but they agreed to take me because Buzz vouched for me and paid the $1,000 in cash for my 7 day stay.

"I'll pay you back."

"Just get well and you do the same thing for someone when you can," Buzz said as he headed out the door with Billy.

"Thanks."

"No problem."

As the nurse started my physical, I started to look around the room. On the wall was a plaque with the 12 steps of AA, a picture of Bill Wilson and Dr. Bob Smith, "co-founders of AA" it said on the bottom of the plaque. There was a big banner that said "Let GO and Let GOD for today".

"You will be her for 7 days, Joe. No phones. No TV. No outside influences. You need to sit and talk and figure out how you are going to change your life. You're in pretty tough shape. Your blood pressure is that of man of 50 and you're only 30. You must have been an athlete because a weaker man would most likely be in the cardiac ward of a hospital. You will have to watch your diet. We'll get you started on a healthier diet and give you some lessons in meditation so you can get rid of the anxiety that Buzz said you exhibited in spades when he went to your apartment a couple of weeks ago. Okay?"

"Sure," I said. What else could I say? I was in protective custody for a week. My expenses were covered. There was no bar on the door. I could leave anytime. So I closed my eyes and fell into a deep sleep."

The old nightmare seeped into my brain. Once again I was in a cave and the ceiling started to collapse on me so I ran as fast as I could to get out somehow even though there was not a door to be seen, just a light of some kind, a soft light that kept drawing me to it until I was awake, heart pounding, sweat covering my whole body and screaming like a donkey dropped into a crusher at a garbage dump or a soldier wounded and screaming in pain until the morphine was pushed into his body and he fell back unconscious of the pain.

Two people came running down the hall. I screamed, "Who are you? Where am I? Don't hurt me anymore, please. I'll tell you what you want to know. Please don't beat me anymore," I screamed as I curled up into the fetal position determined to protect me manhood and as many parts of my body as I could from the rubber hose I knew was on its way.

An angel's voice floated into my consciousness: "Fear not Joey. We are friends; we will help you; we won't beat you. Now, slowly let yourself relax. Ok. I'm going to give you a vitamin shot. It will make you feel much better. You are perfectly safe. Ok."

I looked up between my arms in the direction of the soft voice speaking to me. I could feel her hand rubbing my back just like Mom did when I was a child and fell off my bike and scrapped my knee. She was simply magnificent: blond, blue eyed, perfect skin, with gleaming white teeth, small lips and a smile as wide as the ocean.

"Who are you," I asked.

"I'm Sally Wells and I am your nurse for the next five days from 4 to 12 here at the Stepping Stone sober house. You're here because you have a drinking problem. Your friends brought you here because they were afraid you would die without some medical help. You have been here since yesterday and you just woke up."

"Can I have drink?"

"No. You can't drink alcohol anymore, Joey. It's not good for you. It's poison for you."

"Won't I die now?"

"I hope not," she laughed. "God, the paperwork would take a couple of days to fill out if you died today. Please don't die today. Wait until after treatment. Who knows, you might even want to keep living a little longer once the booze and junk is out of your system. Okay?"

"Okay" I said with a sense that it would be okay and I could be happy as she seemed to be once again.

I went back to sleep, woke up famished. Sally brought me a plate of eggs and buttered toast, orange juice and coffee – really steamy and strong coffee—and I devoured it all as if I had not eaten ever before in my life. I was still hungry but Sally said, "No more, Joey. First, you have to come with me to an AA meeting in the main room. We'll see how you feel after the meeting. If you are still hungry I'll get you some more. Okay?"

"Lead on, Sally, me girl" I said in my best, fake Irish brough.

"You'll need to work on that brough, Joey. My daddy was from the old sod. You need a lot of work to convince me you're from the old sod. My Daddy had plate that said, "An Irishman is not drunk as long as he can hold onto a blade of grass and not fall off the world.""

"I like him already, Joey said.

"Well, Joey, I'm sorry to say he died in an alcohol induced convulsion when I was six months old. That plate was the only thing he took with him when his family brought him to America from Ireland when he was 10 years old."

"I'm so sorry, Sally."

"Me to," she said as she sat me down in the front row next to another resident who, like me, was dressed in a blue sweat shirt, blue sweat pants with PBA on the side and sandals without laces; all donated by the

NYPD when they changed to more visible yellow and red sweats at the academy.

Buzz was sitting at the table in the front of the room of 50 or so men and women. When he saw me he got up and come over to shake my hand and say "I'm glad you made it. The day nurse said you were nip and tuck for awhile. You're a lucky guy. You have a second chance. Hope you take it. I'll talk to you after the meeting. Okay?"

"Sure, I'm not going anywhere. I'm recovering from the flu, remember."

"Yeah; I remember," Buzz replied before walking back to the front table.

Buzz tapped on the microphone and called the meeting to order by reading a mission statement that ended with the "only requirement for membership is a desire to stop drinking." I wondered if I "really" had a desire to stop partying, but I decided to listen. After all this guy had put up $1,000 in cash to get me treatment I couldn't afford and it would have ruined my life if I had been put in a hospital and had my physical condition subject to scrutiny by an insurance company and human resource folks. I'd have been kicked out the door like Mat and May and Larry; they all got fired one year to the day after they were hospitalized for alcohol and drug abuse.

"The world is a cold place" Daddy always said as he "knocked me around and you better learn it now instead of later." I took it until I was fourteen and as big as I am now. Then, I threw him through the front window when he came at me with his almighty belt, wanting to beat me up because I broke a dish when it was my turn to clear the table.

By the time Dad got home from the hospital a few days later I had moved in with my friend Mike's family. The next time I saw Dad his body was stone cold. He got drunk and stumbled into the path of a car on dark a country road near Duluth, MN, a mile from his favorite gin mill – a smoky, wooden building filled with his kind of people – drunks who laughed and fought with one another over which football team was the best or which baseball team or hockey team deserved to be on top.

Buzz started to speak: "I had my last drink on July 4, 1989. It was a beer just before a fight broke out at my favorite watering hole in Manhattan and I got tossed in the drunk-tank for the night. It was a pretty nasty place. Any of you folks been there too" he said as he raised his hand. "Oh yeah," the fellow next to me said as he raised his hand.

"So," Buzz said, "most of you know how ugly that place is to be. I'm going to skip past that mess and tell you about the guy who came to help me the next morning. He was a minister at the church of a friend who I had called to beg for someone to pay my bail and get me out of there. He saw me at my worst and he got out of a warm bed to come help me. I'm pretty self-centered and this kind of help is rare so I figured the man deserved a hearing.

He told me:

> "When I was a young pastor, I was assigned to a Church on Long Beach Island, New Jersey. There was an airport nearby and the most influential member of the parish had a son who was paralyzed from the waist down. This young fellow was an avid aviator. He owned and operated a small plane, flying from the local airport where I was called on too many occasions to help folks injured when a plane hit the wires not too far from the airport. The young man's name was Joseph P – nickname, Joey. Joey often invited me to go for a flight with him. I was reluctant but I had a feeling it was necessary to accept his invitation or I'd look like a coward of some kind or a man with little faith. After all he had been flying from the same airport for 5-years without an accident. Where was my faith?
>
> One day I said, "Okay, Joey, Can we go after Sunday service?"
>
> "You betcha," he said with that Minnesota expression that makes New Yorkers laugh like you just did."
>
> I was really nervous when his Dad picked Joey up from his car and carried this paralyzed from the waist down young man and placed him in the pilot's seat. Then, I got in."
>
> "You ready," he said.

"Oh yeah," I replied fearful I'd wet my pants before we got off the ground and my heart nearly stopped as we went up over the wires that had captured so many planes in the past year.

"Well," he said, "Joey and I became great friends and we went for a flight on many Sunday afternoons. I got to see more the ocean and surrounding cities from the perspective of a man in a small plane less than 5,000 feet above the ground."

Then, he said to me: "Buzz – to get the benefits of a full life we have to take a chance. You have been given a second chance. You're alive and you can live sober. You can live a better life. I hope you will fly the path AA offers you. It's got to be better than bouncing in and out of that drunk-tank."

My friends, the pastor had his Joey fear and I had my "can't live without booze fear."

Happily, my friends, I never turned back and have never had a drink, a drug or spent a night in the drunk tank since that Day that Minister I barely knew got my sorry ass out of jail and shared his story with me about Joey.

I hope you all have the same experience after hearing the story that Matt of the 47th Street noon time big book meeting will share with you tonight. Matt…the floor is yours."

I didn't hear a word that Matt said. My mind was spinning.

I was thinking of all the times I had said I will change but didn't, all the times I promised myself and others that I would quit drinking so badly but didn't. In fact, it occurred to me I never really committed to put alcohol aside. I had quit for a year a couple of times in high school and college but I never really said, "this is it and I'm off the sauce until I die because it keeps making me do stupid and dangerous things and hang out at dangerous places."

Sally winked at me as I left the meeting after a long talk with Buzz about what I might do when I leave this place. I just don't remember anything I said to him. In the morning all I could remember was the sanity of the statement that it was best to just "not drink today" and see what the world would bring your way as well as accept the present results as okay.

One guy at the meeting had said, "I had one eye on yesterday, one eye on tomorrow, so I was cockeyed today." I laughed out loud at his comment, a belly laugh that had not been part of my life in a long time- an authentic laugh that welled up from the navel and enveloped the whole body.

Buzz said, "Maybe you laughed so hard because it described how you were living your life when you were running from bar to bar to try to make sense of life and your place in it?"

18 months later:

After dinner with the guys from my regular Monday night AA meeting on 22nd and Park Avenue, I wandered through a book store, picking up a copy of *Joan of Arc* by Mark Twain because one of my friends was as big a fan of Mark Twain as I was and told me that Twain thought this was the only book he had written that was worthwhile. Twain, according to the book jacket, said 'She was the most remarkable woman in history." Such great praise for what I had always thought was a psycho-girl by Twain piqued my curiosity. I decided to settle down for an hour a night for the next few nights until I finished it.

My life had really changed since I was let out of the sober house and stopped drinking, attending a AA meeting a few times every week just to make sure that I could tell someone I was keeping on the track and trying my best to practice being honest, open-minded and willing to change and let go of whatever was going to make me a morose, cynical, joke telling guy who tossed down martinis and imported beers and wines like a crazy man – turning into a crazy man.

I was much stronger, some 40 pounds lighter and muscular rather than flabby. I was running five miles and day, nearly every day with a bunch of guys and gals from the neighborhood who I had met at meetings or in the mini-marathons that I ran for a variety of causes – breast cancer marathons had become my favorite because I always met at least one woman who I'd meet for dinner a couple of times. Sadly, none of the women I dated really held my attention for long. I was not really looking for a long time relationship, just fun and a bit of sex. The women I met were not really hot for just a fling: the dangers of HIV and other STDs made everyone wary and cautious unless, of course, they got drunk or high on some drug or another and just let the rational mind evaporate.

The one thing I noticed was the girls I met were usually glad to see I didn't drink or drug. Some were put off, thinking I was some kind of head case or fanatic – like a Baptist preacher's son from Minnesota or something like that – who just was too rigid or frail to be worth getting to know. On the other hand, all the women I dated were at least 30 so they had experienced a wild ride with a drunk driver or some guy who bent over in the curb and threw up after too much to drink. One lawyer my boss introduced me to was glad I didn't drink because she was handling family court cases and in too many of those cases the guy got drunk and beat up his wife or girl friend.

Over dinner on our first date she said, "Sex without booze is real sex—liberating sex that can last a long time without the help of Viagra, especially," she continued," if the guy doesn't smoke."

"Really: You know I don't smoke."

"Oh yeah," she said.

We went to her place before desert and proved her theory. When I went home in the morning after eating her special cheese omelet and a roll in the shower, I was weak in the knees. She called later and said, "I'm bow-legged. See you tonight at 7?" "You betcha," I said.

She was my first real sexual relationship after a year of trying to just get my life back in order. It lasted about six months and ended when she went to Paris on business and returned with a French Nobel in tow; a fellow lawyer and a guy who was ready to commit to life together. His family owned a vineyard. They had met at a wine tasting and he simply swept her off her feet. Since we were not living together, I told her to feel free to toss my sweats in the trash and that I would be available for lunch if she needed to talk. Then, I hung up and screamed into the noisy New York traffic surrounding me as I tucked my cell into to my pocket.

Buzz said, "Sorry, Man. I guess she wasn't the one, the soul mate you thought she was. At least you hadn't given her the ring."

All I could say was, "Fuck. I have to start dating?"

"Yeah," Buzz said, "unless you want to be a celibate single. Take my word for it, celibate single sucks. I did that for about 6 months when I was 35 and totally tired of the dating scene. Then, one day I met Carol. After that, I was on with life, happy, even fulfilled because she was the real soul mate I was waiting for or the one that I was ready for because I had grown up and accepted the idea no one is fricking perfect—just human. I liked everything about her."

"So, if you can do it without a drink, I can too?"

"Yep, you will meet the right woman at the right time but you have to be there, fully present to appreciate her and see her in your life."

"Thank you Buddha."

"You're welcome smart ass...." He laughed just before I ordered desert – an apple pie ala mode with chocolate syrup, a dietary delicacy I had not eaten in more than a year to try to calm the sense of loss within.

The next afternoon, I met Sally Wells as I was completing my jog from 30th and Park to Wall Street and back. She was just strolling down Park on her way to work. I fell in next to her and we chatted about nothing except what a great day it was and how she was busy with new people at the sober house.

"It seems the bad economy is getting a lot of people to get straight and sober before they lose everything and the patients are a lot younger too. These new drugs are just knocking them down a lot faster than when you were scoring and boozing," she said.

"Well. I'm glad to hear the biz is good. I don't miss that life at all. It was so fricking chaotic, not to mention scary when I woke up in some of the places I woke up," I quickly shot back, probably a bit too quickly because it felt like maybe I was still embarrassed by the life I had led and wanted to assure her a bit too firmly that I was a new guy.

"You want a coffee," she said.

"If you can handle the sweaty mess in a public place."

"Not a problem for me," she laughed, "remember the crazies I work with."

As we sipped our coffee, Sally looked me in the eye and asked, "So, tell me Joseph"

"No Joseph. Only the cops and doctors call me Joseph."

"Ok. So tell me Joey, is sober better?"

"Oh yeah."

"Okay. So, Joey there is a question I've wanted to ask since I first met you, but I wasn't sure."

"Sally, you can ask me anything. How could I have a secret from you? You saved my sorry ass, didn't you?"

"Ok. So here's the question. What caused all those scars your back and legs? Were you tortured by someone?"

I put my cup down and thought about getting up and walking away because this was subject I never really discussed with anyone, but this was Sally, an experienced ER nurse, a friend, someone who had saved my life. Still…

"If I tell you, I'd have to kill you," I laughed.

"Oh. Come on. It's me. Don't go hiding behind that joking bit that keeps you stuck in the hole you dug yourself into."

"Ok. Here's what happened. My Dad was a mean guy. He beat me up as a kid. He stopped when I went to school because the welts would show up in gym class and they might raise questions. Then, I was captured by some bad guys when I was in the Secret Service and they – those cartel guys from south of the border – took a bull whip to me. Fortunately, the good guys arrived before those bastards killed me. Some of the surgeons thought they could fix them, you know, make them disappear, but I had no interest in going under the knife again."

"Jesus," Sally said. "Do they hurt?"

"Not anymore. Not anymore" I replied.

"So you carry a gun so those guys won't get you before you get them?"

"No. They are gone. They sleep with the fishes, as Vinnie said in the Godfather. I carry a gun because it makes me feel safe."

She looked up at me with that gaze of I'm going to ask but she stopped and said, "Thank you for telling me. I'm so sorry no one came to your rescue when you were a child."

"Me to: want a dish of ice cream?"

"Oh god, I'm going be late. Another time, ok. Walk with me to the house?"

When we got to the sober house, Sally asked me to brunch at her house on Sunday afternoon and I accepted. She gave me a hug and soft kiss on the left check. Then she was off, turning back with a big smile.

God, I was glad for the invite. Sundays were always a drag in the city and I had nothing planned except a run and lie in the embrace of the New York Times Magazine after lunch with some single guys I knew. Lunch with Sally, at her place, had a lot more promise than discussing sports and the 12 steps, divorce tactics and how to get the best deal for alimony, child support, visitations and all the other nonsense that is part and parcel of the old divorce process. I sure preferred lunch with Sally to lunch with guys like me who were in the search for the soul mate-mode while seeking some sort of financial foundation that felt more stable than steering a ship at sea on a windy, rainy day without a landfall in sight and a broken rudder.

Sally's home was an old brownstone in the 30s near Park Avenue. It was so big I just assumed there would be some 3 or 4 doorbells because there was no way she could afford to live in place like this on her own, but when I got up the stairs I saw there was only one bell. I shrugged my shoulders, put a big smile on my face and punched the bell. In a couple of minutes a very tall guy answered: "You must be Joseph," he said in a very British accent. "I'm the in-law, Mary's husband Harold, not the competition," he laughed. "Relieved?"

"I am. Where is Sally?"

"Through there to the kitchen mate."

Sally was busy chatting away when I entered the kitchen with flowers in hand. She gave me a big hug and thanked me for the flowers, then introduced me her sister, her niece and two of her girl friends from nursing school. With a Perrier in hand I was shunted to the living room to meet the guys while the girls got "the gossip" out of the way they said, almost in unison, as I was ushered out.

"This whole place is Sally's?" I asked Harold.

"Yes. Her folks left it to my wife and Sally but we wanted to live in Vermont so she got to keep it, live in it and pay half the taxes until our daughter Sarah turns 18 and needs money for college in about 3 years Then, we sell and the two sisters split the proceeds. Pretty cut and dried, I'm afraid. They never even did battle over it. No drama because their Mom kind of made sure the deal was done before she died a few years ago --Lovely woman, best mother in law I ever had, plus, she was the only one I ever had."

We went downstairs where a couple guys were playing pool and watching a baseball game between the NY and Chicago. Tim was a NYC cop, dating Sally's friend from nursing school. George was a reporter for the New York Times specializing in crime reporting but scheduled to move to the general news desk on Monday dating the other girl.

Tim noticed the sidearm under my left arm. Warily he said, "I see you're armed. How come?"

"Oh. I always carry. I'd rather have it with me than at my apartment where some burglar might take it. I'm ex Secret Service. Want to see my ID?"

"Actually, I would."

When he was satisfied, he said, "Why don't you lock that thing up with my weapon? It will make the girls much happier, especially Tim's girl who works the domestic violence desk in the 15th."

With guns away we played a heated game of pool with the cop and the ex cop against the reporter and the in-law who was a surgeon working in a small hospital in Vermont so he and his wife could ski and the children could experience the life of a small town before going off to study in England, they hoped.

We were tied when Sally came in and said, "Okay Boys the games over. Dinners ready. All your secrets are out. The girls are ready for a happy meal and we all promise not to dwell on any of your faults until desert – at least."

"Sally said you're a big fan of Twain," Sally's sister Sarah said.

"I am."

"What's your favorite?"

"Joan of Arc because Twain said it was the only work he wrote that was worthwhile."

"Really? I thought Huck Finn was his best."

"Huck Finn was his most popular, that's for sure, but he said Joan was his best. He considered her one of the most significant people in history because at 17 she was able to lead an army, end the Hundred Years war in a few months, freeing France of the British -- Sorry Harold but England wasn't always such a great country – and she did it all without any education, money, connections or training of any kind. Remarkable, don't you think. She was only 3 years older than your daughter."

"Remarkable, indeed, but surely she was mad and the French were desperate," Harold replied.

"Mad or inspired she was some general and the remarkable thing is that she only asked the King of France to promise to not have the people in her village pay any more taxes after she won back his throne and country. She asked nothing for herself. Isn't that remarkable?"

"I can't imagine a leader of today doing anything like save a country from an enemy for so little," Tim the reporter chimed in as he proposed a toast "to the Soul of Joan and may she infuse her spirit of charity into the souls of our leaders."

"Fat chance," the cop laughed, as we all lifted our glasses in a toast to Joan and a toast to Mark Twain. Then, at Harold's insistence, we lifted our glasses in a toast to the special relationship between America and England.

Before the table was cleared, Sally looked at the watch and said, "Joey and I have to walk a couple of blocks to get that special ice cream I forgot to get. You guys clean up and we'll be right back.

As we walked back with the ice cream, a guy walking toward us stepped in front of us, pointing a knife in our direction. "Give me your money," he said, his hand shaking.

"Sure. Honey will you hold the ice cream while I get my wallet for this guy" I said as I handed the ice cream to Sally, reaching back as if to get a wallet. Then, I simply grabbed hold of his right wrist and hit him as hard as I could in his Adam's apple, holding on to his right wrist as he fell back onto the ground. With my knee on his chest, I took the knife from his fingers.

Sally called the house. Tim came a few minutes later, put the cuffs on the mugger, called the station and few minutes later the guy was on his way to lockup. Tim told the officers, "I'm going back to the house for desert. You guys take the collar."

Sally was still shaking when we got back to the house, hanging onto my arm all the way home. "Jesus, Joey, you saved me from that knife wielding crazy."

"It's my job to keep you safe, Sally. Hell it's just pay back. You saved my life, didn't you?"

"I did, didn't I? Still, thanks, and you get an extra scoop of ice cream on your desert."

"It's a deal," I said, hoping for a bit more, but an extra scoop of ice cream was a good start, especially since it was my favorite --chocolate chip mint.

Sally asked me to stay when the family left. It was still early afternoon so we went for a walk, only this time I had my piece with me. I didn't feel as vulnerable as I did with the knife wielding mugger without my metal strapped to my side.

I could feel her squeezing my arm pretty hard when some guy started to walk toward us, especially when he had hooded sweatshirt on like the mugger from earlier. It was an alert that I used to assure her it was okay, even when she was telling me she had a dream of selling the house in the city, moving to the town of Snowmass, a little place a few minutes from Aspen, where she could have a dog, a couple of babies and work as a nurse in the local hospital that was always looking for people to work during the winter months in particular when the skiers and the tourists broke their bones and cracked their heads while skiing or snowboarding.

"And the summers are simply magnificent; the mountains are like a canvas in the Louve, filled with breathtaking colors."

"Sounds pretty good," said. "Wonder if they could use a guy who knows guns, suits and security in such an idyllic place?"

"Sure. You could be a tutor. And there are great AA meetings up there. Folks from New York and LA come there all year long. It's – what did you say – Idyllic for a guy in recovery with skills like yours."

"You know I'm a carpenter, plumber and all around fix up guy."

"Really"

"Oh yeah, but first, I think we need to check out our living and playing together skills."

"Hey. I'm up for it," she laughed.

"Me too, "I replied as we embraced under a tree on 14th.

DRONES ATTACK D.C.

President John Bartlett entered his 2nd four year term on January 22, 2020, after capturing 67% of the vote, with nearly 72% of registered voters going to the polls.

He ran as a "peacenik" – a nation builder. His new policy was "rebuild America by cutting back on military forces, worldwide. To the conservative GOP wing of Congress his view was as big a threat to the future as the American Revolution was to King George III in 1776.

"Sovereign nations," President Bartlett said, "should be free to become what their people want. Change could come about by armed revolution, the ballot box or a military coup. In each case, America is not required – I repeat -- not required --- to act as a surrogate paren. A nation's political future is its own responsibility. There is no constitutional imperative in the U.S. Constitution saying any nation must become a democracy like ours or that we must help them achieve Democracy.

"I will not let our sons and daughters become cannon fodder to solve the political problems of other nations. Washington and Jefferson warned us to "avoid foreign entanglements". We forgot their good sense when we invaded Hawaii, tossed out their royal family, and took over the Island nation for the benefit of Dole Pineapples as part of our Manifest Destiny mindset."

"Thus, in the spirit of Washington and Jefferson I have ordered the withdrawal of all US troops from every nation hostile to us. Within a year, military forces in Asia and Europe will be cut in half. America will no longer be an empire builder like the U.K. that our forefathers tossed from our shores in 1776.

Let me be perfectly clear: Islamic extremists kill one another over what some see as theological differences that others see as power plays based on their group's desire to control the wealth and people of their nations. This administration has decided to "Let them kill one another until they tire of killing one another."

During my administration, we will no longer have relations with any Islamic nation until that nation has a Constitution that allows freedom of religion and courts of law that are based on human rights as defined by our Constitution and/or by the UN Charter on Human Rights.

We will not support, do business with, or have diplomatic relations with any country that permits the whipping and stoning of men and woman, sometimes even allowing the raping of women for marrying the person they love and not the person their village elders or parents want them to marry.

President Bartlett explained:

> "The delusion that America could create democracies like ours with force of arms as Bush, Cheney, Rumsfeld proposed is as obvious as the snow falling on us today. Kings and Military regimes still rule in many parts of the former Persian Empire. The religious fanatics on both sides have refused to stop killing one another because they cannot agree which version of Islam is the "right" version.
>
> I will not put one more American life on the line to save the life of some other nation. We will let these folks fight it out, kill one another until they get tired of killing one another and choose peaceful negotiation rather than mutual murder to resolve their differences.
>
> We have plenty of energy to operate our growing economy for a century or more, enough sources of energy in surplus to withstand the stoppage of oil shipments from countries in the Middle East.

"My fellow Americans," President Bartlett concluded, "We enter a new age, an age where our needs will come first, when our national infrastructure will be rebuilt, our children's educational needs attended to in a more robust way, and, if we do this right, our tax rates will fall as our indebtedness and interest expenses tumble."

Tomorrow, I am sending a proposal to the House and Senate that will make sure every American has a stake in America's future, asking the Congress to require that every working person pay a minimum of 5% of their earnings every April, 15th.

The 5% tax will apply to all taxpayers with an income of $100,000 or less. For those with incomes over $100,000 a flat tax of 15% will apply to all incomes – corporate and personal -- with no tax deductions for anyone.

In this way the richest and the poorest will support their government to assure the Constitutional Guarantees that this Federal Government is required to provide."

President Bartlett's comments rocked the lobbyist world in DC – a community that earned, on average, twice the national average and was growing at 3 times the rate of the rest of the country. This growth was achieved because companies and lobbyist groups gathered in DC for a seat at the table when budget dollars were distributed by all Departments of the US Government as part of its Multi trillion dollar annual budget.

- Cutting the US military in half would free up $350 Billion for construction projects in the USA, projects long held back because of the size of the US Defense Departments budget.
- Embassies in Muslim nations constantly attacking and berating America as "occupiers" and "Satan" would be leased by Switzerland at $1 a year to serve US citizens visiting those countries.
- All CIA employees would be removed from Middle Eastern and Muslim nations.

- Any US citizen employed by a US company in any Islam country would be required to sign a waiver saying "I agree to work in this war zone and do not and will not expect any help from US forces if I am captured by hostiles in this Islamic country."

The isolationists that New York papers referred to as the "Let us dress in britches again muskets gang" in the most "conservative" and dominant wing of Congress agreed to one provision that "sticks in my craw" Speaker Bain proclaimed after President Bartlett explained why he was focusing on US needs rather than the needs of the rest of the world.

With Speaker Bain's support, The GOP House agreed to a Dem controlled Senate proposal that a US based company could no longer keep its taxable profits overseas for as long as it wanted – a hole in the US tax code Congress had refused to close for decades.

Under this provision US based corporations had accumulated nearly $6 Trillion in taxable profits offshore by 2020 without paying any tax because the corporations only had to a pay tax on those profits if they were returned to the USA as they were in 2005 @5% instead of @ 35% tax rate.

So, President Bartlett asked Congress to require all US based companies to pay taxes due on their overseas profits at the end of each quarter; and, for good measure, no company would be allowed to pay less than 15% of its profits in federal taxes each year – a number that was approximately 2.5% below the "effective" tax that US corporations paid on average after all legal deductions were allowed under the current, often referred to as "convoluted" and "mysterious" tax code. He also proposed a moratorium on new tax standards for citizens and corporations for 3 years as a way to assure the "transition to sanity" as the President Bartlett supporters called his proposed changes in taxes.

Finally, President Bartlett declared his intention to allocate 5% of all Federal taxes and fees collected each month to pay down the principal on the national debt, reducing interest payments and giving the US dollar a chance to once again reign as the most favorable currency in world trade.

These financial changes satisfied the super liberals in the Congress as well as the super conservatives because both got an issue for the 2022 mid-term election that would appeal to their bases in a nation that was as gerrymandered for re-election as it had been in 1808 and 2008 when a Democrat was elected President and a super conservative GOP majority won control of the US House.

Aspen, Colorado:

Henry Coal and his brother Harris, co-owners of a $80 Billion oil and gas consortium they had built because of their foresight to invest heavily in North Dakota when "Fracking" opened up the enormous gas fields in that state. The Brothers were leaders of the "Muskets Party" in Colorado where their company was headquartered.

They listened to the speech of the newly elected "fricking liberal-commie-asshole president" as they described him to friends and colleagues, in horror.

"That son of a bitch," Henry exclaimed as the speech ended. "He is actually going to do what he threatened the last time we saw him. I thought he was just blowing smoke up our ass. It will cost us Billions if he succeeds. Shit. How do we get this nonsense shredded? It will cost us billions!"

"Hard to say brother: I think he's gotta go. He's not motivated to stay in the Middle East, pushing our troops and weapons into the area!" Harris replied, raising a fresh glass of bourbon to his lips, "He will kill our companies in the weapons business and threaten our oil and gas interests. It's not acceptable. It's time for the nuclear option."

"So we call Bo and tell his it's a go?"

"Yep," Harris replied as a big smile filled is puffy, red face, as he flared his rather large, red nose.

New Mexico

"Bo: a.k.a. Boregard Waters, a retired 42-year-old fighter pilot who had spent his youth in the skies over Iraq until he was shot down and tossed into a prison for nearly a year, living like a trapped rat, lucky to have survived brutal treatment from an enemy with little regard for his life or wellbeing unless he said America is the enemy and ought to go home when his captors asked.

Bo was one of those prisoners who never gave in to his captors. His granddaddy had been a soldier in the war in the Pacific, captured and wounded, surviving the Battan Death March – a lucky man who never stopped eating after he came home until he passed away at 87 when the heart in his 300 pound body just blew up while he was sitting at a family bar-b-que devouring his third plate of ribs.

Bo had voted for President Bartlett twice, but he never really expected to hear what he considered "capitulation to the godless" as he liked to describe the whacko terrorists who killed without mercy in the name of some god or another at the behest of some Iman or preacher or demigod like the current Presidents of Pakistan and Afghanistan who Bo saw as "Hop heads, hooked on white powder sold to children, so they could keep paying off crazy-religious- whacko- guys with guns to stay in power and salt away Billions in bribes."

When the phone rang, Bo smiled. It was them- "The Cossacks" - as he called the Coal brothers who pulled the oil from the ground and used the money to take America back from the peaceniks and the commies who had no respect for those men and women who fought and died and limped around the world on iron legs after serving their country in bitter wars between the US and the Muslim crazies who fought with the viciousness of a junk yard dogs and these religious crazies who, like the Viet Cong in his Daddy's Day, never surrendered, preferring to let children blow themselves with bombs than withdraw from the field.

Bo was horrified at the potential death of America and its dream if Bartlett pulled the plug on America's military might.What did my friends and brothers in arms fight and die for if not to see the dream of America available for everyone in the world?

For Bo, Bartlett had become a traitor to ideas that drove America, a man who forgot the suffering of the men and women who fought and died or got seriously maimed fighting to free Iraq and Afghanistan.

"Yes."

"Bo: Harris here. It's a go."

"When?"

"Today, during the walk!"

"Funds transferred?"

"Courier will be at your door in a few minutes. Plane at the airport and ready to take you anywhere you want to go."

"Ok."

As he set down the phone, Bo slapped his hands together like a man wanting to wake up a room full of sleeping children. He even slapped himself in the face as he walked to the front door to see if the courier was on his way up the drive. Sure enough, the motorcycle was just rounding the corner and starting up the drive. Bo put his jacket on to cover his holster with a 9mm-Glock, safety off.

One million dollars in US $100 bills was intact, as was the $20,000,000 in bearer bonds, denominated in Swiss Francs and Euros, with 6% coupons so Bo could spend them anywhere in the world with little hassle because banks would treat them as cash.

Bo went to his shed, pulled back a false wall in the middle of the shed and fired up a sophisticated computer system. He pulled out the codes to a number of drones sitting on the tarmac at Andrews, outside the nation's capital and fired them up.

Quickly the drones were headed for Washington, DC at altitudes of 100 and 500 feet. Bo figured two could fail or hit a building, suggesting there was a mal-function on the system, rather than a deliberate attempt to kill President Bartlett and block his attempt to turn America into a more peaceful nation.

When 5 drones headed toward DC popped up on D.C. radar, U.S. Air Force planes scrambled to stop them. Jets scheduled to entertain the crowds lining Pennsylvania to cheer America's newly elected President were sent to stop the invaders. Phones buzzed as the president's protectors quickly pushed him into the limousine dubbed the "Brick" because it was considered unbreakable.

Bo watched three drones shot down by planes and missiles, one hit a building and one drone crash into Pennsylvania Avenue within 100 feet of the "Brick" should turn President Bartlett and many of his entourage into dust. Landing that close to the "Brick" made it breakable with 10-pounds of C-4 in them.

It had been tougher than Bo planned to aim the drone. He had to shoot at a moving target because the Lojack ® like device had not been installed on the "Brick" by the inside man at the White House, so Bo led the Brick as he would a deer running in the forest and crashed one of his drones into the middle of Pennsylvania Avenue.

"Mission accomplished!" Bo sent in an email to the *Brothers of the Revolution,* a militia style organization he joined a few months earlier as James Johnson with an IP address registered in Alabama, the message routed through an internet café in Colorado outside Denver.

Bo set a timer device to a bomb that would completely destroy his shed in one hour after he left on a Lear to London as Mr.Henrie Teller a diplomat with a Canadian passport, granting him passage into Europe without clearing customs.

Washington, DC – same day.

In DC the media stood in stunned silence, unable to get back on its feet because many top reporters were injured or killed when the drones exploded near the President and people lining Pennsylvania Avenue to get a glimpse of the President as he strolled along on his "march of triumph, a conquering hero" as Box News liked to describe these strolls down Pennsylvania Avenue after the President and Vice President took their oath of office. Several reporters were killed.

The streets of DC quickly filled with armed men in uniforms, as ambulances rushed to the site of what the Press Corps immediately called "An Attack on the President just after he declared a desire for world peace and less American arms and dollars spent on the hot spots of the world".

Tom Phillips, head of Secret Service Protective Services, swiftly assembled a team of additional agents for the Speaker of The House and the Secretary of State because it was likely they would be sworn in as President and Vice President as soon as his men could get one of the Supremes to the Rotunda in the Capital where all the political well-connected and fund raisers for the President were gathered for a lunch to congratulate President Bartlett on his re-election after his walk of triumph down Pennsylvania Avenue.

Speaker Henry Bain was not a friend of President Bartlett.

The Speaker did not agree with Bartlett's "America First" mindset and the Speaker felt the President was too tough on business. He was a libertarian, but he played Conservative in the GOP caucus because it was that stance that got him noticed, applauded and promoted as a party line guy who could be counted on when a brawl over some prickly piece of legislation came to the floor for a vote.

Speaker Bain was known as member of the "go along to get along" school of politics. His greatest fear was losing America's position as the country with the most powerful military in the world and his position as Speaker.

"We need guns to keep our butter fresh" was Speaker Bain's favorite closing line on the campaign trail in his Congressional District in Northern California, where military contractors were dominant employers.

"Look," Speaker Bain told President Bartlett a week earlier, "Soldiers stationed around the world keep the enemies of freedom on a leash."

Bartlett replied, "Let's see what the world looks like in 3 to 5 years, Mr. Speaker: that leash is too expensive."

Secretary of Defense Pinero walked up to the Speaker shaking his head, his hands on his ears looking like someone who did not want to hear what he was hearing as news of the President's impending death notice was whispered around the room.

"Mr. Secretary," Speaker Bain said: "Before I am sworn in I want to hear from you that all ignition switches on all drones in our arsenal have been removed from all drones. I don't want another lunatic with computer skills to use our own drones to kill any more people in the capital or anywhere else in America. This is a god-damn disgrace: some son of a bitch just murdered our commander in chief with weapons from our own arsenal, manufactured by our own people, on the streets our own country. We need to turn those fucking pieces of metal off-- and now. Okay?"

"Done" DOD Secretary Pinero said, as he texted the order to all commands from his encrypted i-phone.

"Mr. Attorney General," the Speaker said: "Find these bastards. Fuck the Constitution. Just find them and kill them and let me know when it is done."

"Sir" the AG said as he walked down the steps to the subway in the Capitol with the Speaker and the rest of the cabinet as directed by the Secret Service contingent assigned to the Rotunda.

A few minutes after the Speaker had started to act like the new President, President Bartlett entered the Rotunda through a side door. He stood in front of a CNN camera to tell the world: "I am okay. My wife is okay. Sadly, the Vice President and his wife and too, too many civilians are not Okay. They have been murdered by cowards and cutthroats. I promise America will find these killers and squash them."

The Rotunda crowd went from tears to elation, giving the President a standing ovation and great shout of "Hurrah!" "USA, USA".

Speaker Bain and the Cabinet were turned around and escorted back to the Rotunda.

By dinner time, an all agency task force gathered at FBI Headquarters. Marvin Springer, an experienced investigator, a supervisor at Secret Service, a friend since grammar school of President Bartlett would lead the team. He seemed a perfect leader. He was trusted by President Bartlett. He had led a number of DOD teams that had captured or killed terrorists while serving in Afghanistan and Pakistan. For seven years he led teams sent to capture notorious criminals.

Marvin Springer looked every bit like the perfect agent. He was 6/2, 200 lbs., rock solid. He pressed 300 pounds in the gym 3 times a week. At the age of 42, Springer looked and acted more like a 20 year old on his first assignment; a man with energy and impatience, anxious to please himself and his superiors by finishing his tasks on time, tolerating few delays or excuses from underlings or himself.

One of his closest comrades in arms from what he referred to as the "old days" was Bo Waters, a contemporary who had saved his life on an operation in Iraq in 2010.

Marvin looked over the room of investigators assembled in one of the main auditoriums of the FBI, his head moving back and forth like a man in mourning, his eyes glazed over from disappointment and fear for his family and his country.

"Folks," Marvin said in a clear voice. "President Bartlett is my friend. He was a man I grew up with in a small town in Alabama. He is a patriot and a dear friend. The attempted murder of my friend after his re-election as our President and commander in chief is an outrage that will not stand, that cannot stand. The murder of nearly 50 of our citizens gathered to celebrate our democracy is simply unacceptable.

Now, we are charged with finding the bastards who did these murders. We are charged with bringing these bastards to justice as quickly as we can. We will not fail. We cannot fail. The world is watching us. We will get these bastards. There will be no inter-agency fighting over this one. Anyone starting a turf war will be transferred to Anchorage and assigned to snow removal. We cannot fail. We will not fail. Now, everyone who is with me on this commitment stand up; the rest can leave and no one will think any less of you because this will be a 24/7 all out assault like investigation in the U.S. and around the world. No holds barred.

I'll be back in a minute. I have a call from President Bartlett."

As Marvin left the room the room erupted in applause. Not one man or woman moved from their chair. It was the crime of the century and they all wanted to help find the killer or killers of the VP and innocent civilians on the streets of their city.

"Mr. President," Marvin said.

"Marvin. Can you do this? Can you be objective?"

"Sir, I'll find the bastard or bastards and I won't waste time or money until they are in a cage or in the ground."

"Ok. Keep me up to date. I want to be the first to hear about your progress. Ok?

"Yes Sir."

"Come to the White House for breakfast tomorrow morning. Let's discuss what needs to be done and what you intend to do. See you at 8."

"Yes Sir. We should have a plan by tonight."

"Good. I'm glad you're on this one Marvin."

"Thank you sir, I appreciate your confidence."

Next afternoon:

President Bartlett met with heads of all intelligence agencies in the Situation Room.

Everyone rose as President Bartlett entered the room and took the chair at the center of the table. He had decided to take this seat during his second term because he had never liked sitting at the head of the table, remembering how people who took that power seat in meetings when he was an investment banker did so as a means of intimidating others. He really hated to have to scrape and bow to the "biggest// swinging dick" in the room as they used to say when he was making his fortune on Wall Street.

After nearly dying he intended to shake up the troops and operate in a manner that suited him better.

"Ladies and Gentlemen," President Bartlett began. "We need to get the bastards who murdered so many of our men and women and children. These wonderful people must be avenged. The nation needs to see us as competent. It took ten years to get Osama. It's now 2020. We have better investigative techniques and we need to get this guy or people in a year or less or the nation's standing in the world will begin to fall further as the key country in the world. We need to assure our people we know how stop home grown terrorists. So, let's see what you have learned. Jim, you're first."

"Sir," General Scott began, "We tried to find out how anyone could snatch one drone from Andrews and use it to attack DC, let alone five armed drones. We can say that based on the size of the crater at the kill site, the killer used about 10 pounds of explosives per drone. It seemed impossible.

So far, Mr. President, we know these drones were delivered and held as reserves for the US Forest Service to use in the event of a forest fire or to find lost souls in the mountains of West Virginia, Maryland and Virginia. They were delivered to Andrews and placed in the reserve pool area five days before they were used to attack you.

Their papers seemed in order, Sir, but when we back tracked the orders we discovered several anomalies. The person who ordered their delivery was not real. The folks who signed for them at Andrews are real. The guards on duty who signed for these drones remember the delivery as being as normal as could be. The drones did not appear out of the ordinary."

"General, please, how were they armed and taken over?"

"Sir: Three days before the attack two men appeared at Andrews with orders to service the drones for the Forest Service. Their identities and papers were verified. They were on the roster of scheduled visitors. Security folks scanned their IDs.

One fellow was Dennis Thomas, a former member of the NSA and reputed to be one of their finest technicians; a fellow who had worked with our drone folks in New Mexico when we searched the world for Bin Laden. Mr. Thomas was clearly capable of secretly attaching the explosives to the Drones and operating them from a remote area. He could secretly program a drone to be operated by him or an accomplice.

"He was DOD?" President Bartlett sighed, shaking his head in disbelief.

"Yes Sir. He has found dead in his apartment last night. He died of a heroin overdose. The needle was sticking out of his left arm. He was dead on the floor of his bathroom. A suitcase of cash found in his closet contained $500,000 in hundreds."

His accomplice could be a man known as "Mr. GO" – the go to guy if there was an anomaly in the operation of the Drone program. Smart Guy, holds patents on pieces of the drone program that make them target accurately.

"Seems" is the operative word here because Mr. Go. – His real name is Mr. Boregard Waters.

Mr. Water's garage was blown up about 2 hours after the attack. His home is in Santa Fe, N.M. Our forensic teams said they found a lot of computer equipment in the garage debris but none of the evidence gathered so far can prove the software on the system was designed to operate a drone or a series of drones. IT experts are still searching the debris but they are not too optimistic. They think the main ingredients of the system could have been taken away from the scene before the explosion.

Most importantly, Mr. President, the bodies found at the scene were identified by DNA as local burglars; petty thieves with long records. It appears they opened up a gas line. The gas line apparently blew up when the fumes were ignited by a cigarette or a lighter that was found at the scene.

We are looking for Mr. Waters because facial recognition software picked him up as one of 1,200 possible folks who have been trained in the world of drones and are battle tested—men with the hubris to commit such a crime, according to the profilers. Most the 1,200 men and women have been identified and FBI agents are interviewing them as we speak.

We can't make a clear identification because the man never spoke. He wore a professional looking medical bandage around his neck and lower jaw so we can't get a clear picture of his jaw line and he had a patch on his left eye. The eye scanner has identified the man with Mr. Thomas as a "Clarence Patton" – an expert in computer science who died of a heart attack while camping in New Hampshire a month earlier.

If Mr. Waters is the man who committed this crime, we have a real problem. He won't break cover unless he wants to. He was trained in special ops. He is smart, tough, battle tested. He was awarded a silver star and two purple hearts for action in black ops as a member of a Navy Seal team operating in Afghanistan. He was there for 3 years. He served with Marvin, even saved his life on an operation according to Marvin. Marvin has been informed of our suspicion but Marvin thinks we are nuts to expect Mr. Waters. He said, "Bo is a patriot!"

"Jesus, "Chief of Staff Quist piped up: "How could a guy like that go so wrong? Marvin is probably right. Who else do we have?"

So, Mr. President we suspect – and it's only a suspicion – that someone, perhaps Waters, directed these drones from his shed in New Mexico and attacked D.C.

I must, however, report that we found no evidence to suggest he is a terrorist or tied to any terrorist group. He may not be the guy but he sure fits the profile from a skills point of view and his body type and facial features suggest he might be the one. It's only suspicious. We need to talk to him. Thus, we put out a worldwide warrant for him."

"The FBI director has details on our search, Sir."

"Thank you General. I am almost relieved it was probably an act of domestic terrorism like Timothy McVeigh instead of an Osama like plot because no one wants another Iraq, Afghanistan war. We just can't afford it until we get our house in order. Director Mints?" President Bartlett said.

"Sir: We only know Mr. Waters has not used any of the credit cards or moved any money from his accounts in the US. We have asked all the overseas banks to let us know if he has any account in their country so we can track him down and pick him up with the aid of the CIA or DOD or Interpol. We will sort out jurisdiction after we find him."

President Bartlett stood. "Get Waters, but keep looking. He's only one of 1,200 folks that "sort of" fit the profile and the facial recognition. Someone could have used plastic surgery to get him to fit the profile. That may be the guy the in garage at this Bo's house? Find him Marvin."

"Yes Sir."

Walking back to the oval office President Bartlett turned to his chief of staff Quist and said: "How in heavens name could some Seal become a killer of so many of his fellow Americans? It just doesn't make sense unless he was a guy who felt the reduction of the armed forces as envisioned in my acceptance speech was an act of treason or really, really stupid. I just don't get it. There was no suggestion of fanatic in his evaluations or in his performance. What the fuck happened to this guy? Find out. Tell the FBI profilers to take this guy apart piece by piece, day by day, and find out because if someone like him can turn against the USA then we have a real problem with our people. And frankly I just don't buy a guy like this could have pulled off this sort of "expensive" undertaking - - it cost millions to find, steal, transport and get past U.S. security the 5 Drones that took off from Andrews. It's got to be a larger conspiracy. Peel back the onion. Find the whole group."

The Isle of Mann, off England.

"Flight 197 you are cleared for landing."

"Roger" Bo replied as he turned his Challenger into the proper vector for landing at a private airport on the *Isle of Man*, an airport preferred by folks from many parts of Europe who had cash to hide in local banks from their tax hungry governments.

Customs officer Barkley noted the pilot was met by the head of the local bank. He marveled how a man who moved as slowly as the older gentlemen descending the steps of his aircraft could still have a pilot's license, but his papers were in order and he was just landing for a dinner with J. Wilson, President of the Royal Bank of Scotland branch in town. There was no need to check luggage for the "obviously" eccentric French speaking pilot traveling on a diplomatic passport.

When Bo's aircraft headed for Zurich, Bo had $5,000,000 less in bearer bonds. In Switzerland, he met a banker who took his cash and bonds, giving him a black American Express card, a Visa card with no limit and a check book with a balance $900,000 because Bo wanted some "walking around" money to find a place to rent for 6 months for cash as he decided what to do with the rest of his life.

Bo's new identity was that of Mr. Henrie Teller, a French diplomat.

His photo showed him as a blond, blue eyed male with a shaved head, wearing a diamond stud on his left ear, age 42, weighing 200 lbs, 6 foot tall.

When he got to his rented chalet outside of Zurich, Bo put on a black wig, took out the contact lenses and put on his normal glasses with his natural brown eyes peering into the universe.

"Looking good," he told himself as he removed the wig thinking out loud, "I'll just let the hair grow back. No rush. I'm not going anywhere soon."

During the next 30 days, Bo received an envelope a day from the states and England. Inside each envelope was $50,000 in Euros or Swiss Francs which Bo deposited in his safety deposit account in Zurich under the name of Henrie Teller.

It was awkward and tiresome to get a hotel room, changing his identity before going to the bank but it was better this way because he could make sure no surveillance cameras at the bank would get him with recognition software – a system he had used to capture various criminals when he worked undercover for the Secret Service and later at the CIA.

A week after arriving in Zurich, Bo saw a picture of himself when he was granted access to the Forest Service Drones at Andrews Air Force base on the news. He was described as someone Interpol wanted as part of a team that had robbed a bank in Athens. A reward of $100,000 Euros was offered for information leading to his capture because, according to the report, Bo had been a member of the gang that stole $5,000,000 Euros from an armored truck during which four people had been murdered, including a Greek policeman who sought to stop the heavily armed criminals. It was exactly what he had expected: a cover story to find the fellow who had actually attacked America profiled as a bank robber.

Running his usual 7 miles the next morning, Bo carried his smallest 9 millimeter inside his baggiest sweat shirt just in case someone from his past, the police or a killer sent by the Coal brothers to clean up this loose end came after him. The Coal brothers expressed their anger in a text to the number he had used to communicate with them before the attempt on President Bartlett. They were really angry he had missed and did not send Bo an additional $20,000,000 because "you missed you dumb shit" according to their text. His reply: you bought the cheap ones and your spotter never put the Lojack® on the car.

A bright spring day greeted Bo as he stretched for several minutes at the start of the path through one of the cities many parks, paths filled with other runners. His legs felt a big heavy this morning and his concentration on his breathing seemed to fall by the wayside as he considered how to treat this public outcry by police for his arrest and conviction for a crime he never committed. Someone, but who, had fingered him as a suspect for the attack on DC. Why didn't they just say he was an assassin instead of a bank robber? Who was behind the blackout of the truth about the attack on America?

Bo pushed these distractions out of his mind when he sensed another runner moving more quickly than most coming up on his right side. He slowed his pace, put one hand on the pistol in his sweat shirt and stepped off to the right side of the trail, looking to his left to see if the threat was really a threat or just a hot shot runner -- one of the many hot shots who had raced pass the older guy during the past 30 days in Zurich.

A younger woman slowed down and walked toward him, her hands at her side, her steps casual. She was a beauty – blond, blue eyed, trim, small breasted, dressed in pair of pink running pants, matching shoes and a bright red sweat shirt that seemed a bit too baggy for a woman so well attired in every other way.

"Excuse me," she said in French with an obvious Parisian accent. "I don't want to be forward but I see you here every morning for the past few weeks and you never seem to laugh or chat with anyone. This seems so sad, so I thought I would say hello and ask you to join me for a coffee and croissant when your run is over. Is that okay?"

"Sure," Bo laughed.

They continued the run chatting about Paris and Zurich in French, then switched to English when she realized he was able to also speak English because of his work in the US for a few years as a geologist for an oil exploration company in North Dakota.

"So, Yvonne," Bo asked after a few minutes, "when does it become okay to eat all the pastries you want without gaining a pound? You see I can laugh and I'm not sad. Do you feel better now?"

"Of course, Henri, I am glad you are not a sad sack in this beautiful city on this beautiful morning."

They parted after agreeing to meet at the entrance to the park trail the next morning at 7:30 so they could run together. "I always feel safer running with someone" Yvonne said.

"Me too, Bo laughed." Of course, in your case, I am happy to be the sweating knight protecting the beautiful princess from the fiery dragon," Bo laughed as he turned to run up the street back toward his chalet at the other end of the running path.

At sunrise the next morning, Bo ran the length of the trail to see if someone was setting up to get him or where to be particularly careful in case Yvonne was actually the shooter; although, his belly said she was okay, his training could not be pushed down, especially now that his disguised face was all over the airwaves because the banking crisis in Greece made a $5,000,000 robbery in broad daylight with the murder of three civilians and one police officer one of those stories that increased ratings. He smiled as he remembered propaganda school's rule: the front page and top story is always based on the notion of "if the bleeds, it leads".

The next two weeks of running with Yvonne was a wonderful distraction. He started to appreciate her humor and her fragrance. On Saturday morning, Bo asked Yvonne, "Do you like to eat at fine restaurants or do you like pizza at the local family owned place?

She laughed mischievously, replying, "Oh, you want to do more than run together and be my sweating knight."

"I'm up for more."

"Okay. Let's have a pizza on you, but then you need to go to a charity event on me. Will that work for you tonight? Say 6:30?"

"Your wish is my command, Princess."

"Black tie, no running shorts" she called to him.

"Oh my god, you are a demanding taskmaster! I hope the rental place can be that quick," he shouted back as he rounded the corner and started to run up the street to get to his motor bike and spend some time seeing where she went and who she met with after their breakfast.

As he rounded the corner he saw Yvonne getting into a hired limo with another person in the back seat. She seemed quite animated as the car took off, her head facing her traveling companion, her finger raised. She seemed to be yelling at him.

Noting the license number, Bo turned for home. Once home he checked the license number, noted the name of the car service, and called to reserve a car for the evening.

Bo slipped a small 9 mill pistol into a special pocket in his jacket so he could defend himself against someone who might come at him for a close up shot while he ate pizza at Mr. Christy's place for lunch. It was a favorite haunt for the younger bankers of the city who wanted to grab a quick meal and a glass of wine before going back to their computerized investing game-theory based quant tools, pushing to generate a quicker and more successful formula for increasing income for their ever demanding clientele. Bo loved quant talk and often would use his phone hearing aide to listen in on the quant talk of some of the younger bankers.

One banker in particular seemed to be a step or two ahead of the other bankers. Her colleagues called her "Herr Doctor." She looked about 25 years of age, with very distinctive long red hair falling half way down her back, hazel eyes, very long legs and small breasts. He noticed she stayed very still when she spoke of banking projects but got very animated when discussing how her soccer team was on a winning streak and would get the world cup soon. A South African citizen, he overheard that she came to Zurich after graduating from the London School of Economics with a Ph.d in mathematics with a specialty in the design of "big data" statistical analysis formulas for determining how markets, worldwide, could be moved if the right markers showed up simultaneously -- a provocative thesis, Bo thought as he finished reading Herr Doctor's dissertation a few days after he first heard her mention her views to a colleague over lunch who said, "That seems like a whimsical thesis because of the volatility and variance of the markets worldwide, including the time separations of markets", dismissing her idea with the shrug of an arrogant professor who was hell bent on depleting the enthusiasm of an original and revolutionary idea that might rock markets.

"He is a fool," Bo said to the space around him as her critic finished his paragraphs of scorn.

"Yes, he is" Herr Doctor said as she turned to Bo at the table next to her. They both laughed, mocking the professor's unwillingness to really listen to the younger colleague who Bo was quite certain had more brains and savvy than the short, chubby and balding fellow sitting across from her.

The professor tossed a twenty Euro note on the table and stalked off like a man who had been turned into the court jester by a child and a stranger in a sweat shirt and gym shoes reading a copy of *The Guardian*.

"I'm sorry, Miss. Did I offend your uncle? I hope he wasn't your boss or some client who can do you any harm."

"Oh, No. No problem," she said in a very clear voice. "He and I work together. He wants me to toe the mark and agree with his views of statistical evaluations. I can't because he seems to think in two dimensions instead of three: a graph with one line is his favorite bailiwick as my math professor and mentor used to say."

"Ah. You are a math-brat. An investment advisor I suspect."

"I work in the back rooms. Now and then I speak to clients, but not too often because I am too young so they only bring me out of the storeroom when the client is younger and not as inclined to dismiss someone without a bit of gray in their hair."

"Ah. Well. Their loss then," Bo replied.

"You come here quite a lot don't you," she laughed.

"I do. Thank you for noticing. I am addicted to their pizza, especially their goat cheese and spinach."

"Me too: What's your name, by the way."

"Henrie Teller, a citizen of France, living exile so I don't have to deal with Parisians who make me so irritated because they think my French- a version of which I learned as a boy in wine country – is not, what do they say, ah yes, Refined and Pure French – an arrogant lot those Parisians."

"I seem to have hit a hot button in your library of prejudices," she laughed.

"You did: Would you like to try a slice of this pizza pie?"

"No Thanks. I'm quite full. I'm Michel Martel, by the way. Glad to meet you Mr. Teller."

"Oh please. You can call me Henrie. I hate the formality of this country. I keeps people so distant, don't you think."

"Ok, Henrie, you can call me Michel, except, of course, if we meet at the bank then you will have to revert to the Swiss formal of Heir Doctor Martel. And yes, I agree, this place really is too, too formal. Everyone at work, for example, calls me Herr Doctor Martel. I like that because the Swiss value education and if you are a "Herr Doctor" then you have an opinion worth listening to even if you are just a cute, young thing, as the boys like to say behind my back."

"Good enough," Bo laughed, giving her a high five like back in the day when he was in college at Oxford, studying French and Geology so he could make his fortune finding oil in French speaking countries of Africa.

"Boy that was a good pizza," Michel said as she picked up her legal paper sized briefcase. "See you next Wednesday, if you're in town, Henri."

"Oh, I'll be here. An old guy like me – I'm 42 by the way – would never miss an opportunity to share a pizza and conversation with as magnificent a creature as you; especially, one who appreciates the elegance of mathematical formulas".

"Oh. You are a math crazy too?"

"Ask me next week, how big a crazy; but, yes, I am addicted to elegant mathematical explanations for the way the world works from the sub-atomic to the ambulatory.

The Charity Ball

When Bo picked up Yvonne that evening for the "fund raiser" he was thoroughly smitten, feeling as good as he did when he picked up his date for the senior prom in high school. She was stunning; dressed in a long, blue cocktail dress by some famous designer. Bo noticed she wore no makeup but lipstick and her smile was a captivating as her comment: "You clean up pretty good, cowboy."

"You too running lady; but, I really miss that locker room sweat aroma and the oversized sweat shirt."

"Touché Henrie! Are you ready for a night with the well heeled who want to save the planet and preserve the arts?"

"Don't know but if that's what it takes to walk in a room with a beautiful woman on my arm, I'm game."

In the limo Yvonne told Henrie she had a terrible fight with one of the organizers right after they had breakfast. "The pig wanted to sell Grand mama's painting by Monet as "absolute" instead of with a reserve of $500,000-- a fair value offered the family by the Louvre a few years ago when France was feeling flush and wanted to get all its art work back as a gimmick for increasing tourism. I told him most emphatically NO. I said if he does offer it absolute it will not be offered this evening. I told my attorney to send him a letter to that affect as soon as I got home. He has relented but he is not going to be very friendly this evening. He is the kind of man who insists on what Americans like to refer to as a "my way or the highway" guy."

"What is his name?"

"Ah. Atkinson – Roger Atkinson. He is the chairman of this evening's gala because his wife is a Rothschild. She loves the sea. She is the guiding light of the organization. He rows the boat because he has nothing to do but satisfy her."

"Nice Guy, "Bo said. "Can't we get away from him?"

"Doubt it. All seats have been arranged."

"Ah. Well, Yvonne, we will just have to do our best not to punch the guy in the nose."

"His very big red nose, "she laughed, smiling brightly, squeezing his hands in hers, pleased to see Henrie was not some up tight conservative guy like Atkinson but the empathetic guy she thought he was.

At the party, Bo noticed one of the Coal Brothers was in the room, the older brother Hank as his friends called him. He was a bit surprised and wondered what to say when he was greeted as Bo.

Hank walked over to Bo as he stood in line for drinks while Yvonne went off to make sure Atkinson had heard from her family lawyers and had instructed the auctioneer to begin bidding at $450,000.

"Excuse me, Monsieur," Hank Coal said to Bo, but I have not seen you at our other fund raisers."

"It's my first. I am a guest of one of the regulars."

"Ah. Hank Coal is my name," Hank said as he extended his hand to shake with Bo.

"Good to meet you, Mr. Coal. I'm Henrie," Bo said as if he was a complete stranger "and I am here because I am very interested in saving the seas of this world from rapacious and greedy oil men who would suck the life from the ocean until the last barrel of oil was pulled from it."

"Really: I am one of those oil men," Mr. Coal laughed.

"You look more like a banker; Armani tux and all and you don't have the kinds of blackened hands and scruffy looking nails most of the oil men I've known."

"You are funny guy, Henrie; perhaps, we should share a table tonight and debate the merits of the oil from the sea issue."

"What table are you at?"

"Number 4."

"Ah. I'm at table 7."

"Some other time, then."

"Perhaps," Bo replied as Yvonne returned with her Aunt Emily.

"Well Henrie, I see you have met one of our greatest benefactors. Now I'd like you meet my aunt Emily, my father's sister."

"Younger sister," a white haired lady with perfect nails and wrinkly skin, carrying a polished black cane with a gold casting of an elephant at its top added to Yvonne's introduction.

"So, are you going to tell stories of Yvonne's young life that she doesn't want anyone to know," Bo asked in a soft voice that made Aunt Emily laugh.

"A conspiracy to tell all while she is not listening is that the game you want to play young man?"

"Conspiracy – a quaint but accurate way to make sure you tell all about your exquisite niece, Mademoiselle."

Emily took his arm and said, "Evy, you take care of business while I have a heart to heart with this young man."

Bo turned to Yvonne, shrugged and walked away on the arm of the arm of her Aunt Emily, smiling at the favorable response her Aunt Emily had toward Bo.

"So, Yvonne," Hank Coal said, "Your new friend is an interesting fellow. Have you known him long?"

"Not too long, but he is a friend of the sea so I hope he will, in time, become an important ally in the battle to keep whales from going extinct and the planet getting in that place that required Captain Kirk to go back in time to save the earth."

Laughing as he walked away, Hank Coal said: "Good one, Yvonne, Good one."

When Yvonne woke in the morning, her arm felt numb. She had been supporting Bo's head all night after passionate love making. She smiled remembering how her body simply vibrated with delight as he seemed to have an endless boner that he shared with her in more positions that she could remember.

"God you are a great lover, big boy," Evy whispered into Bo's ear in a very, soft voice. "You are an inspiration," Bo replied as he rolled over, looked her in the eye and pulled her closer to him.

"Again?"

"Not yet.... I just love to feel your body on mine. Your skin is so smooth and you smell so good I just want to eat you and devour you until I am without an ounce of energy, Evy............you are the best"

"Compared to?"

"Compared to no one, silly girl; you are simply a dream come true to this slightly jaded older guy."

A couple of hours later, they woke up and decided it was time to eat and catch up on the world before getting back in the bed and simply hugging until they felt their bodies needed a shower, a hot tub and a massage to wear away the exhaustion of weary muscles before getting back in the sack for the evening.

"Decadent Man: It's 11 in the morning."

"So: What did we miss? Is there something of real worth out there?"

"Not really, Henrie, except, of course, the fresh pancakes and sausage I intend to make as soon as you let me go free."

"Ah. Food, home made by a sexy lady beats sex with a sexy lady every time", he laughed as he pulled the covers off the bed and sauntered into the bathroom for a hot shower and, hopefully, a robe of some sort to wear around Yvonne's apartment until his phone showed him if any anyone had been in his home while he was out.

While she was in the shower, a courier arrived. Bo answered the door with his small nine millimeter in his jacket pocket.

Carefully opening the package, Bo placed the Monet he had purchased at the auction on the hook it had been hung from before Yvonne had offered it to the auction.

Yvonne shouted with delight when she saw it: "Oh Henrie, Henrie how could you, how did you ever get this back to me? Were you the mysterious buyer?"

"You are a quick study, Evy. It didn't seem right to see this family heirloom in some other family; especially, after your Aunt Emily explained the history of the painting to me and the way your parent's fought in the courts and with the WWII restoration tribunal to prove this painting was your great grandmother's – a gift from the artist himself to her as young girl when he was a unknown. It just didn't seem right so I bought it for you."

"You were pretty sure we'd be here last night?

"Nope: I wasn't sure of that at all. In fact after talking to Aunt Emily I wasn't sure you were any more ready to take up with me than I was to take up with you."

"Really: and what did Auntie Say that made you feel I was so ambivalent?"

"I liked her so much I thought I might have to court an older woman?"

"And how do you feel this morning."

"So good I have decided to save an older woman experience for another day – maybe for a day when I am an old guy."

"You are too good," Evy said, as she rubbed a finger full of pancake batter on his nose, kissing him softly on the ear before going over to the painting and planting a kiss on it as she had on most mornings, envisioning the beautiful painting of her great-grandmother, a gift to her as a twelve year old child, her spiritual companion.

"God I was dumb to offer the painting as an auction item. I just don't know what came over me, Henrie. I love that painting. I guess it was just one of those dumb things people do sometimes. I don't know how to repay you for such an enormous gift."

"Repay? Don't even think it. The joy I see in your eyes is all the thanks I'll ever need."

"But it was so expensive. Six hundred thousand Euros is no small matter. Are you that well off?"

"Well enough. It will not break me or cause me to skip a meal, Ok."

"OK" she smiled. "I will treasure even more than I have in the past" she said as she put a chocolate strawberry in her mouth, lingering for several moments as her eyes moved down along his torso.

"You are a vixen," Bo laughed as he lifted her in his arms and strolled leisurely back to the bedroom.

"A pre brunch, brunch" she laughed.

After brunch, Bo and Evy went by Bo's house for a change of clothes, and then he drove her to a private airport on the outskirts of Zurich where gliders, small planes and balloons launched.

"Yes. I am a pilot. That old guy will pull us up to 3,000 feet. Then, you will pull this red lever and I will turn to the left and he will turn to the right. Then, we will simply soar on the updrafts until you need to pee."

"A once classy guy, just crashed and burned," Evy laughed. "By the way, we may be up there all day because I have a very large bladder."

"Too much information: Let's go," Bo laughed as the line between their glider and the Cessna started to tighten, pulling the glider into the sky.

Evy marveled at how calm she felt with Bo as pilot of a glider – a plane without engines had felt impossible until a few minutes earlier when the cannon like sound split the air as the tow cable, separating the glider and tow plane, fell away.

She smiled as the simple sound of "swoosh" surrounding the glider slipping through the air penetrated her consciousness, lifting her sense of well being and connectedness with the cosmos just as Bo had described how he felt the first and last time he was at the controls of a glider. "It's like being a bird," Bo told her. "You're free of the earth and machines, at one with the physical laws operating the universe, your only guide a piece of string that signals you by going up straight when you are in an updraft. Then, you circle and rise on the thermals until the updraft ends or you get outside its vortex. Magical is what gliding is for those of us who get over the illusion that only machines fueled by some sort of lubricant can transport us from point A to B."

For an hour Bo created a roller coaster in the sky and Evy laughed as if she was a youngster of ten years again, sitting next to her father as he ferried the family in his sea plane from their home in Paris to their summer house on a fishing lake in the French alps, with a stream that they would go to and fish for trout, her father's favorite pastime.

Bo felt his cell phone vibrate to warn him someone was in his home. He flipped on the security home camera app and watched as three men, all armed with pistols with silencers, moved methodically through his home. In less than five minutes they were gone, leaving a small camera behind on the coffee table as a memento to their visit as well as a warning to Bo that he was under surveillance.

Bo and Evy had a pizza at his favorite spot before retiring to her home for the evening.

Over breakfast, Bo told Evy he had to fly to the U.S. the next day, but before he left they could have a morning run and she could meet someone to run with her in the morning.

On the way to the park Evy said, "I wish you had told me so I could go with you. It's difficult to see you go. I've gotten used to having you around in the morning – and at night; of course, I seem to sleep more deeply with you next to me. Can't you delay a week or so?"

"I'm sorry, Honey, but my friend may not be alive that long. I'll call and be back as soon as I can. Come on let's go for a run."

When they got to the trail, Herr Doctor Michel Matel from Christy's pizza was stretching.

Bo waved and introduced Evy to Michele as the "little math genius who graduated from the Sorbonne and is well versed in the art of eating pizza."

"Ah. You're the pizza girl he told me about. The speaker of French as a true Parisian, just like me."

"Guilty, on all counts," Michel laughed as she and Evy started to chat in French, racing ahead of Bo on the trail.

Arizona Desert:

On his flight to Juarez from Zurich Bo calculated his next steps against the Coal Brothers. He was now certain they wanted to kill him so there would be no chance of his turning himself in if his conscience got to him and his oath as a soldier started to scratch at his conscience, compelling him to confess to his conspiracy with the Coal Brothers to kill the President and get a fellow in the Oval more simpatico with the Cossack's view of an armed America.

Perhaps, Evy and his Teller identity had to go. He was now known to the Coal Brothers as Teller so if he did not act quickly he could be tracked down by their team of killers -- mercenaries for hire and well trained it appeared from the very deliberate way they went through his apartment leaving almost no evidence of their visit. Still. He really felt a connection, a very strong bond with Evy; she was superior to anyone he had met in many years. She actually made him happier than anyone else had done since his wife had been murdered along with his daughter and son by a terrorist's bomb when they flew to the Middle East to join him for a vacation while he was serving as a CIA operative seven years earlier.

Their loss dropped him to his knees, making him feel like a man who had been stripped of any point or purpose to his life, a man who wanted to simply take revenge on the killers who erased the best parts of his life. Shortly after the funeral he resigned from the service and moved back to the home in Santa Fe, New Mexico that his wife had inherited from her parents – "A perfect place to raise the children and we can live there for nearly nothing – just taxes" was how she convinced Bo to say Ok, even though deep inside of him there was a sense that it was wrong to live in such a neighborhood, a neighborhood he could never afford to live in if her parents had not died and left to her as their only surviving heir.

Over the next three years he searched out and killed the man who planted the bomb on his wife's plane while the man was walking the streets in Yemen, a free man because the government would not extradite him and the U.S. was reluctant to extract him because of the uproar it would cause in that region of the world.

Visions of the death of his wife and children still haunted him when he flew on a commercial airliner. He sensed their fear when their plane simply blew apart and they found themselves falling to earth in a broken airliner. He woke as usual with sweat pouring all over his body as his flight neared his destination, his heart pounding like it did at the center of a five mile run up a mountain before it would settle into a smooth and regular rhythm. He told himself: "I am not falling from the sky. It's okay to open my eyes now."

In Juarez, Bo passed through security without incident because he was traveling as Mr. Teller, a French diplomat.

At a storage unit in El Paso, a unit rented as Mr. Teller, Bo changed into this desert gear, armed himself with a pistol and hunting rifle turned into a semi-automatic weapon and started his trip to Santa Fe, NM through the desert in a specially equipped jeep that would allow him to maneuver at night and not worry about running out of gas before he got home. It was a long trip but it made sense because he wanted to be thoroughly impregnated with dust from the desert when he got home just in case anyone was waiting to talk to him as an expert on Drones.

In Arizona, he turned into the desert and started on his trek toward Sedona, before his drive to Santa Fe. It was a dangerous part of the trip because there were a lot of agents looking for immigrants and the coyote's who promised to navigate folks from Mexico safely though the desert.

After sundown, Bo moved away from his campfire and jeep, leaving a blanket set up as if there was someone sleeping in it. Early the next morning, Bo heard some men walking toward his campsite. One of them said in Spanish, "Ah. We have a car. Let's shoot the asshole and get our package to the buyer before breakfast."

The men walked up to the campsite and fired three times into the puffed up sleeping bag.

"Shit. They are not here; must be going for a morning dump: let's get the car going.

"Bullshit; I'm hungry. Let's eat and then get out of here. They probably ran away when they heard the shots."

The men stirred up the fire and started to makes some coffee, happy for their good fortune and confident they could make even more money when they sold the Jeep back in Mexico or to their contacts in Arizona when they delivered the young woman tied to Bo's jeep so they could eat in peace and not worry about her.

Bo called out: "Hey fellows, what's up," in a very calm voice.

Both men jumped up, turned toward Bo with weapons drawn, but Bo was ready and simply shot them both dead, their shots going straight up as they fell back onto the desert floor.

The young girl looked up at Bo as he walked over to the bodies of the two men, took their weapons and dragged their bodies into the desert, letting them roll down a hill into a batch of cactus below.

As he untied the young woman, Bo spoke in calm tones, in Spanish, assuring her "You are ok now." Then, he gave her a blue sweat shirt and matching running pants so she would be warm and stop shivering until the sun came up.

She told Bo, "Those men took me off the streets of El Paso last night. I think they must have slipped me some kind of knockout potion. My boy friend was hit in the head with a baseball bat as we walked to his car in the parking lot after dancing with friends at a cantina. They said they were going to sell me to some gringo. Are you that Gringo?"

"No. Not me. I'm a French Diplomat. I was just camping in the desert and the people who leased me this jeep said I should be careful in this area of the U.S. What is your name?"

"Maria Gonzales. And yours?"

"Henrie Teller and I will get you back home, but what happened here you can't tell anyone. Okay. Well, you can tell your parents someday if you want but on one else."

"Never: Mr. Teller, Never."

On the way back to El Paso, Henrie gave Maria an encrypted cell phone to call home and arrange to meet her parents in a restaurant they knew half way to El Paso. She told him she was violinist and wanted to go to the University of New York so she could be close to Juilliard and, perhaps, in time, qualify for a place in Juilliard and become a member of a famous orchestra and see the world while traveling with other recognized artists.

"Mr. Teller."

"Please. Maria. Call me Henrie. I feel so old when you call me Mr."

"I'm sorry, Henrie, but why would you want to camp in the desert? It seems odd for a man of your obvious education to want to wander in the desert."

"Oh. I was recapturing my youth. I was in the French Foreign Legion. We did a lot of time in the desert. I grew to love it. I loved the variety of plants that I could eat if I was lost or if I was wounded and had to get back to my unit over a long stretch of desert. It's a beautiful place, the desert. Cactus is tasty and nutritious. I love to hear the birds singing in the morning as they emerge from their nests in the holes in the bigger cactus. I don't like how cold it gets at night, but I love the heat during the morning hours and how it gets you to nap in the afternoon as the temperatures change. It's a change of speed and context that gets my mind open to new ways of thinking about the world and my place in it. It's probably the same for you when you get totally involved in a piece of music that you simply love and enjoy to play."

"Ah. It is exactly the same, Henrie. You are such a smart man."

"I'm a lucky man, Maria. It's all genetics. I can play the saxophone and feel like a man riding a wave, but I'm a hack compared to the greats who have an ear, probably like you on the violin. You're already first violin in the local orchestra so you're gifted. You should be able to fulfill that dream. I hope it works for you."

She looked at him and said, "Thanks to you I now have a chance. Oh. Here are my parents," she smiled as she rose up to meet them in the parking lot.

As he said goodbye to Maria and her parents he asked Maria to please play her favorite piece of violin music and put it up on U-Tube so he could see her play. Her parents said, "Of course, but is there no other way we can thank you for saving our daughter?"

"No. Seeing Maria play her favorite piece on the violin will more than enough of a reward for this small service I was able to perform," he said as Maria and her family hugged him goodbye.

Santa Fe

When Bo drove up to his house in Santa Fe, he was greeted by two FBI investigators: Special Agent Sharon Sloan, a lovely woman with long blond hair in her mid-thirties, and Special Agent Jim Parker a fellow who looked like a line backer for a professional football team.

"Mr. Waters, we have been trying to find you. You seem to have disappeared from the Earth for a few months. Where have you been?" Sloan asked.

'I'm sorry. FBI: Why are you looking for me?"

"Can we go inside to talk?"

"Sure. I'll put some coffee on but as you can see I am a mess. All this dust and dirt is from a few months of wilderness hiking in the deserts of America. It's a great experience, if you haven't tried it. Lose a bit a weight and get in touch with the stars and Mother Earth; very healthy."

"I'm sure it is," agent Sloan remarked. "You only take this back pack, a rifle and pistol for a few months wandering the desert. Isn't that a bit dangerous?"

"Not really. You just have to avoid the areas of the desert that are really close to the border so you don't run into those nasty coyotes that the papers describe as the scum of the earth who often rip off the folks who have paid them to provide safe passage to the States."

"So you stay in the deserts that are 50 miles more from the borders?"

"Very good, Agent Sloan; you are a quick study. So, tell me what happened to my garage. It looks like it burned to the ground. Do you happen to know how that happened?"

"As a matter of fact, Mr. Waters, that's why we're here."

"Really: Crime has fallen that much in the last few months? And please call me Bo. Everyone does."

"Fine, Bo it is. So, Bo no one called you about this fire."

"No. They couldn't. I turn off my cell phone. I only have a solar powered one with me if I get snake bit or a break a bone and can't get it fixed on my own. That's the whole point of the wandering the desert without all the modern conveniences."

Bo's phone rang. His neighbor left a message: "Bo. This is Jim Martin. Call me. We need to clean up this mess in your back yard. Marian wants to put our house on the market and it won't be easy with the eye sore in your back yard. Oh, my son called to say the two guys killed in your garage are known burglars. It seems they broke a gas line and lit up. Ah the dangers of smoking. It's good to have a sheriff in the family. Thanks for cleaning up the mess. You know Marian. Welcome back. Hope the desert treated you well."

"When did you leave?"

"I left the day of President Bartlett's inauguration. I heard him take the oath of Office and make his promise to create a more peaceful world in the car radio. Then I was off to test my metal against Mother Nature. How is he doing? Is the world a safer place or is the Congress saying No because they don't want to give up their military bases and all those jobs connected a stronger military in our country?"

"Well, Bo," Agent Sloan started to say as she put down her pen and take a careful look at Bo, noting his authentic smile and peaceful demeanor as he scooped up his Cheerios with the enthusiasm of a teenager who had just gotten off a diet and was finally able to enjoy the food he had longed for during his period of disciplined eating.

"Yes" Bo asked.

"Well, Bo, you missed the worst crime on our shores since 9/11. Someone tried to kill the President and his party as they walked down the street after the inauguration. They missed but killed 53 people, including the VP and his wife, a lot of Secret Service folks and reporters. They were attacked with Drones."

"Jesus! Really?"

"Really: Some lunatic or gang of lunatics sent a couple of deadly drones into D.C. trying to murder the President, his wife and friends as the President strolled down Pennsylvania Avenue. They missed the President. His limo saved him. It's really sturdy."

"Jesus! Have you caught the bastards and strung them up by their balls, Agent Sloan?"

"Not yet. We got one we think, but he was dead when we got to him. He was a former DOD guy, an expert on drones and he was filmed entering the site the drones flew to D. C. from."

"This sounds a like spy novel. The guy does the crime, and then the guy gets killed so he can't blow the cover of the killers who funded the operation."

Bo got up and walked over to the coffee pot, pouring himself another cup.

"So, you're here because I used to operate on drones, fix drones, even got a patent on few of the fundamental parts that are used to make drones, particularly the guidance systems that give these babies pin point accuracy. You want me to examine the drones or examine your findings on the drones to see if maybe I can see something the others haven't seen yet?"

"Something like that," Agent Sloan said.

"Actually," Agent Jim Parker, said, "we have problem that only you can solve for us. You see the photos taken of the men who maintained these drones at Andrews show the man we found dead and a man who looks a lot like you. Indeed, facial recognition software suggests it could be you; although, the guy wore an eye patch and a bandage over his jaw so we couldn't get a clear view of his jaw line."

"Well what about finger prints and eye recognition systems. Don't they still use those to clear folks who have access to secure areas of with drones? As I recall those systems were all going to be on line when I got out of the service seven years ago. Hasn't that happened, yet?"

"Afraid not, Bo," Agent Sloan said.

"Well, that's fricking irresponsible. How dumb can these folks be? Not enough money I suppose Agent Sloan?"

"That's right. These characters were very clever. They only wanted access to some drones that were allocated to the Forest Service, not to the military. They were going to be used to find people lost in the mountains and map the terrain of the mountain ranges and shorelines so the Forest Service and Department of the Interior could get the best possible view of the conditions of the terrain in the mountains and along the Atlantic. They were there for a three month project. Then they would be moved to another site further west to conduct the same mapping. Security for this group of drones was really light."

"So, let's see the photos of these guys."

"Ok. This fellow is dead. The others – all experts on drones aren't even close to the second guy. Here's the second guy. Looks a lot like you, don't you think."

Bo picked up the other photo and said, "That's Jimmy the "Gimme guy." We called him "Gimmee" because he had no patience and would always say, gimme that you bozo, when someone wasn't fast enough to fix a problem. Great guy when I knew him: how did he die?"

"Looks like an overdose – Heroin."

"Poor Bastard," Bo said as he rolled his fingers over the photo and said in a quiet voice, "Rest in peace "Jimmy Gimme": you were a good man. I already miss you and those great jokes you loved to screw up. I can't imagine him a murderer, especially, Bartlett. Jimmy was a peacenik, worked for DOD for the money."

Sloan looked at Parker in quizzical way, almost asking could this guy really be this out of touch and this sincere.

After turning Jimmy's picture over, Bo looked carefully at the photo that was supposed to be him. He carefully picked it up, reached over for a magnifying glass and spent several moments examining it.

"Ah." Agent Sloan, "Did you notice the eyes on this guy are blue and mine are brown. The nose isn't mine. Mine has never been broken like this guy and my ears are much closer to my head than this fellow."

"We noted all that Bo, but still how many guys have your level of knowledge of drones? And your garage had very sophisticated computer systems but no hard drives were found in the debris left after the fire."

"Come On, Sloan; a kid in high school could program a drone. The Cloud has all my data. I wouldn't bother with a hard drive. That's just too primitive."

"Will you let us look at the cloud records for your account?"

Getting up, Bo said, "Look it's been good meeting with you but I have other things to do today. You've already looked at the cloud for my account. CIA/ DOD/ NSA have blanket permission to investigate my computer records because I signed an agreement for them to do so when I resigned from the Secret Service and CIA. So, I suggest you folks get back to investigating. Find the bad guys and put them to death. I like the President. I voted for him. If I can help let me know, but, you know I'm retired and you have plenty of good people."

"Ok Bo, but one last question," Sloan commented as she started to gather up her papers.

"What is that?" Bo remarked in very impatient voice.

"Is it true that President Bartlett let your father out of jail and that resulted in your mother's death at his hands when Bartlett was a prosecutor?"

Leaning back in his chair, Bo took a long sip of coffee before he responded to the question. Finally, after a minute or so of silence, Bo said: "Yes. He did it when I was overseas so I could not protect my mother from that bastard."

"Still, you voted for him?"

"Hey. He was young and hampered by the stupid limits of the laws of Alabama. He could not keep him in prison any longer than he did. Do you remember the asshole that was running against Bartlett? He was a nitwit. I could never vote for a moron in the Oval Office. As for my dad killing my Mom back then, it was not that difficult to find Mom when he got out. Her murder was the result of a system done haywire. Still is, as I understand it."

"Where is your Dad, now?" Agent Sloan asked in an off handed way as she continued stuff her papers into her bag.

"I'd guess he is dead or in prison somewhere and don't refer to him as my Dad. He was a father the way Dracula is a giver of life."

As they left, Agent Sloan gave Bo her card. "Call if there is something else or if you have any ideas of avenues for us to pursue to find these killers and I'm sorry we had to ask about your Mom."

"Sure, but let's be honest, if I call it will be to ask you to dinner."

"Ok then." Sloan said as she moved toward her car, blushing as if she was a youngster asked out by one of the hot guys in high school. Her partner, Agent Parker, said, "That interview was like a first date, Sloan" as they drove away.

"Yes. But we have a motive. He was still pissed about his Mom and he knew it was Bartlett who let his Dad out. We will have to put a full court press on him. He is a slippery one and there is no point on giving him polygraph: he knows how to beat them. I'll call the local office and make sure team is put on him 24/7 for the next 3-months; full surveillance and full coverage of all his communications, including interviews with anyone he meets with right after the conversation takes place."

"You think he did it?"

"Oh yeah, but I don't know who funded him or where he has been holed for the last few months. That's the real $64 question. Who knows? Maybe I should ask him to dinner and see if he is less guarded than he was today."

Aspen:

Bo landed at Denver and drove to Aspen, leaving home less than an hour after Agent Sloan and Parker left. He traveled as Henrie Price, an investigator from Interpol, wearing sunglasses as he entered the airport and surveillance areas and contacts making his eyes green instead of brown. He was passed through the trusted traveler gates, his one carry-on would be scanned so he gave his weapon to a TSA agent who gave it to the Captain of his flight for return when they got to Denver. However, the Captain gave the weapon to the Air Marshall on board his flight, arranging for the men to sit together for the flight from Santa Fe to Denver.

The drive to Aspen from Denver was tedious, although the scenery was spectacular, the snow covered peaks reminding him of Switzerland and Evy. His missed her more than he thought he would. She seemed to be constantly in his thoughts, often making him wonder if he really had to gun down the Coal Brothers so he could return to her and not worry about the Cossack's agents hunting him down and killing her as well.

He met a rental agent, paid cash for one month and moved into a three bedroom condo, with a trail that allowed him to ski to the chair lifts at Ajax and walk to town. It had a group hot tub that he immediately took advantage of when he arrived, noticing how much his muscles seemed to stretch out and get soft as spaghetti. He decided to follow the examples of others, jumping out of the water and rolling in the snow before diving back into the hot tub. "Perfect" he shouted as he felt the benefits of the hot water his body, a distinctly tingling sensation that seemed to lift him right out of his skin.

While getting new skis two weeks later, an Aspen police officer entered with two coffees and a couple of bagels. The officer put down the coffee and, as usual, looked over the crowd in the store.

"Bo? Is that really you," the officer laughed.

"Joey? An Aspen copper. Can't believe it," Bo shouted back, walking toward him in his stocking feet. The two men hugged like brothers.

"Put your shoes on, Dummy. Let's go get some breakfast and catch up," Joey laughed.

"Still the observant smart ass I see," Bo joked.

Over breakfast, Joey explained how he had fallen in love with a woman in New York City, gotten sober in AA, and decided to move out here so he and Sally could raise their children in the mountains, in a town where the locals all knew each other and they would experience a small town atmosphere.

"Small town: are you kidding. This is the world's gathering place for the movers and shakers of the planet."

"Yeah: but the skiing is great and who cares who is zipping down the hill next to you? I don't. Sally doesn't. And the kids, just 3 and 4 years of age right now will be able to have the experience of skiing on the finest snow on the planet. Not a bad compromise?"

"You're right, of course. Is there much crime around here? Can you stay busy enough? It's not like back in the day when were chasing those counterfeiter guys for the Secret Service."

"Jesus, Bo. I don't need that kind of excitement anymore. I'm glad to give tickets to guys like Donald Trump or stop the limo for one of the Coal Brothers when his guy runs a light so Coal will be on time, then watch Coal walk the last couple of blocks instead of sit in the limo steaming while I fill out the ticket. – I did that once. Then, the chief said, "don't do that again" after the Mayor called to complain about that new guy causing trouble for one of the city's benefactors."

"Same everywhere, Joey: Money talks, Bullshit walks as our leaders used to say back on the Potomac."

"Indeed. Can you join Sally and me for dinner tonight? Will you be here?"

"I wouldn't miss it. Can you get us a table at the old Palace? Do you have enough juice for that?"

"That's an easy one: the owner is good buddy. Let me call right now. Can you come to the house after, see the babies and sit around to share a bit of history with Sally. She often wonders what my world was like before I got sober and started to live a normal life."

"Of course: I wouldn't miss it for the world; unless, of course, my leader calls and sets me on some other path."

After a day of skiing on Ajax mountain, Bo walked over to meet Joey at the Palace restaurant in the center of town; an older structure, restored to its original state after a fire destroyed it when wild fires zipped through town, devastating nearly a third of the town.

"Hey," Joey called out when he saw Bo walk in the door.

"Hey," Bo called back as he approached the couple, noticing the wife, Sally, was as beautiful as Joey had said.

Sally gave Bo a big Hug and said in a stage whisper that made several heads turn: "Thanks, for saving my Joey. You are my hero."

"Easy girl," Joey laughed, "he's a charmer you know."

"Who cares," Sally laughed as she punched Joey in the arm before kissing him on his ears.

Dinner was a joy for both the men. They had not seen each other for nearly 10 years, keeping in touch with Christmas emails every other year of so; although, Bo had been quiet for nearly five years after his wife and children had been killed by a terrorist while traveling to meet him while he was serving in the Middle East.

Joey turned to Bo after Sally excused herself and the two men poured their coffee: "Are they off the planet?"

"Oh yeah: I got them after two years of investigation. State didn't have the balls so I got'em; picked up Farsi, went black, entered Yemen and took out that bastard and a bunch of his guys all training in a camp in the desert. Was lucky I had the training to go black."

"Did it feel better when you got them?"

"Wish it did Joey. It didn't. I still feel empty without Kathy and the kids. When I start my morning run I always say: "Morning my loves." I think they travel with me – a halo of sorts to keep me safe; makes me depressed and reckless some days, but not too often."

"I tell you Bo, I can't imagine my life without Sally and the boys – they make all the BS during the day bearable and my nights home playing with the kids or laughing with Sally are the real joy in my life. Never knew what I was missing until I got my head out of the bottle. It's been 10 years now and I feel like I can really appreciate the life I have and the people in my life – even you my friend."

Sally walked back with the owner of the Palace in tow because he wanted to meet the man who had saved Joey's life so many years earlier. He too had been a soldier, serving in Iraq during the Bush years, earning a visa to the US for his heroism and later becoming a U.S. citizen.

"You did a good thing saving this character so Sally could meet him and get him to live in Aspen. Then, Sally won't admit to it, but she saved my life after a terrible car crash. So, my friend, you see, you actually saved two lives that night many years ago. Yes, Joey and I are in your debt."

"Thank you, but please, he would have done the same for me. By the way, the food in your restaurant is magnificent and I'm a tough critic, even a chef of some skill so I don't say this lightly."

"I am grateful you enjoyed the meal. Can I get you folks anything else?"

"No. I think we are fine," Sally said and the others nodded.

Bo turned to Sally as the owner walked away: "Hey, come on, you don't have to praise me to the whole world. Don't get me wrong. I enjoy the applause but let's just not discuss it anymore. Ok?"

"Ok," Sally said with a look of disappointment because she wanted to tell everyone.

The next morning Bo rang the bell at the Coal Brothers home on the outskirts of Aspen. The guard asked if he had an appointment. He said, "No, but the boys will want to talk to me. Just ask them if they can see Bo for a few minutes."

A few minutes later Bo was led into the library of the Coal's 4,000 square foot home – a classic mountain home filled with art from around the world and a spattering of Elk and deer heads shot by others by displayed by the brothers to show their manliness.

"Bo? Isn't it Henrie?"

"Bo, will do."

"What can we do for you" the younger brother asked.

Bo took out a phone and showed them a video of three men roaming through an apartment with guns with silencers as he explained: "These three fellows were in my home the night after we met at that charity event. I found one of them: His name is Hans Manchee, a fellow well known to the world of European assassins at the CIA."

"Really," the younger Coal said.

"Really: And here is a bit of what he told me," Bo continued as he showed Hans tied to chair, looking like he was about to collapse and die from the look of fear on his face.

"My name is Hans Manchee: It is 2020, April. I was hired to find and kill a man called Bo by an attorney for the Coal Brothers. He said Bo was a detail that had to be erased. The fee was $50,000 if I could do it within 24 hours. I went to his home. He was not there. I was unable to find him before he found me. I am now at his mercy."

The brothers were silent when the video was turned off.

Bo said: "So you know. Hans is fine. Now call off your dogs or this will go the authorities at Interpol, along with a document that explains how you and I committed a crime that will not be forgotten. If I don't die of natural causes, all the details will be automatically conveyed to the world's media, Interpol, FBI, CIA and NSA, Wikipedia, New York Times, USA Today. Your money won't protect you. You know what I am capable of so don't ignore this warning."

Getting up from his chair, Bo turned to leave. Before leaving he said to the brothers: "See you both in Hell."

At the Aspen Airport a chartered Challenger was fueled and ready to fly Henrie Teller to Zurich. His papers were in perfect order and as a French diplomat allowed him board without any luggage inspection.

"Another rich guy on his way to Switzerland in that Challenger," the young lady behind the counter at US Charter said to her colleague. "Good looking. Think he's attached."

"Don't know. I saw his papers. But who cares. He's French and those guys are Never-Ever attached. A Mistress is as natural as breathing for what my Daddy calls "Frogs", she laughed.

Back at the Coal Brothers house, the brothers got more and more enraged at the threat that Bo had made. Before Bo left their driveway, the older brother said:

"We need get that piece of arrogant shit gone and get his fucking records. Tear up his house in Santa Fe and Zurich. We can't afford to let that little prick think we can be shut up and do what he wants. Find the data or burn his properties to the ground."

"No," the younger brother cautioned. "He's too wily to keep the papers at home. He's got a lawyer or CIA contacts or a bank vault somewhere. Have our computer spies find out where he has been, who he has been talking to, who he knows. Get this girl in Zurich to talk. She has no idea who he is. Tell her. Get her to turn on him. Send in a couple of phony agents – women and see if they can get anywhere with her. Maybe she will work with them to help him. Let's be cautious. Remember that scum bag at Wikileaks and that Manning guy and the Snowden guy. We'd be cooked if he told someone like that."

"Alright, but I'd rather take down the two houses as a show of defiance to that little shit and let him know we are not going away anytime soon. He needs to know he is not in charge."

"But, brother, he is until we get the info he has hid."

"Fuck………..I hate to say it but you're right. I hate this. We should have taken him out the same day as the Bartlett attempt."

"Yep: Big mistake."

Halfway to Europe, Bo is awakened by a call on his cell phone. Herr Doctor Michel Martel sounded breathless with sadness in her voice.

"Henrie?"

"Yes."

"Evy is gone. Burglars shot her in your kitchen. Three rounds to the chest. I found her 10 minutes ago. The police are on their way. What can I do? Jesus, I just want to sit on the ground and cry, maybe get a gun and shoot the pigs that did this – if I only knew."

"Easy, Michel: I'll be in Zurich in about 6 hours. I'm on a charter so I'll be out of the airport quickly and to the house as fast as possible. Can you stay with her? I can't bear the thought of her being alone like that. Just don't touch anything. The police will need a pristine crime scene. Jesus; I feel like the world just ended. She was my love. I was planning to spend my life with her – have kids, do the whole domestic way of life and die in old age after a life of wedded bliss with grandkids around."

"Okay, Henrie. I will stay but I have to be in the living room. I can't look at her anymore. She was a beautiful person who had become a wonderful friend during the weeks you have been away. I feel a huge hole in my life right now."

"I know what you mean. Did they shoot her in the face?"

"No."

"Thank God…… At least her Aunt Emily can see her at the wake. Tell the police I will take care of the cost of funeral costs, etc. See you in a few hours. I need to just sit and cry for awhile."

"See you soon, Henrie. I'm so sorry I have to be the one to tell you."

"Me too: See you soon. Take care of yourself and Emily."

"I will."

Arriving at his home in Zurich, Bo was confronted by police. They let in his home after inspecting his papers, noting he had been in the air over the Atlantic when Evy was killed. As requested he looked to see what had been stolen, what items might be missing because they had decided it "was probably a robbery gone violent by some druggie" as the lead investigator told Henrie. Nothing was missing.

Bo was grateful that her body was gone from the house being watched by her brother at the mortuary because her Aunt Emily had insisted and she personally knew the commissioner of police– a family friend whose parents had helped her family get started when they escaped from the Nazis when she was a young girl.

The funeral was held the next morning. The Commissioner and Mayor told the coroner to do their investigating; taking whatever samples they might need so "Evy's Aunt Emily can put her to rest in the traditional way."

A detective took Bo to the coroner's office at Aunt Emily's request so he could say his goodbyes in private before her remains were brought to a gathering place where family and friends would say their last goodbye to their beloved Evy.

Aunt Emily described Evy to her friends and family as "a dynamo, a force of nature that could not stop finishing a project once she started, a loving child who "never – ever failed to call me on my birthday or the birthdays of her mother and father – even when she was a student in Paris. More than once she would simply appear at my house for breakfast on those birthdays because she knew I was particularly sad on those days. She would let me tell stories of her father's youth and her mother's youth and telling those stories was so uplifting to my spirits that I could almost forget the terrible lose our family had suffered when the black shirts took them. She was a poet: I shall miss her greatly."

Bo was signaled by Aunt Emily to come and sit next to her as she spoke. She held his hand as she spoke, then introduced Henrie as the man that Evy planned to marry: "A man she said was the love of her life, the soul mate that appeared one day on a running trail and captured her soul."

Bo walked the grandmother back to her seat before going back to the podium. He stood silently for a moment – tears running down his face and said to the friends and family: "It's true. I loved Evy. She was a gift, a surprise that scraped away any of the cynicism or skepticism or wariness that I normally use as a filter before getting to know someone. She simply loved life, me and the world she was navigating as adventurously as she could. A few days before she was taken from us she told me she was pregnant – the doctor thought it was twins – maybe one boy and one girl but it was still a bit early to be sure. She was simply delighted. A boy would be named after her father. A girl after her mother; I'll have no argument on this one Henrie," she said.

"I could only laugh at her insistence and said, "Of course: the next set we can name after my parents."

"More? She laughed.

At the internment the lead detectives scanned the crowd, hoping the thief would attend the funeral because they had caught the last burglar-murderer at the funeral of a victim. That fellow had been a former boyfriend of the victim and could not keep from attending the funeral. When the victim's sister saw him on the fringe of the crowd she told the detectives. They took him for coffee and in less than a few days found so many holes in his alibi, he simply shrugged his shoulders and confessed, relieved not to spend the rest of his days looking over his shoulders for the police and / or private detectives hired by the family to keep tabs on him.

The detectives were disappointed at Evy's internment because only the crème de crème of the Swiss society showed at the funeral and internment. The prominence of the family in the charitable and banking world of the city was well known and respected. Several bankers from

Geneva and London traveled to give some solace to the family, her brother and cousins.

Three days later when Bo met Michel at the usual spot for their 7:30 AM run through the parks of Zurich, they ran along at a much slower pace than usual. Bo told Michel about his plans to get the men who killed Evy. He said, "I was not always an investor. I was trained as a spy and worked uncover for several years in several countries. I had to do things I would not do today, but now, with Evy gone, killed by some mindless criminal, I have decided to disappear, to go back under-cover, to invade the world of criminals and find the bastards. I have their pictures. I have their finger prints. I have their identities. They are not locals. They are from Europe. My friends at Interpol say they are disappeared from their usual haunts, so they are either dead or simply in hiding because the murder of Evy is really the result of an attack on me because of my former life – the life I lived in my 20s and early 30's as a spy."

When they finished the run, Michel turned to Bo, put her hand on his shoulder, stared at him and said: "Henrie – or whoever you are – Get the bastards who killed Evy. They are not worthy of life. I will miss you. Just don't get killed and let me know when you get them. Ok?"

"Deal."

They hugged in the same way brothers and sisters hug, warmly but not with passion.

"Now, "Bo said, "You and I need to have some coffee and a croissant with a lawyer that I have asked to meet us this morning."

At the meeting with the lawyer, Bo signed a quit claim to his house in Zurich. The lawyer witnessed the signature and the deed would be transferred to Michel by 4-PM that afternoon. The lawyer thanked Bo for the business and left. After the lawyer left, Bo took an envelope out from under his sweat shirt and handed it to Michel.

"What is this?"

"Ah. This is One Million Euros in bearer bonds with a 6% coupon. They are yours. This should allow you to do whatever you want knowing there is some backup if you falter. In addition, there are articles of incorporation for an Evy Foundation, funded with $5,000,000 Euros, and dedicated to the funding of education of talented young people from around the world. It's not a lot of money, but Aunt Emily has said she will get donations. It will not be hard to run up the value of the fund and keep it going as long as the family is behind it."

Reading the papers, her hands shaking, Michel said, "Anything else?"

"Yes. You are the President of the Foundation. Aunt Emily is Chair. You two will work together and when she passes, if you are still involved, you will become Chair. By the way, when I told Aunt Emily of my plans, she was first to recommend you as the President and as her successor. She liked you and said Evy spoke very highly of you. Michel, Stay true to her ideals............I'll call when I am out of harm's way."

After Bo left the café, Michel sat for an hour getting a grip on the new world that had just opened for her.

On a train from Zurich to London, via Berlin, Bo posted a video to Michel featuring Maria Gonzales playing a very difficult piece by Beethoven with her school orchestra. He included a note suggesting the organization give Maria a "full ride" to NYU. He also posted a note to Maria signed "Henrie" with a cashier check for $1,000,000 He Maria would use the money to get the musical education that she dreamed of getting when they discussed her future in El Paso.

Reading *the Financial Times* Bo saw a small item that was riveting. It said, "Claude Zatt, a prominent banker in London, was found dead in the parking lot inside his employer's parking area on Saturday morning. He had been shot 3 times in the chest. No money, not even a watch was taken from him. The family suffered a similar loss just two weeks earlier when his sister, Evonne Zatt, had been murdered. A private service was held in Zurich yesterday. The police have no suspects."

Bo dropped the newspaper to the floor, sitting up straight. He remained hyper-vigilant until he arrived at the Paris train station and transferred to the Bullet train to London, upgrading to a sleeper car so he could lock the door and get some sleep. It was worth the additional costs even though it might bring some unwanted attention to the switch to such an expensive accommodation by a man who was simply a detective with Interpol traveling on a inter-governmental voucher, a necessary step so he could travel armed and not questioned about carrying a weapon on a train by the security forces who roamed the platforms and trains as a show of force to discourage criminals, terrorists and pickpockets to stay off the bullet trains of Europe.

At Paddington Station, Bo bought a burner phone to call Michel in Zurich to see what she knew, if anything, about the murder of Evy's brother.

"Henrie: It is good to hear your voice. It is so sad. Aunt Emily is simply broken. She cannot understand. What did the family do is all she can say. It's so unbelievable. Interpol is at her home. The funeral this morning in Zurich was very brief. Aunt Emily was unable to speak. She asked me to read a statement about the boy and how he and his sister were very close and did not deserve to die so violently after a life of service to the community and the family. She is broken. Can you call her?"

"Whoa... How are you?"

"I am lost. So sad, so unexpected, so undeserving: who did you get so angry, Henrie."

"I don't know. I will find them. I can't talk to Aunt Emily right now. I'll call her tomorrow. Tell her I am out of the country and will call her when I get somewhere with a good connection at noon tomorrow, Zurich time. Okay?"

"Thank you, Henrie. I will tell her. She will be just happy to hear your voice. Can you come home to see her?"

"Not yet. It will be awhile. I am meeting with some old friends from the days I told you about that should be able to direct me to these guys. I'll find out what happened but it will take some time. Give her a hug for me. Okay?'

"Okay. I'll be there when you call."

"Good. Talk to you then, Michel. And Michel, be sure to run in the morning. Activity will help but if you can find some strong guy or good friend to run with you. You are close to the family now. You might be the next one to face some trouble from these guys."

"Don't worry Henrie. I am a very good shot and I got a permit to carry from the lead detective on Evy's case, now Ned's case. He likes me so he volunteered to run with me in the morning until they get these guys. He made me promise not to shoot him if he got too friendly."

"He sounds like a good guy. I feel better now. Talk Tomorrow."

At the Tower hotel, one of those regular hotels frequented by Americans in London, Henrie called his old friend and confident at the London Station of the CIA – Beth Poland, twin sister of his wife, Kathy.

"Henrie Teller is calling on a matter of some urgency – a code 231" – he told the operator at the London Station.

"Henrie, aka, Bo I presume?"

"Yep: a long lost soul who needs a dinner partner. Free tonight?"

"The Indian place?"

"Still there on 7th?"

"Yep, good as ever. How is 7?"

"Perfect. See you then."

Bo spent the afternoon with a gorgeous real estate agent looking for a flat to buy as close to Big Ben as he could get –a cash purchase for less than $2,000,000 (US) was the target. Kathy Thompson, not long in the business, said, "No Problem: Need something right away?"

In the next two hours Bo walked through some newer flats. By 4-PM he found the perfect spot within his budget and wrote an accepted offer. He then asked Kathy to find a smaller flat somewhere along Hyde Park so his brother would have a place to run when he moved to town to help operate the new business they were designing.

He agreed to meet the real estate agent at Barclay's Bank the next afternoon and went back to the hotel to clean up for dinner with Beth. In the shower he decided to just come clean with Beth – tell her everything about killing the guys in Yemen who killed his family, taking the money from the Coal Brothers to take down the President and deliberately missing so President Bartlett would live.

Walking toward the Indian restaurant however, he changed his mind. He decided to tell Beth about Yemen, skip DC and tell her about Evy and the murder of Evy and her brother, explaining that he was a friend of the family and was seeking the murderers of the brother and sister because their daughter had been murdered in his home in Zurich and they might just have been after him. D.C. would be left for another day because he was sure Beth would never understand or ignore an attempt on the President of the USA.

In the bit of his stomach, he wondered if Beth was going to bring someone along or even take steps to make sure he was covered when dinner ended. His photo had been on the news from the Athens bank robbery. Since that time his hair had grown back and had grown a well trimmed beard. To add to the rugged outdoors guy look, he wore levies, a sweater with a cowboy roping cattle on it, cowboy boots and a leather jacket with a special pocket for his 9mm Glock.

Beth came strolling in about 10 minutes late, as usual. She gave him a big hug, a long look and said," Bo, Kathy was right. You clean up good."

"Beth – you look great. I'm so glad you were free tonight."

"Now—you're not going to shoot anyone tonight are you?"

"Nah: It's a habit. You never know. We have cracked a lot heads in the past. You just never know if they are going to pop up one day and try to drop you."

"Isn't that the truth: Enough of the bad crap that might happen: What are you doing in London."

"Come on, Beth. Let's order. What's the best? I haven't had good Indian food since the last time you and I were here after that stint in Germany."

Dinner with Beth felt like dinner with Kathy: same gestures, same accent, same eating with gusto and the same penetrating eyes that seemed friendly, but, at the same time, a bit skeptical until questions were answered to her satisfaction.

As Bo explained how he had sought out and killed the terrorists behind the murder of his wife and daughter, he could see Beth's nervousness fall away. She reveled in the knowledge that Bo had done for her family what she and her government had been unwilling to do.

When he finished the tale of Yemen, Beth lifted her glass and toasted to "the sweet taste of revenge".

As the coffee arrived, Beth said: "So Bo. Why London? Why Now?"

"Ah. You always knew the right question to ask. Here's what I need?

"I need a legend, a solid identity like Henrie, but of a man with a sordid background so I can find and kill three men who invaded my apartment and murdered a friend who was simply cooking a meal. The same men I suspect murdered my friend's brother right here, in London three days ago. The family wants me to find them. I want to find them. I'm betting they are professionals taking revenge on this family because of something I did. You know how these vendettas get out of hand and, of course, never seem to evaporate until all the blood lust driving the revenge is gone."

"She was close this friend?"

"Yes. She was pregnant with twins."

"You're the Dad?"

"Yes."

"Jesus, I'm sorry Bo. No one deserves the blood you've seen spilled. You needed it yesterday, I suppose."

"Right again. A US citizen would be best, passport stamped with entrance date of a few months ago at London, etc. I want to go home, some day. I know it's asking a lot but I am willing to pay if I have to. I'll do a job for the agency after I find these guys. You probably need some older guy to do something. Or, we can just keep this between us. It's up to you, Beth. I can get by on Henrie, but I don't think the history of that life will be very convincing to the folks I need to go through to find these bastards."

"You're right. Let's meet Saturday. What's the number I can use to find you?

On Saturday morning, Bo and Beth walked for nearly an hour reminiscing about the wife and kids, the parents who had been so devastated by the loss of their daughter and grandchildren. How her parents had only lived a few years after the loss. Beth was happy with her family and husband. He was an art curator in London. Loved the theatre and taught speech at the local college as well as French and German as second language. Like Bo and Beth he seemed to learn foreign languages they way birds learn to fly.

As they parted Beth gave Bo a package with the legend he would need to be accepted as an authentic bad guy to find these people as well as a profile of the three men who were in his apartment because he did not tell her that Hans was already dispatched to the beyond.

"How did you get so much information on these three guys so quickly?"

"They are suspects in a number violent robberies and one of them is tied to a terrorist organization here in the UK. Manchee is probably dead. He hasn't surfaced anywhere in a couple of months. Nasty guy by the way. The worst of the three, killed without reason."

"Okay. I'll put him as the third on the list and see what I can do with the other two. How come they seem to move so freely in London? Isn't Interpol or Scotland Yard on to them for something?"

"It seems they do a job now and then for the MI 5 or 6. Howard was SAS and Brickman was a smuggler of guns and people. I guess the Ms had use for them so they have them on leash, a short leash and they are under surveillance a lot. You'll have to be careful not to be seen or captured on film by the M shadowing them."

"So, Interpol wouldn't pick them up, even with video evidence of their murder of my Evy?"

"No. Can't; Ms will tell them to back down and the diplomatic folks are as useless as a hammer without a handle."

"So stealth and costume it is. Thank you Beth: I'll be back to you when the job is done. Hugs to all," Bo said as he gave Beth a big hug.

"Be careful Bo."

"Of course: I'm not on a suicide mission."

A week later Bo was standing on the roof across from the favorite watering hole of Brickman and Howard in a area of London known to the locals as Fagin's neighborhood – a neighborhood of 4- square blocks considered too rough to navigate unless you were a druggie and in dire need of fix or one of the bad guys with connections to the really hard core criminal elements of the city.

Bo set up his black tent to protect him from the rain and to set the weapon up that, equipped with a silencer, would take out both men as they exited the door. To make sure he didn't miss their exit a camera hanging from the roof of his three story building was aimed at the front door.

Sure enough, at exactly 11-PM, like every other night that week, the two men emerged with some woman on their arms. Bo took careful aim and killed both men with a round to the head – still in sight because of his infra-red site; he put two rounds into the chest of each man as they lay lifeless on the sidewalk.

As the crowd ran for cover, Bo simply put the weapon and rounds into his guitar case, jumped to the roof of the building that emptied into the next street, walked down the stairs and exited the building onto a street that was crowded with folks at the usual Friday night festival. Bo blended into the crowd. He looked like another musician walking down the street in cowboy boots, levies and a poncho with his guitar case on the way to a gig in the festival.

Bo left the main street of the festival hailed a cab and went back to his apartment.

"Done pretty early, aren't you," the cabbie asked.

"Yeah: a couple of the guys drank too much. We couldn't keep a tune and the crowd went wild. We left to avoid getting wounded by the debris coming our way."

"Sounds like a sensible decision," the cabbie replied.

Bo walked the last three blocks to his flat, meeting no one. In the apartment, he stripped down his weapon and put the expended rounds into an acid solution that would turn them into liquid.

He sent a text to Beth, asking if breakfast at 11 would be ok and she replied, CUT for "see you there."

"That was fast, Bo."

"Your intelligence was excellent. You guys have gotten better since I left."

"Indeed we have: more women analysts now."

"No wonder, Bo laughed.

Beth handed Bo a package with his original U.S. Passport marked with an entry date for London one day after he was interviewed by Agents Sloan and Parker. There was also a first class ticket to Santa Fe, via Washington, on American airlines. Bo gave Beth the car keys. She would take the car back to the embassy and dispose of the pieces of the rifle used to kill Evy's killers.

"I owe you one – a big one – Beth. You call when I can help. Ok?"

"Ok Bo, but I have to be honest. I hope you find a nice woman, get married, have kids and teach them how to ski and camp and sing in five or more languages. Kathy loved that part of you. Your arias in Italian were her favorite. She mentioned it every time we got together – even when we just went shopping for an afternoon. Your voice, she said, was the instrument that captured her heart."

"Those were the days, Beth. Those were the days. I have to go. It's too hard to go there, even now."

"Ok. Be well, Bo. We'd love to see you for Christmas or Thanksgiving – or any time. You are always welcome. And thank you for settling the score with those men who took Kathy from us and your Evy."

They hugged warmly and parted: Bo for the airport and a private plane back to the US, via Washington and Beth to a junk yard that would flatten the car as she watched the body melted into scrap, erasing any evidence of the gun or the man and woman who had used the car.

On the way back to the office, Beth stopped at her favorite little church in London and lit 4 candles for her sister, her two nieces and Evy. In a silent prayer, she asked the souls of the departed to "save him and let him sing again."

Washington, DC

Bo diverted his flight to Iceland to meet up with an old friend, leaving in his bank vault, a package of information that could be published if Bo was found murdered. "It's insurance" he told his former supervisor at Langley when he was in the field in the European theatre. "Guard it well Andre. It's my life line to security in this world infested with the likes of our nation's former enemies."

At the airport he bought a few Icelandic sweaters and shipped them to Beth's family for her whole family as well as two sweaters for Michel in Zurich Aunt Emily.

At DC he dismissed his rented jet and took a cab to the Madison Hotel, a favorite, though expensive place to stay so he could be close to the White House. He liked the neighborhood because it was filled with folks from all over the world, year around. He could blend into the crowd in any kind of dress and there were plenty of places to run in the morning with plenty of open space and views of any incoming trouble.

After checking in he called FBI Agent Joan Sloan.

"Agent Sloan, this is Bo. You interviewed me in Santa Fe a few weeks ago."

"Yes. And you are a hard man to find. You have been off the radar after that meeting. What happened"

"Ah: It's my way. IF you could meet me for dinner tonight I can explain. I'm only in DC for a couple of days and found some information that might be helpful to you in your investigation. Are you free?"

"Tonight won't work, but lunch tomorrow will. Say 1?"

"Sure. It's pretty late notice. I apologize but I just got into town: I'm staying at the Madison. They have a great restaurant. Will that work?"

"Pretty pricey for a government worker…"

"It's on me. Call it business and pleasure."

"That will work. See you at 1?"

"Perfect. See you then."

Agent Sloan arrived at precisely 1-PM, dressed in the same blue suit she wore the first time Bo met her. The bulge of her weapon on the left side was easy for the trained eye and the maitre de reminded her there was a ban on weapons in the hotel, except for Federal officers. She showed her FBI credentials, the maitre de smiled and led her to Bo's table.

"What was the fuss?" Bo asked.

"Oh. The usual weapons stop; a lot of famous people stay here so they are very alert and attentive to anyone who seems be armed."

"Surprised you got through the front door."

"Same nonsense: I don't mind."

They both ordered a lobster salad, laughing about how their tastes were simpatico on this very sunny spring day, a day when the cherry blossoms were just starting to brighten up the city, signaling the end of winter and the beginning of warmer times.

"So Bo, what do you have on our case? What vital evidence?"

"Vital. Did I say vital? No. I said some information – more of a guess really. But, Agent Sloan, to be perfectly honest I just wanted to see you again. I felt we might have had a connection back there in Santa Fe."

"Oh. Bo. You are much too elusive a guy for me. You come and go like Banqo's ghost. I need a more solid guy, a more predictable guy. Although, I must confess I like the way you cook and your house was well organized and clean unlike most of the guys in this town who work all day and have apartments that are as messy as the dorm room of a Georgetown freshman."

"Ok. But I am telling you I am going to settle down in Santa Fe. I've decided that I've been around the world enough. Seen enough new places and had enough casual and short-term relationships to change my ways. Maybe if you're still free in a year or so, we can go out and you can judge for yourself if there is any connective tissue between us."

"Fair enough, but now that the foreplay is over, tell me what you've got."

"Okay. I just wondered if you had looked overseas for that second man, the guy who tricked up the drones from the Forest Service. I wonder because I remember working with a Brit in the Middle East on drones. He looked a bit like the guy you thought looked like me. Indeed, a lot of the guys in our unit used to get us mixed up – some thought we were twins until he spoke. The British accent was very distinctive. Have you looked overseas?"

"We did some investigating, but a lot of the countries only gave us a nominal amount of help. Sovereignty issues and all that: Do you remember his name."

"Sure: We were side by side for nearly a year. He saved my butt more than once and me his. I'm not sure where he is now. That was nearly 20 years ago. I'm not even sure I'd recognize him anymore. Twenty years can do a lot to a man if he doesn't stay in shape and he was a bit of party animal – much more of a party guy than me. He used to say, "I'll be dead soon enough.""

"Was he a drone expert?"

"Oh yeah: Almost as good as me."

"Really: and why didn't you mention this before."

"You know why, Agent Sloan. I was just back from a long ride, after a month in the desert when you laid the bad news about an attack on the President, a guy I really liked as President. Then, you accused me of being the bad guy. Anyway, I think it would be worthwhile to find and talk to this guy. Maybe he knows someone or maybe he is the guy."

"What's his name?"

"Brickman.... Joel Brickman, SAS when I knew him. Probably still is if he hasn't been killed. He was a real dare devil. Try anything. He loved the danger: He said he got higher on danger than cocaine."

"He was an addict?"

"I don't know. He just did some when he could get it when he was on leave, but on duty, he was stone cold sober – about as serious as a guy doing open heart surgery."

Agent Sloan looked around the restaurant and noticed the once crowded tables were nearly all empty.

"Christ. It's nearly 3 – I'm late. I have to go. Thanks. And when will you be leaving town?"

"Some time tomorrow."

"See you" and Sloan was gone, giving Bo a hug, a move she seemed to regret as soon as she did it. It was just an instinct. She did feel a connection to him. It was strange. He was the kind of guy she had longed to meet. Smart, Funny, Strong; a man who served with distinction but never mentioned it in any kind of bragging way. And, best of all – he was a handsome guy who reminded her of her Dad and uncles, soldiers who returned from battle and led responsible lives, caring for their families without a lot of complaining or whimpering – simply enjoying the company of their children, wives, and families most the time.

Bo had to laugh as he watched her leave in a rush. She was a beauty. Smart and very disciplined. Probably a dynamo in bed, but he was sure he'd never find out because she would never let herself get too close to a suspect unless, of course, she was perfectly sure he was completely innocent.

'Maybe Brickman will fill the bill, close the case and give Sloan and me a chance to see if something can develop,' Bo thought as he signed the bill. Noticing he had a boner just from talking with Agent Sloan. Bo laughed and lingered over this coffee until the boner settled down and he could leave without embarrassing himself.'

At 5:30 there was a knock on this hotel door. He put on his robe, his 9MM in his pocket, put down screen on his computer so it would lock up and automatically encrypt all his information and files.

"Agent Sloan?"

"Bo. I came for desert."

"With or without whip cream"

"With, of course, "she laughed as she pulled a small can of real whipped cream from her pocket.

"Great," Bo replied. "I really am hungry and this desert is magnificent."

A few hours later, Sloan said, "Bo—that was really good but I really am hungry. Can we go out or order in or something. I'm starved. It's been a long day and I didn't get a nap like you, you lazy man."

"What's your pleasure? But first I have to tell you something.

"Will it take long?"

"Ever the practical one: No... I just wanted you to know I had a boner when you left lunch. That's a first. I mean you are just a magnificent creature and my response to you is enormous."

"I can see that: Thanks," she said as took his penis in her hand and started to gently pull on it until it simply sprung to full length. "Can we take a few more minutes before dinner? It's a shame to waste a perfectly firm member."

"Sure, "Bo said as she inserted him into her with one hand on his chest as Bo softly squeezed her breasts.

The next morning Bo and Sloan drove to her place in Georgetown so she could get some fresh clothes and show Bo where she lived during and after attending Georgetown, thanks to her parents who wanted her to have a place to live in Georgetown, not a dorm room, while she completed her undergraduate and later a law degree.

"It turned in to a really good investment. Daddy won't sell. I won't move. And the price has soared from a few hundred thousand to a million plus... maybe two. It even has a garage," she laughed, as they turned into the open garage door.

"Not bad for a Fed," Bo remarked as the door closed behind them and the lights went on in the garage.

"Jealous: right?"

"Absolutely: Actually I'm glad to see you live so close to everything

As they entered, Bo noticed a ping pong table, a billiards table, one of those very large TVs, and all the makings of a home office – complete with a couple rifles in a rack above the desk.

"Oh, this is Dad's space. He gets to use it when he is in town or just passing through while I am out of town. He loves his billiards and Mom loves to whoop his ass at ping pong. She was a professional of sorts in college to hear her tell it. She played for martinis. Loved her martinis until she got pregnant with me and stopped drinking and become both a vegetarian and an expert skier. God she loves to ski."

"How's your ping pong?"

"Fair to good depending on the time of day," she laughed as they went up the stairs to the first floor.

"This is where I really live – a master suite, two baths, a gourmet kitchen and a that big dining room table is for the big dinners when Dad and Mom are in town or I throw a party for the folks at the Bureau and others. I do that about once a month; Too much information?"

"No. I'm glad to see you have an active social life. It makes your coming in my direction a great compliment."

"Ah……feeling like a winner are we?"

"Yep," Bo laughed as he pulled her close, starting to take off her clothes as she took off for the shower.

When Bo woke up an hour later, Sloan was sitting up in bed reading a report from the office on her iphone.

The Memorandum was from her boss at FBI headquarters with a CC to Agent Parker:

"Good job: "John Brickman, a suspect, in the attempted murder of President Bartlett, has been murdered in London with three shots from a high powered rifle – two to the chest and one to the head. It could be a cleaning up of details by the folks behind the attempt on POTUS. Brickman's financial records are under scrutiny. So far, our forensic accountant team has found two transactions that could be attached to the murder. One hundred thousand US was transferred into his account a week before the attempt on POTUS and a similar amount was transferred into his account the morning of the attack. The monies are not immediately traceable but initial IT suggests the money was drawn against an account in Zurich at a small but well respected institution known as Zurich Trust. The source of the money was an account of a subsidiary of the COAL Brothers Oil Consortium. Agents will interview COAL Brothers financial executives as well and Bank personnel who track transfers of funds: Looks like a solid lead. Good work you guys. Will know more in a few days: stay on it."

When Bo finished reading the report, he said: "So, if you get a raise and a promotion do I get finder's fee?"

"You're gonna get it all weekend long"

"Outstanding, but seriously this does sound like the sort of thing a crazy bunch like the COAL Brother's friends might just do – they were really pissed about a peacenik president getting re-elected and cutting the budget. Those brothers are always banging on the war drum – couple of draft dodgers like Dick Cheney – never got shot at by some crazy, scared enemy. Don't have a clue about how bad it can get out there for the soldiers and civilians. The Secret Service taught me in catching the bad guys 101 when searching for Counterfeit $ – "follow the money because it never lies."

"We'll see. By the way, I wouldn't have come to see you if you were still a suspect," Sharon said with a bit of a blush.

"So under the covers, is not under-cover?"

"God you are a dude – like a college student- sometimes."

"Good to be seen as a youngster....."

Sharon drove Bo to the airport on Monday. She felt very sad to see him go back to Santa Fe but was smiling when he said, "See you for dinner on Friday. Let's have lobster on the River."

"Call me when you get home?"

"Ok," Bo promised.

On the plane it became clear to Bo that he was going to get the Coal Brothers and they were not going to get him. They'd try but there was no trace – no money trail, no electronic trail, no conversations with the Coal Brothers except the one in Aspen while he was on a skiing vacation. Their body guard might identify him but that could be explained away because Bo had run several seminars at their company about executive security programs and practices.

A text to Michel in Zurich said: "Thx. Project done. See you in London for concert."

In London, Bo went to one of the apartments he had rented under the name of Robert Ferris – a traveling salesman who wasn't home much. In the wall was a secret pocket filled with cash and IDs. He put the cash in a lining in his baggage. For four days he wandered the streets of London. A morning run, a bit of lunch with a former colleague, a dinner with Beth and the kids and one visit to Oxford to see his old stomping grounds and discuss coming back to take a few courses in French Literature because it was so outside the pale of reality he felt his mind and spirit might get re-charged. As he told Sharon, "spending a year reading literature from the 18th century might make me feel better about civilization." What he didn't say was "I'm pessimist about life, love and need to put some sort of a cap on the pain I feel everyday about the loss of my daughters and the two women I loved and lost to some violent thugs."

Back in FBI headquarters Sloan started to follow up on the Brickman information.

She learned that a fellow by the name of Nat Howard was murdered at the same time and place as John Brickman, that the two men were known associates, suspected of often acting in concert. Both men were violent and, based on intelligence tests while in the Service both man were shown to have higher than average IQs, more than a little paranoia and great deal of cunning. "They were likable rogues who often disarmed people with humor," according to the field reports of interviews with family, friends and associates of the two men.

Agent Parker came into Sharon's office just as she was hanging up with Bo with a huge smile on his face. "You find the Hope Diamond?" Sharon laughed at the expression on his face.

"Maybe: Take a look."

"This Nat or Nate guy also got a $100K into his account the day of the POTUS attempt and a week later from the same account of that Coal Brothers subsidiary. It was also to a Zurich Trust Account. That's pretty big money for a couple of burglar. What they were doing for Coal Oil? No one in HR over there seems to know them. They have no record of working for the company. It's got to be one of the brothers – or both they did something for to get paid that much. Our guys in Zurich are digging deeper."

"That's really good Bill, but how do we get to these guys without getting walled out by lawyers and lobbyists, even the AG is a good friend of these guys? He goes to football games with these guys."

"I won't be easy. I'd say our guys in Zurich have to find out who opened the account and who has been to the bank lately from the Coal Organization or its local subsidiary. Can we do that without arousing the ire of the AG?"

"Sure. You think the AG will object to an agent following up, especially in this case, when we are just interviewing someone low on the corporate ladder about a couple of small offshore accounts and transfers of only $200,000. Let's make a request of the folks in Zurich in white collar crime. We can characterize it as possible money laundering scheme that went wrong by some low level employee of Coal, ending up with a street shooting on the streets of London in the raunchy and rancid "Fagin District.""

"That's good Sloan. We can get that one from our regional Director easily. I'll go see the old man right now."

Sharon leaned back in her chair, her minding wandering away from the rush to arrest some crook, fantasizing about how she and Bo would be together when he got back tomorrow. Her life as a crime investigator had felt surprisingly stale during the past week, even though she had broken a money laundering ring and had been in the team of agents kicking in a door to capture the whole team of crooks as they were meeting in the Madison Hotel, just across from the White House.

She placed a quick call to Bo on a burner phone he had given her, got a busy signal so she left a message, "See you tomorrow: Safe travel."

As she went to hang up she noticed a small, lower case "e" in the corner of the screen on her phone – an indication that she was calling an encrypted message to an encrypted phone. "God, he is a worrier" she said out loud. When she got home, Sharon listened to a message from Bo: "Honey, sorry, I can't be there tonight. Gone to Switzerland: Important, back on Monday, will call later, much love."

Michel met Bo at the Zurich airport, hugged him warmly, and thanked him profusely for coming: "Aunt Emily is so anxious to see you before she goes. And, I'm sorry Henrie but she is really going. Her spirit is broken. I can't take the place of Evy and she does not feel too close to other family members. She says they are all too greedy. Evy was the poet among them."

"I'm really glad you got me before I was too far out into Atlantic –that old point of no return because of gas—only so much, Michel. Another 15 minutes and I couldn't have gotten here until tomorrow."

Aunt Emily shooed Michel out of the room. "I want to talk to Henrie alone."

When the room was empty and the door closed, Emily asked Bo to sit close to her on the couch. "Now Henrie, I want you to tell me everything. You got the men who killed sweet Evy?"

"I did: there were two of them. I got them in London. They were really nasty pieces of work. They would have made perfect SS guards; terrible people no one will miss."

"And you Henrie," Aunt Emily asked, as she took his hands in her. "Can you handle doing this? Are you ok?"

"Emily, I have done this before. I was in Special Ops for several years and undercover for several years. To erase swine like these does not harm my conscience one jot I do not have one iota of regret. And, by the way, there is no trail to me and there will not be. A friend helped me erase all traces of me in Europe during that day. I'm out of it completely..... I only wish I had been with Evy when these swine invaded my home."

Both sat in silence for several minutes, Aunt Emily with her eyes closed and Bo with his eyes focused on the photo on the dresser of Evy with Aunt Emily when Evy was a high school student skiing down a slope in Switzerland.

He turned to look at Emily and noticed how much she had aged since they met just a few months earlier at the party Evy hosted to save the whales and other living things from the rapacious and greedy "plunderers of nature and our grandchildren's birthright" as Evy would say on her organization's website.

Emily opened her eyes, squeezing Bo's hands with all the strength she could muster: "Henrie. I thank you. I can leave this world now knowing those swine are gone from the world. She has been revenged and that was something I was not able to do for my parents because the men who killed them disappeared after the war. No one could find them. They must have died in battle or been hidden. It was a great disappointment they were not found and shot while I watched. Henrie, I don't want to sound ghoulish, but please tell me they suffered a little."

"I was a long shot, Emily, from the roof to the street. Both men were dead from the first round to their head and I put two rounds in their chest just for good measure. They fell in the street and lay there for several hours while the police investigated. Based on their records, Emily, no one will care about them. Their funerals will be empty: No one will mourn their passing. We need to simply forget them. Evy is the one we need to remember and it is her memory and her dreams that we have to help come into the world."

"You're right of course. I see why Evy loved you so. You actually know what is important."

Emily let go of his hands as she leaned back in the couch and asked Henrie to get Michel.

"Michel, "Emily said, "could you get that folder we discussed before you left to get Henrie."

"Henrie," Aunt Emily smiled, as she opened the file. "I am going to sign these documents and you and Michel are going to witness my signature. In these documents I give all my fortune to your care, to the care of you and Michel and the Evy World Foundation. My lawyers say this is airtight and the family cannot break it. Michel gets power of attorney. If anything should happen to Michel you become the head of the organization."

"Emily. This is a great honor, but I am leaving Europe. It has not been kind to me. I am filled with sadness just at the thought of being on this continent. It is not where I want to be ever again. So, I would prefer you assign the task to Michel and let her pick a worthy successor. She has impeccable taste in people, and sound judgment. I think she will be about a lot longer than me."

"Oh, Henrie, would you deny an old woman her dying wish."

"Yes. I have to. Michel is the one to carry on Evy's legacy and mission. She has the smarts and she loved Evy almost as much as I did.

They were great friends, though only knew each other for a short time they were soul mates if ever I saw soul mates. Let her do it."

"Very well: Will you sign as witness at least."

"No. Get the butler and the maid to sign as witnesses. They are not part of the family or the legacy so they will be best, unless your attorney is coming to dinner. In that case the lawyer can suggest the best way to sign. But, I must be out of the loop on the paperwork because if the matter we were discussing comes up it would not be good for the foundation."

Michel almost said, "What was that" but she held back as she noticed the look of determination in the eyes of Henrie and the silent acknowledgment of Aunt Emily of the truth of what Henrie said.

After dinner the lawyer arrived for coffee, bringing her assistant along so that Michel and Emily, the attorney and her assistant could sign the new last will and testament of Emily Zatt – a survivor of the death camps in Germany during WWII.

After all the papers were signed, Aunt Emily asked her attorney to get the painting hanging on the wall by Monet. Emily took the painting in her hands, smiled, kissed it softly and handed it to Henrie. "Henrie, this is yours. You carry the family memory for all time. Pass it to the children you have with some lucky woman. Don't be a sad sack all your life. Evy would not want you to sulk and feel so lost that you could not build a future for yourself. Burn a candle for her every March 5th, she said with tears streaming down her face.

Henrie too was crying as he sought to return the painting to Emily but she would not have it.

She asked her attorney to write a note that said, "I Emily Zatt do give this Monet painting to Mr. Henrie Teller – a friend – and husband to be of my wonderful niece Evy who lost her life on March 5-2020 in Zurich. The painting is given to him into perpetuity. It is given in gratitude for his love and friendship. It is his forever. Signed and witnessed by: Emily, her attorney Constance Gerber, and Michel Martel- Ph.d, CEO of the Evy World Foundation.

At the airport, Michel refused to take the painting. "I can't. I can't lie to Aunt Emily if she asked if you kept the painting. Don't ask me to do that Henrie. I can't."

Reluctantly, he boarded a private jet and flew to the US as a French diplomat, Henrie Teller, so he would not have to show any of the bearer bonds or the painting that Emily had given to him, but he thought "How do I tell Sharon I have a Monet?"

One Year later: London

Beth smiled widely when she saw the note from Bo in her early morning mail at the embassy in London. Inside she found a picture of Bo, a woman and two children. His note read: "I took your advice... Thanks. Say hello to Sharon and the twins—Tanya and Sean. Life is good in Aspen. Come visit. Great skiing and we can make room for you and Paul and the children. Yes. I am now a cop in Aspen, working with an old partner from Secret Service days. It's wonderful to get up every morning and see the sun rise over the mountains. Be well. Love to all – Bo."

On her encrypted phone she called Bo and left the following message: "Bo --Got your note. I am very happy for you. Wife and children are gorgeous. I'm betting that Kathy and the twins will watch over all of you and keep all of you safe. See you guys in the spring. Love to all, Beth."

Bo replied: "Thanks. Too bad about our most prominent citizen – the Coal brothers -- lost their lives in a riot in Nigeria where they were negotiating a new oil field. First week of March is best. Look forward to it."

7/29/2014

London: the search for Evy's killers..............

TEACHER LEADS REVOLT ON LONG ISLAND, NY

History shows that the proper word, the proper phrase, spoken at the proper time, by the proper person can be a python swallowing villages, whole cities, even whole civilizations. Examples abound.

"Let them eat cake" motivated the French to cut off the heads of King Louie XVI and Marie Antoinette- the lady who spoke those four words to a confidant while the people of France faced starvation and she lived a life of luxury.

Eight words: *"God made me king :* GOD MAKES NO MISTAKES" -- a notion ruling France until the "God-made-me-King" head dropped into a basket before a cheering crowd as the no longer docile Roman Catholic population, despite the warnings of Bishops and Cardinals who suddenly lost absolute control over the people. Starvation and injustice trumped promises of Heaven, denying the idea that kings had a "god given" right to plunder the nation and its people.

When the heads of the king and his paramour were guillotined, their heads falling into a basket, at the Place de Concorde, in the middle of Paris, the power of "The People" to rule, for better or worse was irrevocably endorsed as a legitimate notion in the hearts and minds of Parisians and like-minded souls around the world.

A Bloody time followed for the people of France, as *"rule by the people"* was seized by ruthless men seeking the same privileges they would deny the former King and his consort.

In time people in France started to feel that "Maybe God doesn't make mistakes."

"Maybe it was a mistake to chop off the head of the King" was heard on the streets of Paris as the people of France suffered through one bloody coup after another bloody coup.

In time a leader appeared, a man of "Gravitas" who promised to put France back on the Road to Greatness – a man of little physical stature from Corsica. This little man, Napoleon Bonaparte, created order and ignited a dream of greatness. His wars eventually turned France into a broken nation with every man between the age of 14 and 60 years either in the ground or a beggar in the streets without a limb or an eye or an ear, their limbs torn from their bodies by cannon balls on killing fields created by Bonaparte's quest for greatness.

Those still alive after Bonaparte's reign suffered daily from the wounds received in Bonaparte's war to establish the Greatness of France, and his own greatness.

In North America soon to be U.S. Citizens declared, *"No taxation without representation."*

With those four words the colonists took up arms, pinned the mighty British Empire to the ground, declared their freedom to practice whatever religion they wanted – a decided change from the rule of Popes and Potentates, Kings and Princes who ruled Europe with iron fists and a rigid social hierarchy, codified and enforced by nobles and churchmen for centuries.

This new U.S. citizen demanded the right to decide what taxes he would pay, what religion he would practice, what laws would govern his daily life. This declaration of freedom from the neatly arranged social pecking order "designed by god" through "birth rights" for upper classes, born to the aristocracy that prevailed in Europe was upended by the new, free to be, U.S. citizens.

In 2018, three words spoken in a small town along Long Island, New York provoked a revolution.

On that extension of New York State into the Atlantic a town's life was changed when the most unlikely of men, a man of some prominence – visibility at least - spoke 3 words as part of a teasing conversation with a woman he wanted to bed and spend months of happy frolicking with in his sheets.

His three words caused a social earthquake among the peoples of a small, quiet, conservative, Christian town where the Tea Party ruled and the local Congressional representative was poised to get the nomination as the GOP Presidential candidate in 2016.

The three words provoking this revolution were *"God makes Mistakes!"*

These three words, spoken in the town of *More Churches than Taverns, NY* located a few miles west of Montauk along the Atlantic evoked a public debate of the sort noted by historians as outrageous and vile, an organized rage that would have led to the Guillotine for a speaker in France before Bonaparte ruled and some order prevailed.

Fortunately, this modern day revolutionary could not, like Joan of Arc, be kidnapped and sold to English Lords by the powers that ran a little conservative town on Long Island –a town so conservative it had changed its name after several heated battles a few years earlier to reflect the fact that there were 16-Churches and only 8-taverns in their town of 16,000 to *More Churches than Taverns, NY* from its former name of *Grant's Crossing, NY* – a name given the community by its founders in honor of General Ulysses S. Grant when the North won the Civil War.

> The conversation that started the battle in the community
> was innocent enough.

Who was the leader of the revolution?

The agent provocateur of this revolution was a high school math teacher by the name of Harold Lutz who had transferred from Manhattan five years earlier at the age of 25. His move was driven to this "oh my goooood it's quiet at night" suburb by the outrageous prices commanded by real estate developers in Manhattan.

In time, Harold was happy with his new situation but this was his fifth summer at the beach community and he was "JUST FRICKING

TIRED" he told his brother of fighting deer flies – a nasty creature that popped up in July, chasing people indoors for one month before the nasty little buggers died off, having sucked the blood of thousands of otherwise not too cantankerous, Christian folks in the town and its visitors.

Harold Lutz seemed an unlikely candidate to lead the charge of social change, but, alas, he was so tired of putting lotion on any part of his body exposed to the biting deer flies one morning when he stopped for his first coffee at his favorite coffee shop –a coffee shop with a special attraction for Harold—a local piano teacher who ran the restaurant in the summer, one Maria Luciana.

This particular morning, for some reason unknown to him, he felt compelled to express his disdain for those damned deer flies.

"So, Harold, how are you on this fine summer day without all those children in class?" Maria asked as Harold ordered his usual black coffee and eggs breakfast.

His reply, as always, "Dark, really hot, with as much caffeine as you can muster. I really need it today".

In a few minutes Maria returned with a bright red "More Churches than Taverns" coffee mug, filled to the brim with the darkest coffee from Columbia that her little diner offered.

As she handed him his cup with a big smile, Harold said in a low, soothing voice he liked to use when trying to coax the skirt from some woman he met in a bar: "You know, Maria, I miss those little brats. They are certainly a lot less bothersome than these damn deer flies. They're driving me nuts, turning my usual happy self into a roaring manic. When I go out in the morning to get the New York Times, they attack me like I was their own personal feeding tube."

"Ooooohhh my God-- you must have sweet blood like my Mother, Harold," Maria laughed. "Maybe you should you drive to the Post Office across the street and get a PO Box like I have. There are few of those nasty creatures up here because of that steady ocean breeze, you know."

"Maria, I don't want to be guilty of heresy or get burned at the stake or anything like that, but when those little bastards attack me – excuse my profanity – but when those deer flies attack me all I can think is

"GOD MAKES MISTAKES." He must because these flies do nothing but cause pain and suffering."

"Oh come on Harold. It's not that bad. They serve a purpose, a useful purpose like all of God's creatures, don't you know. There are no mistakes in God's world—nope, not a one. Why our minister, Rev. Dooley, just spoke on suffering last Sunday when he showed us how many deer fly bites he had on his face – an otherwise beautiful face it was – but last Sunday he must have had 100 bites on his face and neck. He even shaved his head so he could put some lotion on the bites. He looked like a teenager with a bad case of acne who put some of those creams on their zits...He said God doesn't make mistakes........He was a sight," Maria laughed.

"I'll bet he was," Harold laughed, imagining the chubby preacher with a pimply face, every deer tick bite covered with some kind of white lotion.

"Reverend Dooley is a lot more charitable than I am. Maria, I'm going to the town hall meeting tonight and ask them to pump as much fly killing fog on the town as they can. It's so bad, it's clearing the beaches. And, you know, Maria, we need the money out here. We only have a few months to make our economy work, to cover our annual expenses and pay our taxes and pay our teachers, of course."

"Oh come on Harold, aren't you overreacting just a bit too much. They're only flies. We can endure a few weeks of bites. It's better than gassing the town, isn't it? What will people say? You know Harold; this is a very, very, VERY Conservative town. I've lived here all my life and these folks don't like change. They are not like the folks you grew up with in Montana."

"I'd like to agree with you Maria but by God this has to be stopped before the whole city falls into the sea on the backs of these nasty creatures..."

Harold drove off. "I got the last word in on that one," he told the world as he raced back home with words and phrases filling his mind to use at the town meeting after dinner, words and phrases he was confident would win the day and make him a hero in the town. 'Who Knows? It might even get me promoted to assistant principal making me eligible to replace the retiring superintendant of the district high schools, middle schools and K-12 facilities serving the whole north end of Long Island – about 500,000 folks in all with 12 schools."

Maria went to the city council meeting that night because she wanted to hear what Harold had to say and, she hoped, they might share an ice cream at her childhood friends ice cream parlor after the meeting. This would not be a date, exactly, but, she hoped he might actually move a bit closer to asking her on a real date like dinner at Montauk, a bit of dancing under the stars, and, she fanaticized they might even have wild sex on the beach like all those characters in the romance movies she watched every night in her bedroom after grading papers during the school year.

It was summer now and the 33 year old divorcee, still childless, feeling it was either time to either have the baby or forget the mothering bit. She wanted adventure, romance, a night of bliss and groping that made her feel she lost her touch with the earth as the mighty Harold filled her with bliss.

The City Council meeting room was filled to the brim with residents dressed in shorts and tee shirts and other summer attire except, of course, the attorneys representing the city and the folks hired by residents to argue against any changes in the city's taxes. As always the lawyers were attired in required suits, ties and polished shoes, carrying the required leather briefcase that looked like it had been traveling through India for a year or so, kicked by every goat in the country because a brown beaten briefcase spelled "experience".

"This meeting will come to order" Mayor Jim Taylor said at exactly 7PM. He pounded the meeting to order with a great wooden gavel his wife had made especially for him when he was elected Mayor. In the summer it was the only way to get the attention of the crowd buzzing with chatter about fishing and the upcoming weekend festival for those who loved lobster sponsored by the local Micro-Brewer – a subsidiary of the Mayor's saloon on the beach.

Winter meetings of the council were much a quieter because only about a dozen regulars attended the Council Meeting. Mayor Taylor loved the winter meetings: "predictable as the tides" he often told his wife after a council meeting in winter.

Mayor Taylor was a stickler for timely meetings. He abhorred tardiness and slow motion speakers who couldn't get to the point without a 3 minute introduction to their 10 second request or recommendation.

After the pledge of allegiance was shared by everyone in the room, the Mayor asked if the Clerk could pass along the sign in sheet for members of the public who wished to address the Council as he told the audience, "Folks who signed up to speak get 3 minutes and no more – no exceptions, not a one – because there are nearly 30 folks signed up to speak for 3 minutes. The means about ninety minutes, plus, so the Council would appreciate it if the folks signed up to speak will be even briefer than 3 minutes if they can. Brevity and clarity is greatly appreciated."

"Mr. Mayor," Thelma Right, the Deputy Mayor, piped up, "I'm sure the Council agrees with your request for brevity. We need to discuss taxes tonight and I'm sure the folks here tonight want to hear about that issue and make their views on taxes heard by this council."

"I'm sure they do Thelma. Thanks for the support. Now, let's see, who is first on the list of speakers. Ah. Of course, Mr. Harold Jones, our local baker is recognized for 3 minutes. Mr. Jones."

"Thank you, Mister Mayor and Members of the City Council; I am opposed to any tax increase, Period. We pay too much as it is."

With that comment the town's 300 pound, five foot tall baker, considered by all as a pillar of the community, the third generation of bakers in town stepped back from the microphone.

"Well thank for your brevity, Harold," Mayor Taylor said as he read from the list, "Ah. Our local sixth grade teacher, a recipient of tax dollars because he is educating our children, Mr. Harold Lutz."

"Mr. Mayor. I'm here tonight because I've learned these past summers that *God makes mistakes*. What is God's biggest mistake? It has to be those damned deer flies that cut down our population in July and cause economic damage to our residents, including the butcher, the baker and the saloon keeper who can't serve outside in the month of July unless they have a spot on the beach like yours, Mr. Mayor.

So, I am here tonight to ask this council to INCREASE- Increase – increase – our taxes and pour on as much gas as you can on this population as the Health Department will allow you to pour on us and gas these Mistakes created by GOD out of our lives. These flies are an abomination that needs to be erased from our land. Please... Please... Eradicate these nasty little creatures. They are an abomination and a scourge on the land that is harming the people and the businesses in our community -- Thank you."

"Your time is up," Mayor Taylor said, as he rang the bell on his desk and called the name of the next speaker, "Wilma Hitchcock, our local librarian and pastor of the "Heaven Waits" Evangelical Church."

"Thank you, Mr. Mayor. We missed you last Sunday, by the way," Wilma Hitchcock told the Mayor as she began her address to the council, a council she had been addressing for the past 30 years, Wilma had organized the community as Mayor for eight years before Mayor Taylor. Being May was a welcome activity after her husband had been killed in Vietnam as a fighter pilot and she returned home as a widow from the war as a decorated nurse who had been wounded when the Viet Cong got a number of mortar rounds into the military hospital where she served as a surgical nurse.

Wilma was perceived as a foundational character in the community, respected for her service to her country and her devotion to the children of the community –especially the victims of domestic violence – in the town of *More Churches than Taverns*, a name change she had been instrumental in getting passed by the Council and voters when 68% told pollsters they were in favor of the change 5-years earlier.

Mayor Taylor smiled as Wilma walked to the podium because she had "Gravitas" in the city. If she was against a tax increase, it would dead on arrival. He looked forward to her words. He was confident the rest of the folks on the list will just say "Against" or "For" after she finished. This could be a shorter meeting than expected, allowing him to get home early and go fishing at high tide with his brother, Mort.

"Members of the Council," Wilma began, "I'm flabbergasted by what one of our teachers just said about *God making Mistakes.*" That is simply the dumbest and most sacrilegious things I have heard in this room. Mr. Lutz should be sent packing because he does not see the Wisdom of the Bible and does not reflect the values of the people of this community who know with certainty, God is perfect and God does not make mistakes" she said with the same emphatic tone Supreme Court Justice Roberts used when he declared that the Affordable Care Act was Constitutional as a tax.

"These deer flies," she turned to tell Mr. Lutz, "serve a purpose in God's world and I would absolutely oppose spending a plug nickel on gassing God's Creature – even a creature as irritating and difficult to deal with as those creatures that are part of our annual "deer fly infestation".

"And, Mr. Mayor, as a nurse who served the medical needs of this community for decades I would tell this city council that our people, our children and our visitors don't need to be gassed just because the deer fly is a bit of irritation for most of us but a "big enough irritation" for our local math teacher to seek a gassing of one of God's creatures – AND US."

Wilma then turned to where Mr. Lutz was sitting next to Maria, pointing her finger at him, she said: "Shame on you Mr. Lutz. Grow Up! Find God!"

Turning to face the City Council, she smiled sweetly and said: "Thank you for listening Members of the Council".

As she returned to her seat a great round of applause filled the room, applause started by Maria's preacher, the Reverend Dooley.

Sensing the mood changing in the room, the council stood and joined in the round of applause until Wilma was seated after being embraced by several of the folks near her and on the aisle as she returned to her seat in the last row.

Mayor Taylor asked the Council to gather in a circle and said, "Look, this debate is going to change. How about asking for a show of hands on tax increases, closing the public hearing and start the debate about items on the budget?"

The Council nodded approval:" It's going get real contentious now that God is in the mix," one Council Member said.

When the poll was taken, all but 5 people in room were opposed to a tax increase.

The Mayor closed the public speech portion of the meeting, inviting folks to send a letter to his office outlining their opposition or approval of tax increases.

"Wait a Minute," "Wait a Minute!!!" the Reverend Dooley repeated in his most booming voice as he marched up to the Microphone. "This is an outrage. We are citizens. We have the right to speak our mind. This Council has posted an agenda. It has to fulfill that agenda or this Council Meeting has to be canceled. Besides: I think the people want to hear from Mr. Lutz and about Mr. Lutz's notion that God makes mistakes. Really: How can a man like this be allowed to teach our children?"

"Hang on there, Mr. Dooley. We live in a Democracy so a citizen can say whatever they believe," Harold shouted back.

"Look Lutz, if you're right and GOD MAKES MISTAKES then the liberal crazies in this country will say," kill every fetus that isn't perfect and let the sick and old and dying who cost so much to keep alive be gassed – like those deer flies you don't like – so the society can have more money to enjoy the good times, to travel and entertain themselves like a pack of heathens and pagans guided by a moral compass as broken as the moral compass that ruled in ancient Rome where people cheered as gladiators killed one another for the entertainment of the crowd. HITLER PUSHED THAT AGENDA! -- Lutz."

"Nonsense, Dooley" Lutz yelled back. "An all knowing, all perfect god is illogical. If man is made in the image and likeness of GOD then GOD has to be a mistake maker, just like the rest of us –Dooley!"

"Blasphemy," the Reverend Dooley, shouted back.'

"Nazi," Harold Lutz shouted back as he walked out the door with Maria pulling him along so this shouting match would end, they could get that ice cream cone

and fulfill her fantasy of a night in the sheets.

A few hundred feet from the meeting, Harold said: "Oh, it will be okay Maria. Those noise makers want to keep their tax exemption and their right to tell people what to believe and what to do. They won't come after freedom of speech because they might lose their freedom of speech" Harold exclaimed, his heart pounding like the first time he slugged his brutish Dad and kicked him down the stairs with such force an ambulance had to be called to the house. His rage put his Dad in the hospital long enough for his Mom to get a restraining order, file for divorce, get a permit to carry a firearm, change the locks and get an ADT alarm for a new house, moving Harold and his two brothers to Long Island, NY so the ex could not ever harm her or the boys again.

"Harold, can we get an ice cream now?"

"Sure, but why don't we get a pint and go to my place so we can avoid any of that nutty religious crowd who will probably go to Mac's for ice cream and coffee to discuss how their God is perfect."

Smiling, Maria said, "Is your place close enough to walk?"

"Sure. Isn't everything in this town?"

Maria, faking ignorance of his address, had to smile because she already knew the answer. She had driven by his place every morning and afternoon, wanting to simply knock on the door and ravish him.

Walking along the coast road with a pint of chocolate chip mint, Maria and Harold acted like a couple of teenagers on their first date because it was their first date. They saw each other every morning and all day long at school and the restaurant but on this moonlight night they strolled along, listening to the roar of the ocean, speaking in softer voices than usual.

Harold took her hand saying, "Maria, I'm really glad you were there tonight to get me out of there. I really got too hot. I'm going have to win the lottery or get a new job because that Wilma Hitchcock is like a junk yard dog when she gets a bone in her mouth she won't let go. I'm screwed when my contract comes up if she doesn't forget tonight."

"It's ok Harold. The parents will defend you. We're New Yorkers! We don't like being told what to do. The people will defend you, especially the parents of the kids in your classes. They love you. You always get high five's from the kids. I hear it all the time from the kids. They like the way you treat them and respect them."

Harold smiled, and then he simply leaned in and kissed Maria with a verve and passion he had not felt since his first night of sex in the college dorms at MIT. She put her hands on his face, pushed him back gently, winked, and pulled him to her with all the passion and energy she could muster.

The ice cream was nearly melted by the time they stopped having sex and decided to go for an ice cream break.

"You are amazing, "Harold said as he gently ran his hand over her belly, plucking his finger into her navel and turning it around until she started to laugh.

"Oh Please, I haven't felt this good in a long, long time."

"Really," Harold smiled with a smile that filled his entire face.

"Oh Harold, you are such a boy. Come on let's get that ice cream, have a little coffee and go til dawn," Maria laughed as she wrapped a blanket around her body and headed for the front door where the bag of ice cream had been dropped when they entered the house, just before he picked her up in his arms and carried her to his bed, as she bit his neck giving him a Hickey – the first she had delivered since high school.

When he got up in the morning, Maria was gone. A note on the pillow said,

"I enjoyed you. Like to stay but there is a restaurant to run. Drop in – coffee is on the house. The note was signed ML Maria."

Feeling lucky, Harold bought a lottery ticket when he picked up his New York Times. It was his first and the prize was $440,000,000.

As he bought the ticket he told his student behind the counter at his father's store: "Charley, I'm buying a ticket even though the mathematical chance of winning is one in a Zillion. I just feel lucky this morning." "It's okay Mr. Lutz. You gotta be in it to win it, as the advertising says."

"Quite so Charley, Quite so," Harold replied as he pocketed the ticket and headed off to Maria's diner.

Maria's diner was crowded with the early morning Friday crowd that had driven out from the city, leaving at dawn to miss the insane and tiresome afternoon commuter traffic when it seemed every single person in Manhattan headed out to the Hamptons area for a weekend of pot, alcohol, a hookup for a great weekend of sex or just to lay on the beach, read a book and brush off the pain of a lost love, a lost job, a tiresome existence surrounded by tall buildings and the noise reverberating from taxis and impatient drivers clogging New York's city streets.

The beaches of Long Island were sanctuary – places where the cacophony of the city was replaced by the steady rhythm of the sea pounding the shore in a discernible pattern that somehow soothed the soul and helped tired trend setters from the city drop their pretenses, stop the prancing required on city streets and switch to a casual, relaxed stroll along the sandy shore of the Atlantic – a repast more restful than that drug induced feeling of euphoria that fills a brain during a hit of high test marijuana- the 1960's Acapulco Gold on steroids.

Maria smiled as Harold approached her in the restaurant, directing him to a reserved table in the corner so he could calmly read his newspaper, devouring the news in the same methodical way he would most likely consume his usual two poached eggs, a patty made with grandma's recipe, two pieces of rye toast, orange juice and coffee.

He smiled, following her to the table, looking at her back-side as he would a piece of fine sculpture by Rodin, noting her back end was supple, swaying in perfect rhythm and inviting. He restrained his desire to simply rest both hands on those two perfectly shaped cheeks as he had with enthusiasm the night before.

"God, you are a beauty", he whispered in her ear as he sat down.

"And what can we get this morning for our town's most talked about teacher?"

"Pancakes and Bacon, I think."

"Something new for Mr. Two Eggs; did something happen to alter your appetite?"

"It did. I feel lucky. I even bought a Powerball this morning. My first and if I win you get $2 Million and Charley gets $2 Million so he can go to MIT and you can do whatever you want."

"You are too generous," Maria laughed as she rubbed her hand softly on his shoulder, before walking away to fetch his coffee.

The Mayor walked in a few minutes later and sat across from Harold.

"Harold, you really opened a can of worms last night. Can you just write a letter to the Editor and apologize to the Reverends and end this dispute? I'm afraid you don't know just how hostile these folks can be? They've been running this town forever. They'll slice you nuts off in the name of Christian Charity. Please recant. It'll make my summer so much easier."

Harold took a sip of coffee and a bite of warm, running over with raspberry jam piece of rye toast, his head bobbing left and right as if he was weighing the decision, calculating how he would respond to the Mayor's request.

"Nope: can't help you out Mr. Mayor. This is a free country and those bigots – they are you know –should not be allowed to slap down and publically humiliate anyone who doesn't genuflect in their direction."

"Is that really your final decision," the Mayor said as he let out a deep breath, imagining the battle that Wilma and the ministers would launch if Harold did not genuflect in their direction.

"I'm afraid so, Mr. Mayor."

"Shit. Come on Harold. I you don't recant we're gonna have big old gun fight in this town. Oh Well. I can see your mind is set....May the best side wins," Mayor Taylor said as he got up and shook hands with Harold.

"See you in the ring, I guess" Harold replied.

"Yep, Guess so. Call me if you change your mind," the Mayor said as he turned and walked out, shaking hands with about a dozen folks before getting out the door.

Maria came over to Harold's table sat down and took a sip of coffee before asking Harold: "What did the Mayor want?"

"He wants me to recant – like some heretic before the Inquisition. I told him: NO Way. These bullies have to stand down because I will not recant. That's just plain nonsense. It's the 21st Century for god's sake, Maria."

"I guess it's not going to be a quiet summer, is it?" "No. I'm going to the beach to read this book on "Brilliant Blunders" about folks like Einstein who learned from their mistakes and how it improved their contribution to their field of study. It should be fun. Want to have lunch or should we have a late dinner because it's Friday and the crowds are on their way to disrupt our serenity?"

"Dinner sounds good. How's eight. We can go to Randy's for a bit of seafood up in Montauk. He's a friend. They'll hold us a table on the sea.'

"It's good to know people who know people of influence."

"It is," she laughed as she picked up his bill and tore it up: "This one's on me because you are a celebrity and folks will fight for the opportunity to sit in the table where the battle lines were drawn that turned our little town's summer into a donnybrook -- But you, my friend, can buy dinner." "Wait a minute. I just gave you a promissory note for two million dollars. Doesn't that count?"

"When I get that check, I'll buy," she laughed.

48 Hours after the City Council Meeting the small office of Rev. Wilma Hitchcock was filled with 14 of the 16 ministers in town. Two ministers were out of town on holiday and the local Catholic priest sent his regrets because he had to represent the parish in a sexual abuse case in a Manhattan courtroom.

Every minister agreed. They had to do "something" about Mr. Lutz. The Reverend Dooley started by apologizing to his fellow ministers for the rather unsavory, screaming match he had at the Council meeting; "I was just so disturbed by that man's lack of respect for the word of God, I couldn't stop myself from crying out. It was undignified and I certainly didn't appreciate the story in the Beacon describing me as a man with a lot of pent up rage who forgot that America was a place of "religious freedom", including the freedom to not believe in any kind of religion. We need to get him fired or converted... PERIOD."

"Oh, it's okay William," Wilma said. "We all know your heart was in the right place and that little SNOT of an editor has been snotty on the subject of religion forever. I first met him in the hospital after he fell out of the tree near Mrs. Wilson's home when he was in grammar school. He blamed God for not making him stronger. He's just snot; No one pays him any mind, do they."

All the preachers agreed: "He is a pain in the ... I won't say it, but you know what I mean," Reverend Healy of the House of the Divine Word said. "But look we have to decide what to do about this Lutz boy. We need to get him back in the Church or get him out of the school, don't we? How can we let him get the status of hero – rebel with the children in the middle and high school where he is a very, very popular teacher...? And parents love him. He is a bigger problem than those deer flies he wants us to gas into oblivion."

"Hold on George", Wilma piped up. "My elders want him fired ASAP but they are nervous about the publicity and they fear some lawyer will read the story and get Mr. Lutz to sue us for infringing on his right to say what he wants in the public square. The fear of a lawsuit is really big for a solid majority of the elders. We just don't want a battle in the papers and the courts that could reflect badly on our town. What do your elders think?" Emily asked the assembly.

After each preacher reported on his congregation's viewpoint about Mr. Lutz, Reverend Healy – the oldest of the preachers and leader of the biggest and newest Evangelical church in town stood up and said in an unusually strong voice –"It seems agreed. We need to dump this Lutz. He has to be gone. He has to be made an object lesson for our children and the people of our community. We just can't afford to let him be, to let him continue to teach our children or to gain any notoriety in the press. Let's see if we can get the Principal – she is in your church isn't she Wilma? -- To push this guy out for some other reason in the fall. In the meantime let's just treat the shouting match as reported in the local paper the result of a hot night and broken air conditioning in City Hall."

The men and women in the room responded with a "good" and a "no way, we can ignore his attitude toward the Word."

Wilma Hitchcock looked at her watch as she tapped on her desk top to get the attention of the assembled preachers before suggesting a minute of silent prayer and meditation about "How to save this boy and our congregations from unwanted bad publicity."

When everyone fell silent, Emily said: "This Lutz fellow is a virus we need to knock out before it gets so big we can't contain it. As a first step I'd like to suggest that we each ask our congregations this Sunday to write a letter to the editor of the *Beacon* next week saying Mr. Lutz has to apologize to Reverend Dooley and the community for his behavior at the City meeting. If he does, we forget him. If he refuses we push for his firing due to unacceptable behavior in his treatment of others"

Rev. Healy smiled in the way a crook smiles when he sees a way to explain why he is innocent of any crime, complimenting Wilma for an excellent way around the fear of a lawsuit that seemed to paralyze his elders and himself while he was still trying to get the money needed to finance his new church and the house he had just built around back of the Church with a view from the second floor porch of the ocean over the dunes – a view that he had dreamed of having ever since his parents moved to town, buying an inexpensive home nearly one mile from the beach when he was in kindergarten.

"So, Wilma, if I understand you correctly, we should ask people if that kind of shouting in public is bad manners and should not be practiced by a fellow who has a Ph.d. in Mathematics and is supposed to be a Role Model for our children because this approach will free us from the charge of trying to attack his right to express his religious beliefs in any way he wants.".

"Exactly, George – bad manners of the kind Mr. Lutz displayed that night should not be acceptable for one of our teachers."

Everyone nodded in agreement. Emily's approach could help avoid a lawsuit while putting Mr. Lutz on notice.

Wilma thanked everyone for coming and excused herself to perform a baptism for a new baby in the congregation. "Her father is getting deployed to Afghanistan in two days and this was the best time for the family to gather and celebrate the new life."

Every preacher smiled, noting the beat goes on and the congregation was one member richer and one family was more likely to stay connected to the Church because as they learned in the seminary, "Folks are creatures of habit. Get someone hooked on the church early and they stay connected."

"Thank you for coming and please stay as long as the coffee and buns last. Mrs. Harris will be available if you need more of anything," the Pastor Emily Hitchcock said as she left her office, smiling to herself about how much fun it would be to take this arrogant teacher down a few pegs, while solidifying her position in the community as the "go to" negotiator when trouble rears its ugly head in her home town.

Sunday morning – Two weeks later

Maria and Harold slept late, waking in each other's arms at Harold's place after a very satisfying night of great food and dance at her friend Patty's Place in Montauk. The Lobster was superb. The wine perfect and Patty had made sure they got the best table in the house, overlooking the ocean on the upper balcony of Patty's.

Harold snored, very loudly and Maria turned him over with a whisper of "Keep the fire alarm off, Mr. Noisy." He laughed, gave her "the finger" and turned on his side, falling sound asleep in a moment. His snores were too much to bear so Maria got up and went to the kitchen. It was time to take a cool and calculating evaluation of the apartment where Harold ruled and read the *Beacon* to see if the community was going to ask for Harold's head.

When he woke an hour after Maria, Harold pounded his chest like when he was boy, imitating a gorilla in a Tarzan movie just after having sex.

"Oh my God, You are such a boy."

"Aren't you lucky – a boy who can sleep over, play with your magnificent body and not put you in jail for having sex with a minor – That's what we math guys call a "Twofer" – sex and no penalty," Harold shouted to Maria before he got up and ambled in the direction of the smell of hot coffee and a breakfast in his kitchen.

Maria laughed at his getup – "You are a real clothes horse, Harold."

"You like the fig leaf?"

"I do, but get a robe so we can eat breakfast without me just pulling you down on the floor. I need some energy."

"Oh my, so this is the danger of hanging out with an older woman."

"You are a bad boy," Maria laughed as she took him by the hand and ran back to the bed".

Over brunch, Maria said, "Harold, you have to recant. The letters in the paper are really, really hostile toward you. The ministers did their work. You'll get canned for sure.

Listen to this: "Mr. Lutz has shown no respect for the belief systems of the people in *More Churches than Taverns*.

As a result of his insult to our community he is not qualified to teach our children, anymore. Clearly we would not have hired him if we had known of his disdain for the belief system of this community. Fire the man." And the next: "Heathen's don't belong in our school rooms. Send him packing." And Harold, all these folks are well known on town. They are the backbone of the town. Thankfully the Mayor and Superintendent didn't submit a letter – yet. But they will."

"Maria, I'm not going to recant because that's what people did when the Templar's roamed the Middle East killing the folks who wouldn't convert to Christianity. I'm going to fight them. I'm not going to just fall over because I don't agree with them. That's the act of a coward. You'd never respect me if I did that and the students would learn a terrible lesson."

"Will you consider it?"

"I have. I'm done with considering."

"Where will you go? What will you do? I don't want you to move to another city or part of the world because of this."

"Maria," Harold said in a soft voice as he took her in his arms, "I'm not going anywhere without you and that's a promise I don't make lightly."

"Really?"

"Absolutely: I've wanted to be with you since the first day I saw you in a piano recital at school. I loved the way you moved and how you ripped into the music with great passion and precision. You were magnificent... I mean, really magnificent, even breathtaking."

"Ok. I get it. You do like to go on..........."

"It's one of my most endearing qualities, don't you think."

"I do." She said putting her arms around his neck before a passionate kiss.

The phone rang.

"Charley – what can I do for you."

"Dr. Lutz. Someone bought the winning Powerball ticket in my store. It was early in the morning so I wonder, did you win?"

"I don't know, Charley. I haven't even looked. What were the winning numbers," Harold asked as he looked at his ticket, then he read off the numbers: "4 -7 – 8 -10-28-22"... Any good, Charley?"

"Good..............Shit ....it's perfect. You won. You won the whole damn thing --$420,000,000 before taxes—about $240,000,000 net. You can tell those stupid ministers to stick it up where the sun doesn't shine, Doctor Lutz!!"

"Charley: Are you playing with me."

"No Sir." Look it up on Google."

"I'll call you back."

Harold went to bathroom where Maria was reveling in the memory of the greatest breakfast she could remember when Harold slipped in behind her and shouted, "Maria we won the fricking lottery – we are rich beyond my wildest dreams. Charley called. I was the only winning ticket and get $240 Million after taxes. You get two million and Charley gets two million. Beyond that, I'm not sure what to do."

"Hire a great lawyer, my love and stick it to the Ministers, but first you have to stick it to me......"

"Amen............Amen............Amen" he sang as he lifted her up and she put him into her.

A week later:

Reginald Pender, of Boston, was best known as a lawyer's lawyer – a street fighter and a brilliant attorney who had argued several cases before the U. S. Supreme Court. He loved cases about the rights of people to say what they wanted and not get jailed, even if they were advocating ideas considered offensive by the nation as a whole. He had argued for and against the folks on the right who wanted to abolish government and let every state operate as it wanted, essentially shredding the Constitution in favor of rule by state constitutions – dropping the office of President, US Senate, US House of Representatives and Supreme Court, as well as all Federal Departments – especially the IRS. His client wanted to keep the Defense Department in tack and funded by taxes collected by each state so they could satisfy the benefits due to America's Veterans of Foreign Wars.

One client said the Social Security funds should be returned to everyone with a "legitimate" Social Security account so workers who deserved those funds could decide how to use them. This would be the only sensible ending for the "entitlement" segments of the "bloated budget of the USA" Mr. Pender argued on behalf of his super rich client, William Blake, CEO of the Blake Oil Consortium, a man with a net worth, according to Forbes, of $15 Billion.

Mr. Pender was seen by his colleagues as a man who loved his toys. He also devoted 10% of his time and money to support the "innocence project" – a project started by a law professor some years earlier to give his students a clear sense of how the U.S. Legal System works and an opportunity to right the failures that cropped up now and then in the system. Since Mr. Pender had been involved in the Innocence Project some 20 men and one women had been freed from "death row" because the evidence presented was proven false –DNA testing had come a long way since these folks had been convicted and because the evidence in their case had been preserved, newly improved DNA testing was able to show the killer was someone other than the prisoner.

On Monday morning, Harold called Mr. Pender and arranged to see him to discuss his case one week later when he had the money in hand from the NY Lottery folks and had a clearer idea of what the Reverends and School District would do about his remark that "*God Makes Mistakes*".

When they met in Boston, Pender gave Harold a very firm handshake, welcoming him into his inner sanctum, an office equipped with most objects that sailors would have: a large painting of the *Titanic* from the early 20th century hung on wall facing his desk.

"Yes, Mr. Lutz I am a sailor."

"That's pretty obvious," Maria said.

"Now Mr. Lutz and Ms. Luciana, is it?"

"Call me Maria."

"Good. This is my associate Jasmine Jones. She is the rainmaker on the Innocence Project; she is a graduate of your alma mater, Mr. Lutz. She went from science to law after she completed a Ph.d. in Biology."

"Well," Harold said, "can we get down to this. I'm very upset. This is the letter that the School Board just sent me," he commented as he pulled it from his pocket and handed the note to Pender.

As they read the letter Harold noticed how different the folks in Boston were compared to the folks in the town of *More Churches than Taverns*.

Pender was dressed in a 3 piece dark blue suit, probably Armani, costing $5,000 or so and Ms. Jones was in a light blue Chanel suit costing somewhere in the same range. Harold and Maria were in casual wear; although, they had both made it a point to wear a jacket so they could get in the better restaurants in Boston for lunch without a debate.

The letter Harold gave to Mr. Pender said:

"Dr. Lutz,

The School Board is concerned about the remarks you made at the City Council because they do not fit with the general belief system of the people in the community at large.

So, although you have an excellent record as a teacher, we are not going to renew your contract unless you can amend your comments and speak in a manner more consistent with the belief system of the *Community of More Churches than Taverns.*

We will need to hear from you before Labor Day. If you cannot agree then we will void your contract after the next school year. Between now and then you will be paid and have full benefits as if you were teaching, however, you will not be allowed on the school grounds or have access to any of the library services and other services normally used by teachers as part of class preparation.

Mr. Lutz, we look forward to your reply.

Signed,
Paul Baker, Superintendent

PS: Attached is a letter from the ministers regarding your comments to the City Council?

Letter to the editor:

We request the School Board either remove Dr. Lutz from the teaching staff of our local high school or Dr. Lutz apologize to the city at the next Council Meeting for his comments that *God Makes Mistakes* and his desire to have the Council authorize the spending of tax dollars to "gas" the pesky flies that attack our city for a few weeks every summer.

His remarks were intemperate, unkind, without merit and a direct assault on the spiritual sensibilities of our community.

Signed,
ALL Pastors of Christian Churches in the city of *More Churches than Taverns, NY.*

When Mr. Pender looked up from the two letters, he shook his head and said:

"Harold, I'd do this one for free. When you first called I thought you were some kind of a crackpot with cash, in need of therapy. But these letters and this editorial have clearly changed my mind. Now, you seem to be the most-sane guy in that town. These pastors remind me of Nazis and the thought suppression police of Stalin's Russia. How could these characters get so much power in the 21st Century in New York, of all places?"

"Here's what I want to do, Mr. Pender."
"Please, call me Reggie or Reg, like all my friends because you and I are going to spend a lot of time together on this one."
"Fine, Reg. Maria and I have discussed this and here is what we want you to do.

We want the School Board blocked from firing me for some "unkind" remarks outside of the school. We want to sue the School Board and each of the Ministers for $3,000,000 for slander and an attempt to get me fired, plus $20,000,000 in punitive damages per Minister. We want the name of the town changed from "*More Churches than Taverns*" to "*Read your Darwin*" or its former name *of Grant's Crossing.*

Oh, you should know we have no intention of being thrown out of town by these bigots. We plan to stay, to marry, and to raise our children in this town."

Squeezing Maria's hand, Harold reached into this pocket, extracted two checks and handed them to Mr. Pender and Ms. Jones. "The million dollars to your firm is for 1,000 hours of billable hours @$1,000 and the check for $2,000,000 is for the Innocence Project – mark this donation as anonymous on the books."

Pender and Jones smiled as they put the checks in the LUTZ File Folder – a large red folder with notations that said, "A crazy city versus a sane citizen."

"Oh" Harold said: "We thank you for providing the flight over and the car from the airport. I think we agreed we could get pretty attached to travel by private jet without lines or doing battle with travel agents."

"Yes," Maria said, "it was a great way to travel and we look forward to the trip back after a few days here in Boston. It's such a wonderful city and Harold wants to show me around MIT and meet with some of his buddies and the professors who helped him get a Ph.d. in Math at MIT. It was some accomplishment – a great accomplishment, actually, and we are very happy to have him teach our kids."

"Yes. You know, I wondered why you chose to teach high school. You could work anywhere in the world. I saw you graduated at the head your class at every stage of education. A Ph.d.at MIT at 23 in math is very, very impressive."

"Well, Reg, I always wanted to teach high school math because I thought it would be important to get youngsters turned on to math like I was by my high school teacher – Professor Winkler – a professor from the local university who taught us because he wanted us to get as excited about math as he was…"

"Winkler? You learned math from Winkler –the Noble Prize in math Winkler?"

"Yes. He told us he knew Einstein and worked with Einstein once a month on a unifying theory for the universe. He thought they had done it. Einstein and Winkler were doing the final proofs of the theory when they noticed an error in the center of their computations. A plus that should have been a minus – a basic mistake in algebra flattened their theory. They had missed the basics and had wasted their time for nearly 6 months as they continued to finish their work. Winkler told me: I decided to teach high school math so I would keep the basics in mind – all the time. I loved his understanding of math and his humility."

"So," Pender said," You decided to teach high school to find the next great math guy or girl rather than make a zillion in whatever think tank you wanted to join or company or government entity? Is that it?"

"Yes. Now why this town? I love the ocean. I love Long Island. It's in my DNA to be close to the ocean. This little town, however, has changed since I moved there 5 years ago. It's gotten really stuffy and impressed with itself. The ministers have gotten so much power they changed the city's name. And now they want to throw me out because I don't agree with them 100%........."

"Maria: what's your view of all this? You were born and raised in the town, weren't you?"

"I was, Reg. And I can't disagree with anything Harold has said about the town and how it's changed. It's really sad. I'm with him 100% and, like Harold, I want to live out my days in this town. More money doesn't motivate me to move to some fancier spot on the Sound. I like the town and it's convenient to the city – one train ride of 45 minutes and we are in the city. It's perfect. The big bucks just let us take more exotic vacations if we want, or get to some warm climate during the winter if we want until our children are in school and we have to go like everyone else and accommodate our vacations to the school schedule."

"Are you ready for the hostility you could face when word gets out that you and Harold are an item?"

"I don't know. But it can't be worse than the nonsense I had to put up with when I got divorced from the son of the biggest car dealer on the Island; that was about as nasty as it could get, especially when all the details of his gambling, whoring and pouring on the cocaine – even chasing underage girls came out in the local paper. God the town treated me like an idiot for ever marrying the guy and then I was a dunce for not being able to control the crazy man. So, I'm not really concerned. Heck I've got enough money to just lay on the beach and let the folks run the restaurant during the summer."

"Well this is different Maria," Jasmine said. "This time the city's religious folks won't feel sorry for you or feel the need to support you. They'll be hostile to you because you will supporting Harold in a way that can strip them of their power and a lot of their money if a court directed verdict finds in our favor."

"Have at it guys. Harold and I are ready for the firestorm. We are really in agreement on this one."

Harold piped up: "Look, we are prepared to do battle. If they drop their attempt to fire me and change the name of the town to "Read your Darwin" I'll donate a new soccer field in the memory of my younger brother, Ned. He was killed in a car accident outside of town 3 years ago. Maria and I intend to stay but we don't want to live with this kind of religious tyranny. It's as if our little town in New York State was a cow town in the Texas Panhandle where some folks think the world is 10,000 years of age and the Rapture is right around the corner."

Over lunch it was agreed the $1,000,000 retainer would be used on other legal matters if it wasn't needed for the handling of the unlawful discharge and violation of religious freedoms of Harold by the ministers in *More Churches than Taverns*.

City Council Meeting: August 15th

Harold and his attorneys went to the city council meeting one month after the explosive session that got the ball rolling. The Hall was filled with the ministers and their folks. Maria squeezed his hand as they walked in followed by Reg and Jasmine.

Sitting with the leader of the Ministers was Wilamina Williams, Principal of the High School. She and the Rev. Wilma Hitchcock had been friends since grammar school, even served in the Army together as nurses after the Bush Administration invaded Iraq to get rid of weapons of mass destruction (WMD) as they were called within a couple of weeks after the invasion.

Maria whispered in Jasmine's ear," the ministers and the school principal are in cahoots on this one, I think."

Jasmine was surprised how dressed down the principal was and how well dressed the Ministers were at this public hearing.

Channel 4 newsman, Harry Bent, was there from Manhattan because he got a tip that it was a very hot story – as in lots of hot words could be passed between the "folks of God" and a local "Heathen" the tipster said and Harry Bent loved any story about Churches and the public going head to head on any subject. He was one the men molested as a boy in Boston by a priest so he had a particular interest in turning the knife whenever he could in the "wounds of the righteous" as he often described the religious folks demanding folks conform to their way of life.

"Yes," Harry Bent told one of the folks outside who questioned his crew attending the meeting on the issue of GOD –fearing folks doing battle with a Heathen- 'I surely do enjoy turning the knife in the wounds of the Messengers of God."

"You are disgusting" a *More Churches than Taverns* resident told Harry as he spit on the ground in front of him, before walking into the hall and greeting all the ministers and their supporters.

A minute later, Harry Bent's gopher said, "That was the attorney for the Ministers --and the town -- it seems."

"Let the fun begin. Don't miss a minute of it," Harry told his camera man as they sauntered up to the press table where the Snotty editor of the *Beacon* held court with some of the magazine writers who had appeared at the City Council's hearing on taxes and sewers in a new section of the town.

The Beacon guy didn't know who made a generous offer to build a soccer field on a plot of land near the high school the city had been trying to sell for a couple years. It even came close once, but the town was strapped for cash and could not give the prospective builder a tax break. Tonight, the city council was to discuss the offer but the mayor and members of the city council were being very secretive about the deal.

At 7 PM sharp, Mayor Taylor pounded the gavel and asked the crowd to settle down:" Turn off your cell phones and don't yell out if you agree or don't agree with something someone says."

Turning to the agenda, Mayor Taylor, told the crowd, "The first item tonight is the new soccer field – a gift from a resident – that will not cost the city a nickel to prepare or maintain. The generous resident is our own Harold Lutz. Let's give him a round of applause."

The kids and the parents in the room cheered; the Ministers and their supporters stayed silent. "Let's hear what this Devil worshiper has to say," Rev. Wilma Hitchcock whispered to her friend, the principal,

Wilamina Williams as Harold walked to the podium in the front of the room from the last row.

As he approached the podium Harold smiled at two of the Council members because he had their children in his math class and both children had done quite well. They seemed friendly, smiling as he approached. The Mayor smiled as well. The other members turned pages or looked around the room to see who they knew and one waved back to his wife and daughter.

Harold was dressed as a summer resident, complete with flip flops.

"Mr. Mayor and Members of the Council, I am here to offer the city a new soccer field and swimming pool. They will be built at my expense on the 5 acre parcel behind the high school that lies vacant and is owned by the city."

The room broke into a cheer, with parents and students in attendance roaring their approval.

Mayor Taylor pounded the gavel after a few minutes: "Please, let Dr. Lutz finish. There are some conditions on this offer are there not, Dr. Lutz."

The crowd quieted, people looking at one another with quizzical looks and some feeling like maybe it was silly to cheer.

"Yes, Mr. Mayor", Harold continued. "There are some conditions. First, though I'd like you to know that thanks to Charley Timmins, one of my star students, selling me my first Powerball ticket, I can fund this project with no strings attached on the financial side of the transaction. In that connection, the money – all ten million of it – is in an escrow account with my attorney Reginald Pender and John Murray at the Grant's Crossing Bank. The money can be released to start construction as soon as three things happen.

And, Mr. Mayor, these things have to happen before Labor Day or the deal is undone.

First, The Ministers of this city's churches, including the leader of the suppression of thought group, Wilma Hitchcock, run a full page ad in the *Beacon apologizing* to me and the members of this community for their bigoted remarks about me and the fact that I don't "completely" (a word he used as he lifted his arms to signal quotations) agree with their view of the world. This is about as Un-American and Un-Christian as anything I can imagine.

Second, Mr. Mayor and Members of the Council, the city agrees to change our name back to *"Grant's Crossing"*, a name that is more fitting for our community and reflective of the heritage of the community – a name, by the way, that lasted for 125 years until two years ago when this cabal of ministers – led by Wilma Hitchcock, of course – changed the name of the town to *More Churches than Taverns.*

Three, the School lets me continue to teach math in the high school, canceling their threat to fire me because I don't want to genuflect to the Ministers regarding my God making mistakes remarks.

If this council and school board can accomplish these three goals, the lawsuits filed against the city, the churches and the school board will be dropped and the city can get on with the business it needs to do without having to spend hundreds of thousands of dollars in legal fees, something the city citizens would have to pay.

Those conditions, Mr. Mayor, are *NOT—I repeat NOT negotiable.*

I want to live in this town with the woman I married yesterday, Maria Luciana. She also loves this town and we would like to live out our days here and raise our children" – he said, turning to smile in Maria's direction – "here. But not if this kind of bigotry is allowed to stand as the norm in this community."

The Mayor looked in Wilma's Direction and said, "Thank you Harold. I was delighted to have married you and one of our town's greatest assets yesterday. I am sure everyone in the room hopes we can work this out and enjoy the company of you and Maria in our city for many years to come."

Harold walked back to his seat with a thunderous applause, noticing all eyes had turned to Wilma Hitchcock who glared at Harold as if he was the Devil himself. She stood up and walked with the stride of a soldier heading into battle – ramrod straight on the outside but inside wondering if what she was about to encounter was really worth her life or the loss of a limb or two.

"Mr. Mayor," Wilma started to say, when the Mayor brought down his gavel. "Just a minute Wilma; we have an agenda to follow, unless, of course, the members of the council want to hear from you."

All hands went up: "Let her speak," Reverend Dooley, shouted from the audience before deputies removed him from the room.

"Ok Wilma. Your turn," Mayor Taylor said.

"Mr. Mayor and Members of the City Council, I am once again surprised by the demands of our local school teacher. He thinks his ideas are better than those of the Christian Heritage we have been handed by our forefathers and from the Divine. This is hubris at its worst. I can't imagine anyone asking anything more evil. He simply shows his disdain for the ideas and faith that has shored up this community for the past 125 years. It's that faith that has built this town and made this town the safe place to live that it is. It's our faith that has sustained us, given our children a sense of security and kept this community sound.

Now this math teacher wants us to drop all our beliefs for a soccer field and swimming pool – What nonsense? How childish? How weak does he think we are? Soccer fields come and go. Swimming pools come and go. Our faith is rock solid, not as fragile as the sand on our beaches, eroded by a storm now and then.

Mr. Mayor and Members of the Council, I ask you to reject this gift – It's like giving the first hit of heroin to a youngster by some drug dealer who only seeks to put a chain around the neck of the child and tie him / her to life time habit of heroin addiction. We all know haw that scenario ends. So, I would urge you to reject this gift, raise our taxes by $10,000,000 and let the good Doctor Lutz and his new bride – shame on her for cavorting with this man – move to some other town or some other country where the people have the backbone of well cooked spaghetti noodles."

Wilma turned to the crowd. "Well, where's my applause? Aren't I right?"

The Nos were louder than the Right ons......

Mayor Taylor spoke up: "Wilma – I'm a member of your church, but I can't agree that everyone has to agree with you or me. We have freedom of religion in this country and by God; I'm not going to support your attack on Dr. Lutz or anyone else who doesn't agree with you. It's UN-American."

People cheered the Mayor. When the sound ended, Wilma gave the Mayor a look reserved by school teachers with a mean disposition for children who are out of order and not listening to them and agreeing with the rightness of their instruction.

Harry Bent, the NYC TV News reporter, said for all to hear: "Round 1 Professor Harold Lutz. Yes, Miranda, freedom of speech and freedom of religion can even win in the town of More *Churches than Taverns* – the former *Grants Crossing, New York* – on the shores of the Atlantic.

Mayor Taylor turned to the Council: "Question: How many of you agree with the conditions of Dr. Lutz offer to build the sports facility and change our town's name?"

The entire board raised their hands – even the Mayor.

"Ok then. The one condition we can't control is the reaction of the Ministers, so this city council, on the advice of counsel, will send a letter to the Ministers and request they apologize in the form of a full page ad in the *Beacon* to Dr. Lutz.

"In the meantime, Mayor Taylor continued," I need to take a vote by the Council about changing our name. Counsel said it will be as easy as it was two years ago. So, how many members of the council, by show of hands, agree to change our town's name back to *"Grant's Crossing?"* All six hands went up.

"Well, that's it then. It's now up to the Ministers to consider Dr. Lutz's request for an apology in the form of a letter in a full page ad in the *Beacon*. We know where Reverend Hitchcock stands, but we don't know where the other ministers are on the issue so we will instruct counsel to contact all the pastors in town and we will see where are at the next council meeting on the day before Labor Day. This meeting is adjourned."

Wilma Hitchcock headed for the press table but the Snot at the *Beacon* said "Excuse me Wilma" as he headed for Harold and Maria, following on the heels of Harry Bent and his camera man.

Harold was "breaking news" on NYC news the next morning and evening, even CNN and NBC picked up the story and Jimmy B.- a late night host – used the situation as part of his comic routine at on Later Night.

Harry Bent described Harold as the voice of common sense in a town gone nuts under the direction of a power mad group of Christians and Tea Party advocates who want to shut up anyone who does not agree with them regardless of the cost to the community. It was noted that all the Pastors in Attendance and the School Principal were served with notices that Harold Lutz was suing them. The Ministers were being sued for "defamation" and the School for "Wrongful Discharge"

Harry Bent ended his broadcast with, "Sounds like Long Island has its own colony of Christian Crazies and lawsuits by a well funded local teacher who might just break the bank of the city and the churches in this town of *"More Churches than Taverns"*. More to come as the city's sane people argue the costs and benefits of living under the yoke of Rev. Wilma Hitchcock and her thought police friends…"

Friday:

The Ministers and their lawyers met at Wilma's office to discuss what to do about Lutz because their phones had not stopped since the day after the City Council meeting with most of the Members of the Congregation concerned about the way the Ministers had responded to "The Lutz outburst" a month earlier and how the city was getting very negative publicity in the news media.

"Well, Wilma," said as she rang the bell on her desk: "What's the verdict. What are your people saying? Mine are really unhappy. The elders said, "Get this Lutz nonsense out of sight or find a new church."

Reverend Dooley rolled his eyes as he rose from his favorite chair in Wilma's office – a red velvet, wood chair that was sturdy enough to hold his 250 pounds – "Folks, we need to call a truce. Let the boy have his beliefs. He might come around. We can't block the new soccer field and pool. The people want it. My elders said, "Get this out of the way or we will all be bankrupt. Lutz has a reputation for having very strong will. Once he makes up his mind the folks at school say he doesn't waiver. He is not going away and he has pretty deep well of money. How much did he net on the Powerball? Oh yeah: $220,000,000."

Every minister said the same thing: "Let it go. Write an apology and celebrate the end of an embarrassing moment that started in the heat of the night in city hall without air conditioning after a long day when everyone was tired and not thinking too clearly."

On the front page of the Sunday edition of the *Beacon* it was noted that Minister Wilma Hitchcock and her friend, the Principal of the High

School where Harold taught Math were leaving for a mission in Vietnam because they were "called by God to go forward and help those less fortunate than they had been."

On the back page of the same edition of the Beacon was a full page ad, signed by all the Pastors.

It said:

> "We all support Mr. Harold Lutz's right to believe what he wants and to express those views in our town. We apologize for any misunderstanding that occurred at the City Council on a hot summer's night when the air conditioning was broken. Tempers flared. Loose and intemperate words were exchanged between tired folks at the end of hot summer's day.

We applaud his gift of a soccer field and swimming pool near the high school.

We don't object to changing the name of our town back to *Grant's Crossing, but that decision is the decision of city officials.*

We look forward speaking with Mr. Lutz and his wife Maria as residents and teachers in our town for many years to come, and wish them great happiness in their life together.

Sincerely,

All the pastors in *More Churches than Taverns, NY signed.*

Maria brought the paper into the bedroom along with some coffee as Harold took a shower.

When he finished and walked into the bedroom, Maria said: "Well, my love it's done. The ministers have capitulated. The bloody battle of the summer of 2014 between the rights of a handsome free speech advocate and some dopey bigots is over. You won. It's done. Wilma and our principal are leaving for Vietnam to convert non-Christians. Now, we can start to look for a place to build that house you want with the ocean views so the kids can get up in the morning and hit the surf. How about building it attached to the Restaurant as a one story on pilings of 15 feet high or so? Then, when the ocean runs over the dunes we can be safe?"

"Sounds perfect, my sweet," Harold said as he picked up Maria and planted a Hickey on her neck. "I've wanted to do that ever since you planted that Hickey on me," Harold laughed.

"You bad boy," she laughed, ripping his towel off his body and pulling him back to bed.

SAND CRANES

Sand Hill Cranes are the most common kinds of cranes in the US, mostly residing on the plains of Nebraska and Minnesota, staying near the wetlands. So, when three sand cranes landed on the lawn near my grandmother's farmstead in Wisconsin my grandma started to shake as if she had seen a ghost. Her hands shook like someone put a gun to her face saying, "Give me all your money or I'll blow your head off."

"What's wrong Grandma?" I asked.

"Sand cranes came the day my mother and father died. We were walking in the country and three sand cranes landed on the field across from us. Momma said," Oh Dear, someone is going to die. The sand cranes have come to fetch their soul and take them to a place where they will meet their friends and family from ages past; perhaps, they will even meet their maker, although, honey, I'm not really sure about that one. It's so rare to see sand cranes on our farm."

Then Grandma smiled and patted me on the head and we walked on talking about her parents and how they took care of her, making sure she was always warm and well fed, even in the winter when they lived in that log cabin on the frozen plains of Indiana when she was a girl in early 1900s."

"Wow. Your parents lived in a log cabin like Abraham Lincoln."

"Yep- Daddy built it himself. We had nothing to speak of -- No TV, no phone, no internet, no Facebook for sure and No indoor plumbing, just an outhouse that we would tip over every so often when one of us kids was in it. We played in the woods and went fishing down by the river after school so we had some fish to eat if we got lucky. Of course, back then we used a big fishing net - no rods or single hook operations. Rods are too uncertain and we were hungry."

"Were you as good at checkers back then, grandma?"

"'Oh no -- Dad would wipe the board with us until we got to high school. Then we would beat him, but not too often because he didn't like to lose to us kids. He'd get real mad when we walloped him on the checker board. He'd roar about too much schooling was making us dangerous. Then, he'd laugh and we'd all laugh and he'd applaud the kid who whipped him. Mom would laugh loud as the mule. She loved the way he was whooping and hollering when he lost."

The next day I decided to run away, far-far away, far away. I wanted to be out of the range of surveillance cameras and GPS systems. I didn't want the cops to find me because I had a cell phone.

My dream was simple: get away, get far enough away so I could find an empty place where I could find what it was I could do with my life, where I could live and be happy doing whatever it was that was my passion, a passion as yet not defined and blurred by all the competing forces that bombarded me daily from TV and You Tube, competing with friends on edgebook.com

I rose at dawn, packed my knapsack with a few changes of clothes, and tucked my savings account book in my back pocket. After a hearty breakfast of eggs, sausages and whole wheat toast, topped off with a large glass of orange juice, I said goodbye to Mom and Grandma and set off for the bus to my high school five miles from home in the city just next to the regional transportation hub where my bank had a branch.

I'd go to the bank, get my money in the form of travelers checks and some cash then I'd go to the train station and take the first train that was leaving the station, going west toward the open spaces and mountains in Colorado and California where there were trails to hike and places without masses of commuters and cars and trucks and all sorts of distractions.

I wanted to laugh like grandpa. I wanted to feel alive and happy and in charge of my life, in love and ready to grow into an adult who could "really" make a difference in the lives of others, just like Dad who had gone to save the starving kids in Africa, fixing children with cleft palates like the other doctors in "Doctors without Borders" until he was killed in a burst of machine gun fire by some hopped up thug who attacked the hospital he worked in to steal the drugs their militia needed for their wounded warriors."

I was clear about wanting to be a "significant" person in the world with a long obituary filled with stories about how important I really was during the long life I lived, a man lost, loved and mourned by large segments of the world, a man of legends as remembered as Achilles who helped to conquer Troy, only to lose his life in that moment of triumph despite his protection of the gods -- gods who failed to protect his ankle because, so the legend goes, the gods did not want him to be like them - capable of living forever as their equal.

What did Sisyphus say? Oh yeah," There are already enough gods for the world of men to praise and sacrifice for."

The bank teller almost killed my plans when she asked, "Billy, why aren't you in school?"

"Well, Mrs. Martin, if you promise not to tell anyone, I'll go back to class as soon as I get this banking taken care of. I'm getting the money to give Mom a special present for her birthday and this is the best way for me to surprise her; you know, without having to walk home because of missing my bus."

"Of course; Good idea, Billy; what a great son you are. What are you getting her?"

"Can't say Mrs. Martin because, as grandma always likes to say, "Loose lips sink ships" but, don't worry, she'll tell you within a week."

"Oh good; Okay, just sign these travelers' checks on top and here is your cash. Now be sure to put your receipt for the traveler's checks in a safe place so if you lose them, you can get them renewed."

"Thanks Mrs. Martin," I said with a big smile before I turned to leave the bank and get into the train station where, I hoped, I did not meet another parent of another neighbor or a buddy from school.

Before getting in my seat, I went in the men's room and put $300 in travelers checks inside my hiking book -- an emergency fund just in case something happened I didn't expect. I hid my receipt in the plastic holder with my ID hanging from my neck under my shirt.

I was pretty afraid, but I was young and strong - 18 years old, a high school fullback for two years before I was injured by a gorilla of a tackle from the high school for retards with eating problems and watched my career as a professional football player squashed.

'I'll be okay' I thought as I got on board the train from Milwaukee to Denver, taking a seat in the section up above with a plastic dome so I could see the world as we zipped by across the plains.

My mind started to wander, as I thought about what would be next. What part of the world will allow me to see into my future, as the seers like to say -- where will my destiny place me, where will the fates put me and what lessons will I learn between now and the time I get back home to share the stories of my journey.

Crossing Minnesota I saw a flock of sand cranes - It scared me.

I wondered if something had happened to grandma. I wondered if I should call home and let them know I was okay, that they should not worry or call the police with some kind of an AMBER ALERT, causing grandma to have a heart attack and be carried off on the wings of sand cranes like her Mom and Dad and husband -- a hero in WWII who lost his life in the battle of the Bulge when he saved his buddies lives by attacking and destroying a machine gun nest.

"God she was proud of him," I said out loud.

"Proud of whom, "a young woman asked as she took the seat next to me," her soft brown eyes filling me with an awe and pleasure I had never felt before.

"Oh. I'm sorry; I didn't mean to say that out loud"

"Well. You did. So who was she proud of and who was he?" this lovely young woman asked as she lifted her chin and assumed the kind of determined look I'd often seen in the eyes of a lineman getting ready to take me down if the quarterback gave me the ball and I went for the opening forged by an equally determined tackle on my side of the line.

Acting annoyed I said, "Oh I was thinking about how proud my grandma was of my grandfather because he won a silver star for his bravery at the Battle of the Bulge during World War II. She lives with us -- my family. Often she simply likes to sit in her chair, holding his picture from their wedding day, and looks off into the prairies and the corn fields on our farm -- the farm she inherited from her parents in the home they were married in just a month before he went off war."

She put out her hand and said, "I'm Amanda. That is a wonderful story. She must have loved him a great deal. Did she ever marry another man?"

"She never did. Oh. I'm Billy."

Amanda seemed to calm down after we exchanged names. She even smiled and offered to share an energy bar because there would be no food on the train for another two hours and, as she explained, "I've been busy all morning and barely had time to have breakfast."

I asked," where are you going?"

"Denver. I'm in school there. I'm studying journalism. I want to be an anchor on CNN or BBC so I can beam into millions of homes every day and let them know what's going on in the world. I can't think of a better way to spend my days until, of course, I find the right man, have 3 children and live in magnificent apartment in the Watergate in DC where I will hobnob with the rich and famous and be plugged into the world, seeing everything as it happens, reporting significant events to the world before anyone else -- "the queen of the scoopers" as my best friend wrote in my high school year book."

"And how did you decide that you wanted to be a reporter?"

"Not just a reporter, silly. I want to be the anchor like Anderson Cooper or Diane Sawyer because they make the big bucks, get the best trips to places in the world that are hot, and they go by private jet -- that's so cool, though I might feel a bit guilty about burning so much jet fuel to fly just me and camera man on one plane. Nah; I'll get over it pretty quickly because it will lead to scoop after scoop from the major news areas of the world,", she said laughing at the absurd thought she would embarrassed by being "special."

"Wow," I said. "You've really thought that one through. Hope it works."

"Oh, it will work. What are you going to do, Billy?"

I was really scared to say anything at all. She was so smart and so ready for her life while I was just confused and not sure about what to do. I didn't want to turn her off though, so I took a very thoughtful pose, a deep breath, rubbed my hand across my chin and said:

"I'm not sure. I'm young. I hate to say this is the only way. I may find something else to do that has more appeal for me. So, Amanda, I'm going to wait awhile before I set myself down one path or another. My future is like a zebras roaming the Serengeti plains of Africa; my future is dependent on what I encounter as I go from place to place."

"Oh my, you must be a philosophy major."

"'Not really, Amanda; I'm just too young to lock down my future, too many things can happen."

She must have been put off by my answer because she said, "Billy, it's great talking to you but I have to study for a test tomorrow."

"Ok. Will you wake me up when the dining room opens? I have to sleep for awhile. I'm really tired."

"Sure. But Don't Snore: I'll wake you up"

"Thanks."

I closed my eyes wondering what I should do next. She was really cute and really smart but clearly she was older than I was and she probably had a boyfriend at college so I would just be disappointed if she pushed me aside when we got to Denver. I really didn't want to say goodbye but I wasn't sure what to do. Sleep made sense. I'd decide what to do when I woke up.

---I saw sand cranes lift off the prairie floor carrying me off to place of warmth and lots of water, a place where I was going to meet with a grizzly bear who was without claws or teeth, a harmless blob of fur and fat slimming down because his diet had changed from fish and any other living thing he wanted to eat to berries and leaves and strawberries in the strawberry patch out back of grandma's house and the bird feeders in the suburbs that were encroaching on our 150 acre farm outside the city.

Then a woman with red hair like Amanda's came into sight on the dirt road leading to grandma's house, dressed only in a long flowing white robe, wearing gold slippers and no jewelry on any kind on her arms or legs, just a tiara made of something bright that looked a lot like diamonds but the darkness fell so quickly along the road that the girl simply evaporated and everything in front of my mind's eye went away.

An hour outside of Denver, Amanda woke me up.

"Here's some coffee and a ham and cheese sandwich," she said as she put the food on the tray she had pulled down in front of me.

"You'll love it. It was the best they had back there, the freshest. I hope you're not a vegan or something like that she said with a look of concern crossing her face, her nose scrunching up a bit.

'No. This is great. Thanks."

"Oh good; I'm glad. I wasn't sure. Now, Billy, tell me the truth. Why are you running away from home? What's up? Come on. You can tell me."

"Damn. How did you know?"

"I peeked. I saw the ID around your neck and snooped. I read it. It says you are in Madison High School in some Oconomowoc or something like that in Wisconsin."

"Okay. Look. I am on a journey. I got up this morning and decided to go away, far away, away from all the competing visions of what is good for me. I need some rest, some quiet, some time to decide what to do and where to go for the rest of my life. Dad's gone. Mom is set as a school teacher and caretaker for me and Grandma. I'm tired of being in the same town, surrounded by the same people I've been surrounded by the same people I've been surrounded by for my whole life. I need a rest."

'You mean you're Mom and Grandma think you're in school?"

"Yes."

"And when you don't get home for dinner, what will they think?"

"I guess I have to call them and say I'm okay, won't I?"

"Well, yeah. You better. They will be worried sick. My brother left one day and never came home. We never saw him again. Six months later the state trooper from next door came over and told us he was found in a ditch- murdered by someone. Hikers found him about six miles from home. It was terrible not knowing where he was. Even getting his body back was better than not knowing where he was -- it was awful... You don't want to do that to your Mom and Grandma. Promise you will call them from Denver?"

"Ok" I said as I fought back the feeling that I would throw up right then and there. 'Jesus, How could I have been so selfish, so cruel to Mom and Grandma.'

"Say, Billy, I have an idea. Do you have anywhere to stay tonight?"

"No. I was going to find a youth hostel. Tomorrow, I was going to hike into the mountains and get away from the noise."

"Why don't you come with me to the University? We have extra rooms. It won't cost much. You can be safe and have dinner with my roommate and me and go to some classes tomorrow. See the university. See what it feels like to wander the campus of Denver. Maybe, next summer, when you graduate, you can attend."

"You'll let me do that."

"Sure. We do it all the time. Students come for a weekend to see what it might be like to attend. I'll register you as my cousin and get you the package -- you have some money to buy a food ticket and all that right?

"I have a few dollars. I could afford $100."

"That's more than enough Billy."

At the station, we walked together as if we were old friends as she chatted on her cell with her roommate, Heidi, who was circling the station. I noticed a guy started to run in her direction with a box cutter in his right hand. I turned, picked her up and turned to block the guy with my right shoulder. It was a classic move -- thanks coach -- and the guy bounced off my shoulder, lost his balance and fell face first onto the concrete, his box cutter sliding down the floor until it came to a halt at the foot of a police officer who had just rounded a corner.

The two police officers held the guy by the arms and asked if Amanda and I were okay.

"Sure." I said.

"I don't think so," one of the officers said. "It looks like his box cutter cut your arm. Let's see?"

Sure enough there was blood on my arm. The box cutter had slashed my right arm slightly. It was not serious enough to go to the hospital but the cops cuffed the guy, walked us to the aid station and made sure we got a disinfectant and a band aid.

"Don't want you bleeding on my city, "the older officer said.

At dinner in the dorm cafeteria Amanda described her near brush with death and how I courageously saved her from the man with the box cutter who would have cut her purse off and run away with all her money if I hadn't been so quick to protect her.

I felt pretty good about Amanda's praise until she insisted she speak to my Mom and told her what a brave and wonderful son she had. Then, like a den mother, Amanda assured Mom I would be fine, that she and her roommate would get me back on the Sunday night train to Milwaukee and that they would make sure I didn't get lost -- again.

Before I went to sleep in a room down the hall from Amanda, I opened the envelope Amanda gave me. Inside was a slip of paper with a single sentence.

It read: "In the midst of winter I discovered inside myself an invincible summer" Albert Camus.

On the back of the paper she had written: I'm sure you will find your invincible summer. Have a good night's sleep. No sand cranes on this floor..... Breakfast at 8..."

I got up at day break and went out for my usual one hour run. It was the time of day that let me clear my head and feel the brush of life, the rhythm of the world without all the distractions of the texts and conversations and news programs and honking horns from cars filled with commuters anxious to get to their jobs or drop off their children at school on the way to the office.

As I was stretching, Amanda's roommate, Heidi, approached me. She was in a running suit, her long blond hair tied in a pony tail that ran almost to her waistline.

"Morning Billy: are you a runner too?" Heidi asked.

"I am. I run every morning; rain, snow or sunshine. It seems to keep me sane and fills me with new energy. I love the quiet at dawn."

"Me too: Let's run together. I'll show you the campus. I do a 5 mile run. Too long for you?"

"No. I usually do an hour. Let's go."

"Okay"

As we jogged along the paths of the university, Heidi pointed out the various buildings and where I would have to stay as a freshman when I came to the university next year.

"I may not come here, Heidi. My mom has her heart set on me going to Dad's alma mater, Marquette, in Wisconsin. That way I can stay home and commute. It is a lot cheaper and we don't have a lot of money."

"Too bad, this is a great school, Billy. You know the mountains are near us so the ski team is really good. The trails are so much more fun out here. All the students ski. It's a blast. The weekend campus is up in the mountains. You'd love it. On top of that, we go camping on the mountaintops. The lake where John Denver got the idea for Rocky Mountain High is really popular. Do you ski and hike, by the way, or is that just boring."

"You are far from boring, Heidi. Your eyes are as blue as robin eggs; really clear and, as the poet's like to say, captivating."

"Why Billy are you flirting with me?"

"Guess so. Is it ok?"

"Sure, it's flattering but you know I'm an older woman -- at least two years older than you and you're going back home on Sunday so it's not a very efficient use of your time."

She sprinted ahead of me after giving me a punch in the arm. I let her get ahead and stay ahead. I couldn't take my eyes off her shapely form moving swiftly down the trail in front of me, as the sun rose giving her hair more brilliance. She was right, of course. I was going home. Still. It was only Thursday. I could get to know her better. With that decision made I picked up the pace and a quickly closed the gap between us-- tapping her in the arm when I came alongside and commenting "Gotcha."

When we got back to the dorm, I said "Thanks" and went on jogging so I could get my full hour in before breakfast, besides I didn't know what else to do. If I stopped with her I'd feel like just taking her in my arms and planting a long lingering kiss on her very trembling sweating lips and just never let her go. Then she'd knee me, slap me in the face and I'd be so embarrassed I'd have to leave right after I showered.

At breakfast, Amanda told me how much Heidi enjoyed jogging with me and showing me the campus. She said, "You are a very interesting young guy, with the emphasis on really young guy and something about timing and age and how you clearly described the color or her eyes. She liked that you noticed," Amanda said with quiet emphasis as she patted me on the arm.

Heidi came along with her bagel and coffee and said, "Come on. We'll be late for quant. Joyful Quant - the quadratic equation festival--" she chuckled as we walked out of the cafeteria.

"You'll love this one Billy," Amanda said as we walked into a stadium style room with about 100 students. "Our professor this morning is Christie Lequer, a woman from France who has been hailed as one of the most capable mathematicians in the Western World. We don't know why, but she loves to teach instead of just do research and get published."

"Are there any new students in the room this morning," the professor asked.

Amanda stood up and said, "Yes Professor. We have a visitor. My cousin, Billy Marshall, is here to see if this is the university for him."

"Welcome Mr. Marshall. As a new member of the class I offer you the opportunity to try to solve the equation on the board to my left. It is an equation that often stumps students but if you feel up to it, please come down and solve it."

I felt really nervous, but Heidi had just sat down a few seats away, so I decided to go ahead and show her I was more than a guy who could run well.

"Thank you, Professor. I think I just might be able to do this one."

"Come on down. Let's get it done while the rest of you pass in your homework assignments to the front row."

When the professor turned around, she saw I had finished. She walked slowly over to the board, examined the answer. Stood back and said, "Very good. You have studied quant, then. Are you some sort of math whiz?"

"No Professor. It just seemed logical. Then again, I think I saw this problem in an ancient text about mathematical equations solved by a Greek philosopher in the time of Socrates. My Dad had a book with ancient math formulas and problems in it."

"You are right on both counts, Mr. Marshall. Thank you. If you do decide to come to this university I will be happy to have you in my class."

I got a round of applause, started by Heidi as I walked back to my seat, filled with pride and a bit of embarrassment, wondering why I had not just said "No" as I was thinking so I could be a bit invisible."

After class Professor Lequer asked Amanda and me to stay. She put another problem on the board she took from her little green journal and asked me to solve it. I did. We did another. It was tougher but I got the right answer.

"Mr. Marshall, if you need some scholarship money for school, you have your parents contact me. I have some funds for students who are gifted in mathematics and you seem to have a facility with the mathematical puzzles we mathematicians like to solve and ponder."

She turned to Amanda and said with a wink, "Thank you for bringing your cousin to class this morning. I hope you won't be late for your next class?"

"Actually, Professor, I will," Amanda said, "but I don't mind. I was delighted to see how well Billy performed. I didn't know he had it in him."

At lunch, Heidi said, "Billy. Why don't you come with me on a hike with the Sierra Club tomorrow? We hike up to the lake where John Denver wrote Rocky Mountain High, stay in Sierra Club cabins, have a bon fire, and sing along. We get back Saturday in time for lunch. It's a great group: students, some faculty, some families from the town."

"Well. What does it cost?"

"For you Nothing; I'm the leader of the hikers. You are now -- if you agree -- my official assistant. You get a sleeping bag, food, etc. Your job is to walk at the back and make sure the stragglers get to the camp site. Are you game?"

"Okay, if Amanda thinks it's a good idea."

"Are you kidding? Go. You'll get to see the mountains. It's a great hike and a lot more fun than wandering around the library on a Friday night. You'll get the quiet you wanted under the stars."

"Heidi -- You're the boss. What time do we go?"

"We leave at 9. I will meet you at the front door at 8. And, Billy, you won' t need a sleeping bag and all that, just boots for hiking and the usual stuff including a bathing suit in case the lake is warm enough. We have all the other stuff at the site. It's being flown in as we speak. Okay. See you in the morning." she said with a biggest smile any girl had given me.

My head was spinning and my heart started pounding as I began to dream of how her lips would feel when we finally stopped flirting and got down to the passionate feelings that I was sure were burning in both our hearts and minds.

When I got to the front door the in the morning, ten minutes early, Heidi was already there. She was driving a yellow mini-cooper with a Sierra Club emblem on the side.

"I got you a coffee," she said as she handed me a Starbucks large coffee - "and a bagel as well" she continued as she reached into a paper bag and pulled out a strawberry bagel.

"You're the best," was all I could say as I bit into the bagel.

"Oh please," she smiled back.

At the gathering site for the group hike, Heidi gave me a sidearm and a rifle, explaining again that I would be the backup for the group, walking with a Ranger to keep the stragglers in tow because, it wouldn't be good to lose a hiker to a bear or mountain lion on a Sierra Club sponsored hike, would it."

Heidi introduced Jenny and Darrel Hudson; federal park rangers who would help guide the group and available when we get to our destination to answer all of the questions hikers had about the area. Then, she asked everyone to stay together because the fire spotters in the forest have noticed Bear, mountain lions and coyotes in the area, as well as elk and deer.

She said, "All four of us are excellent shots and will keep you safe but we have to remind you this is wild country and anything can happen. Usually, of course, the animals leave us alone but now and then we get a rogue bear or a mountain lion who decides we might make a tasty morsel so we go armed into the mountains. Okay. Stay together in single file or in twos. We'll stop every hour or so, then we can stop for lunch at noon before continuing a couple more hours to the campsite where we can get a warm meal, even go for a swim if the lake isn't too cold or rest our bones in a hot spring a short distance from our Sierra Club campsite."

We started up with mountain, 20 hikers and 4 hiker caretakers, bound for a camp on a lake that was legend thanks to John Denver. As we climbed I couldn't help but feel a sense of awe for the magnificence of the mountains that I had dreamed of climbing since I first saw them in a video in school about how the world was formed as glaciers melted leaving the world filled with fresh water and mountains that rose as high as 20,000 feet.

My adventure felt like fun. I was simply amazed that I was walking the same mountains the pioneers climbed with all their worldly possessions and no idea of what lie ahead.

"God those first settlers were really courageous," I told Heidi as we stopped for our first break." "Yes they were," she said smiling as she patted me on the shoulder like a school teacher after I had given the right answer to a question she didn't expect me to answer correctly.

As we started on the last leg of the morning climb, Jennifer and Heidi, raised their hands and signaled for everyone to get down because about 100 feet above them on the trail, two deer leaped across the trail followed closely behind by a mountain lion looking for a meal..

Darrell and I both clicked off our safety on our rifles. We stood back to back looking to the right and left for any other critters racing for what was sure to be a kill. We had been discussing how the animal chain works, with the wolves and coyotes and other creatures like hawks and eagles and sparrows feed on carrion left behind after a kill. We were certain that this sort of commotion in the woods would bring the wolves and coyotes to hang around waiting for the leftovers or, and this was our real fear, go for one of the hikers.

After a few minutes wait Heidi and Jennifer got up from their crouch and signaled us to continue. Like us they heard the commotion as the mountain lions killed one or both of the deer.

Suddenly, Heidi signaled us to stop and get down. Then we saw the most amazing sight I had ever seen. The mountain lion strutted across the trail some hundred feet in front of Heidi dragging its kill back to a safer place, probably closer to her young waiting in a cave or another hiding place for her to bring them a fresh kill.

"Did you see how that mountain lion looked at us," Heidi asked me when we got to the campsite. "Jesus, I thought she was going to come right at us. I felt like lobster in a tank watching as the chef decided which one of us to put in the pot of boiling hot water so it could be a meal for some lobster lover."

"You'd have dropped him before he hurt anyone," I assured her as I stroked her arm."

"You're right. I would have," she said as she patted me on the shoulder and moved away to start the camp orientation for the hikers who had just finished a warm meal cooked on an open fire by the folks who flew in on the sea plane that was parked on the lake, attached to the dock.

At dinner I learned that Darrell and Jenny had met while they were serving in the Peace Corps in Guatemala. After that experience they decided to do their best to keep nature preserved and study for advance degrees in environmental science. Both were in graduate school working toward a Ph. d. Jenny was getting her doctorate in biology and Darrell was focusing on Geology because he wanted to learn how the world could be preserved "from the core to the surface" he said. Professor Lequer was also in our group. She too had served in the Peace Corps. She spent her time in Mexico working with the poor who lived along the coast near Cabo San Lucas. I told them I only knew a little Spanish because there was no one to really practice with in the little town of Oconomowoc, Wisconsin. "That's okay. We'll practice on the way down the mountain Darrell piped up.

"Ever the teacher," Professor Lequer noted with an approving smile that made Jenny and Heidi laugh.

"That's why I love him so," Jenny said as she got up and kissed him lightly on his head. "Come on, Big Boy; let's get in the hot tub before it gets crowded,"

"You Bet."

As the camp fire started to fade, Heidi whispered in my ear:

"Come on. Let's go to the hot springs. We can rest our weary bones before we get a good night's sleep beneath the stars."

When we got to the hot springs, Heidi took my hand and squeezed, put her pistol and towel down and slipped into the water. I followed her; my heart was pounding like a jackhammer, the hot water a total relief to my legs and back. Clearly the muscles were much more tired than I thought.

"Oh my God," Heidi said. "I needed this. I am exhausted. Those mountain lions this morning did a real number on my head. I was never so afraid. They were beautiful and natural and I loved seeing them but I knew if they came for us I would shoot them dead without hesitation. I was just glad I didn't have to kill it. Just so glad..."

"I don't know what I would do if that lion would have attacked. Oh, don't get me wrong, I'd have shot it -- eventually. I was just so scared - shaking really -- so I wondered if I could get off a clean shot. Jenny was as calm as could be. She had her weapon sighted for a kill and her hands were as calm as could be. I couldn't believe it. I don't know how she could be so calm. -- You know what she said?" she continued before I could say anything.

"She told me she came face to face with an armed man in the jungles of Guatemala. He was taking her to a guerrilla army camp to be held as a hostage until her parents or the Peace Corps. pay a ransom for her release. As they walked toward the kidnapper's campsite, a black cat attacked her guard. It was huge, a cougar she said, and it apparently went for the man because he was a bigger kill. The guy was fighting to keep the cougar from his neck. His weapon fell to the ground. She said, "I just picked it up and killed both of them. Then, she took a compass from the guerrilla's pocket, his radio and his food and started back to the Peace Corps site."

"The next day she was on a plane home."

We soaked our bodies in silence for a long time. I contemplated the depth of the courage and poise Jenny had in such a terrifying scenario and wondered if I would have as much courage if I was faced with death or killing someone or something.

As I was leaning my head back on the edge of the hot springs, looking up at the stars in a clear night sky, I started to think of John Denver probably soaking in the same hot springs with his true love. I could feel the water begin to part as Heidi came close. She put her arms around neck, allowing me to inhale the aroma of her breath and said," Billy. I was fearful for you. I didn't want you to get hurt before you and I could make love and sleep in each other arms."

We kissed. She took me in her hands and we came together and I experienced a sensation that had never before filled my body, mind or spirit. It was the end of the journey; a miraculous event that, though experienced by billions of humans before me, was as spectacular and unique as a sunrise -- fulfilling as nothing else had ever been.

At dawn, Heidi woke me. "Come on. You've got to see this."

At the lake, we sat on top of large flat boulder and she told me to use the binoculars. "Look to the north. Watch the eagles swoop down and catch their breakfast."

As I watched, she leaned against me and told me of the time two years earlier when she sat on this rock and decided to become a teacher of wildlife management. She wasn't sure anymore which branch of wildlife management she was going to specialize in but when she saw those bald eagles swoop down and pluck a fish from the lake she knew they were far too beautiful to ever be erased by man. She had to protect them and their food supply.

We leaned against each other inhaling our new sense of togetherness until the breakfast bell called us back to our jobs as guides for wilderness lovers from the cities.

The hike to the bottom was much quicker and the folks kept much closer together in case those lions they saw on the way up or the wolves and coyotes going for a bit of dinner from the left over kill were moving along the trail.

I was delighted to be at the back of the pack on the way down because I could see for miles, sensing the width and breath of the plains below, with a clear view of an eagle soaring alongside funky balloons that filled the air as the annual soaring fair started in Colorado.

"This is an airborne circus," I told Darrell.

"It is indeed. You will have to try it when you get back out here," Darrell replied.

"'' I think I'll hitch a ride on one of those maple syrup balloons."

"Bring $150 per person, Billy."

"Ok" I said as I stood for a moment watching the gliders and balloons turn the natural beauty of the big sky of Colorado into a multi-colored circus with characters shaped like beer bottles, Yogi Bear, an old car, a bottle of maple syrup with a rainbow of colors running from its base to its top.

At the base camp, the folks all took pictures of their guides. Some shared phone numbers. One fellow put a hundred dollar bill in my pocket. "Thanks for catching me when I was rolling down the mountain. God, that was embarrassing," he said.

"No problem, Mr. Carson. It happens to many people. I'm just glad you're okay."

As we drove back campus, Heidi couldn't take her hand off my arm and I couldn't take my hand off her leg.

"I'm staying with you tonight," she said.

"You better," I replied." I'd hate to be arrested for breaking down Amanda's door so I could spirit you away on the arms of love."

"Oh you're such a Neanderthal," she laughed

That night I slept without a nightmare and I didn't wake up with a sense of impending doom, thinking there was a burglar in the room like the guys who shot Dad. Sand Cranes didn't fill my head; only sunshine got a place in my head, even if I had to say goodbye to Heidi for awhile, I'd be okay and so would she.

The trip to the train station was very quiet. We barely spoke until she walked me to the train saying," Now you go right home, you bad boy and don't forget to say you're sorry for making your Mom and Grandma Worry about you. And call me when you get home. I want to hear your voice. Okay?"

"Okay Mom. No problem. I just wish I could stay. I like college -- especially some of those hotties in the cafeteria at breakfast"

"You are a bad boy," Heidi yelled as she hit me the shoulder, causing people to turn their heads to see what the "bad boy" looked like and if the girl was okay.

On the ride home, I went from happy to sad, from relief to grief. I wanted to go back, settle up with Mom and the school. At the same time I wanted to go to school with Heidi and spend every night wrapped in her arms, listening to her breathing and her occasional period of ear shattering, loud as a tuba, snores.

When I got to Milwaukee, Mom and Grandma were standing at the gate. I didn't know what to say to them, but I didn't really have to say anything because they just gave big hugs and started to talk about an email they got from a Professor Lequer at the University. The email said, "If Billy gets high grades on his SAT Mr. Carson, the man he stopped from tumbling down the mountain will give him a full ride to the University. He is the CEO of a big sporting goods store. When I told him how good Billy was in math, he said, "I'll pay for Billy's education just like my Uncle Mike paid for mine after my Dad was killed in the war, IF he gets a solid score on his SAT."

As we drove up the driveway to Mom's place, I noticed nearly a dozen or so sand cranes milling around on the edge of our cornfield.

"Oh look," Grandma said. "Twelve sand cranes in the corn. It was the same when your Uncle William came home from Vietnam. He looked at them a long while before he turned to your Dad and said, "I am back in the world" with quiet certainty that made us all sense that our world was back in one piece and he would be alright.'

Heidi laughed when I told her the news. She said, "Oh boy do you know who to save," followed by, "God that's good news. I miss you already. Take the test. Get early admission and start school in the summer -- August is beautiful up here. Okay?'

"Can't wait," I said.

From then on "CU/LU" ended every text.